I0727848

Afterlife

of

Alanna Miller

DEMELZA CARLTON

DEDICATION

This book is dedicated to Dad.
Twenty years ago, who'd have believed I'd ever publish
this?
Not even me..

<h1 style="text-align:center">ONE</h1>

In the end, somehow you end up thinking about the beginning.

"Sabrina called again last night. So did Emma," Alanna said, panting a little as we hurried up the steps. "Then there was someone called Suzette..."

I laughed. "You remember their names better than I can. I'm not sure I could tell you which was which in a line-up. They were all pretty, eager and giggly, until they had their clothes off, when they became about as responsive as a blow-up doll or a cadaver. Would you want to have sex with someone who reminded you of a cadaver?"

Alanna screwed her face up. "I've dissected more of them than you have, but only you could think of messing with one. You're seriously messed up, Nathan. I'm going to get you a blow-up doll for your birthday, if only to keep you away from cadavers and girls whose calls you won't answer. I wonder if they have zombie ones..."

"There are worse things to think about during a cadaver

dissection," I replied, hitching the strap of my backpack higher on my shoulder.

Alanna snorted. "Like which of the female med students hasn't buttoned her lab coat up properly over her low-cut dress? I saw you staring at Danielle last week…"

I lost track of what she was saying, her words drowned out by an excited giggle behind us. The dark-haired girl in the same low-cut dress I remembered from last week charged up the stairs, overtaking us and continuing up. Her skirt was so short I could see that she wasn't wearing any underwear – or not much, anyway. Maybe a g-string, I guessed.

A vice clamped onto my shoulder. God, Alanna had a strong grip for a girl. "So I'll be giving Danielle excuses as to why you're not returning her calls next week?"

I shrugged, rubbing my shoulder as she let go. "I haven't slept with her yet."

Alanna's signet ring caught on my shirt, so she yanked it free, the rosy stone catching the light for just a moment. "I bet she'd agree to do it on the necropsy lab table if you asked her today," Alanna retorted. "You'll be in her skimpy knickers before the weekend's over, for sure."

"I could resist if I wanted to," I protested.

"The day that happens, I'll die of shock," she replied. "I can't wait to meet the girl who tells you to fuck off instead of asking you to fuck her." She jerked her bag further up her arm. "Don't wait for me. I'll make my own way home."

"Where are you going?" I asked, dropping my bag so I could button my lab coat.

"Shopping. I might even get your birthday present if I find a sex shop that does inflatable zombies." She winked and strode off.

I stashed my bag in the rack and pulled out my dissection kit. I knew I needed some more scalpel blades, but I hoped I still had one or two left. Clutching the kit and my file, I shouldered open the door.

"Oops!" the girl without knickers said as her forceps tinkled to the floor. She doubled over to pick them up, showing her bare, skinny arse.

I wondered how Alanna could think of anything but sex in the cadaver labs. With death so close, how could I not want to get a piece of that sweet-looking arse?

Professor White cleared his throat grumpily as he entered the lab, his coat flaring as he strode over. "Miller, uncover today's cadaver. Today, your task is to discover the cause of death. You'll be assessed."

No-Knickers had half her lab coat buttons undone again so I could see her pushed-up cleavage. I grabbed the edge of the sheet and pulled, not looking at the corpse.

"Miller, tell us your first impressions," Professor White instructed.

Her tits are too small, but they'll make a nice handful. I wonder if she gives a good blowjob?

I glanced at the faceless body. "Young, with no white hair or regrowth." My eyes travelled further down. "Lacerations and abrasions to skin on torso and arms. Extensive trauma to wrists and hands. Deep incisions on thighs with further abrasions. Widespread bruising…I would say cause of death is blood loss when some of those incisions pierced veins." I swallowed, trying not to breathe in too much formaldehyde.

"Wrong," Alanna said. "You did this. You didn't protect

me. You let them do this to me. You killed me..." No longer faceless, her corpse sat up, reaching for me with twisted, broken fingers.

I sat up, too, panting with panic as cold sweat trickled down my skin in the dark. Fuck. The nightmares were getting worse. If I slept in pyjamas like I had as a kid, they'd have been drenched. As it was, I just wiped myself down with a towel I kept by the bed for just this purpose and lay down again.

Tears rolled down my cheeks as I reached for the sleeping pills, shaking two into my palm. Without Caitlin, sleep eluded me. One look at her sleeping form beside me would be enough reassurance to get me to relax. But it'd been five years since I'd seen her – five long, lonely years since she disappeared.

I grabbed my water bottle and gulped down the tablets. I wouldn't get sleep any other way when I dreamed about Alanna as a zombie, because she was right. I'd killed her six years ago by not protecting her.

I lay down, waiting for the pills to take effect, hoping my sleep would be dreamless, dreading the endless nightmares when it wasn't, and all the time wondering…was Caitlin alive or dead?

TWO

Living in witness protection is like living someone else's afterlife. Everything from your past life, including your own name, is dead…but you're still alive, forging the future as someone else.

Of course, there'll be times you forget your new name. It was never really yours to begin with.

"Um, that's you," a voice behind me whispered.

Disoriented, I blinked back into the present, lifting my eyes as I ascended to the stage. Barely hesitating, I shook the Chancellor's hand and summoned a genuine smile as she whispered, "Congratulations, doctor." I beamed at the photographer for the obligatory flash before she released me and I escaped to the offstage anonymity I usually enjoyed.

No one knew who I was. Just another graduate with a medical degree, the ink barely dry. I slipped into my seat and invisibility once more.

But to one person, I'd never be invisible.

"I still can't believe it." Dad was waiting for me in the foyer, wiping tears from his eyes. "My little girl is old enough to be a doctor."

I waited until he enveloped me in his arms before I whispered, "You know I'm not. If you'd put the right dates on my school enrolment forms when I first started kindergarten, you wouldn't be here until next year."

"I blame the stress. I was supposed to bring two girls home, not just one." He pulled away and hooked his arm through mine. "She would have been so proud of you today. Let's take the official photos and then go back to my hotel. I think I need to tell you about your mother."

We posed for the photographers, I got to hand back the hideous black graduation gown that made me look like one of the black-draped cocktail tables, and we were free.

We crossed the hotel lobby and Dad jerked his head at the restaurant. "Do you want to go in there or would you prefer if we get room service upstairs?" As I watched, his eyes strayed back to the restaurant.

"Is that the one with the really good seafood you were telling me about?" I hid my smile as he looked at me guiltily. "I haven't had lobster in a while. Let's do dinner at the restaurant."

Given how late it was, the place was pretty empty, so the hostess offered us our choice of tables. Dad pointed to one tucked into a corner and that's where we sat.

I waited impatiently as we ordered and our drinks were served, but Dad didn't say anything. I took a sip of my wine and finally said, "Okay. You've waited for almost twenty years and now you've dropped a hint, you won't say any more?"

He gulped his beer and set it down. "It hurts, sweetheart. The last time I saw her was twenty-three years ago when she was pregnant with you. Barely showing, but her face was aglow. When I returned for my girls, she was cold and buried in a grave I couldn't even visit and you stared at me with her eyes, but you didn't know me." He sighed. "You know, I met your mother at a university. You see in the news about Islamic countries where women aren't allowed to be educated, but she was. She was a graduate student, doing her PhD in chemistry. I never even found out if she finished it. Anyway, we'd found what we thought were some significant gas reserves, but the samples went missing on the way to the lab and by the time we managed to get the survey vessel back to take more, the whole lab had been turned into a crater. We don't know who blew it up – the Americans or the Iraqis – but it didn't really matter. We had a fresh set of rock samples and I got volunteered for lab duty. Someone arranged a lab for me in a university – don't ask me its name, because I couldn't pronounce it then and I don't remember it now – and I was working late into the night, every night, to get all of the samples analysed.

"One night I must have fallen asleep on one of the benches and I woke up to a furious argument I didn't understand a word of. Probably a good thing, too, because I learned later that I'd been called all sorts of things, including an ass." He laughed.

"*Koon*," I said slowly, nodding.

Dad looked surprised for a moment, but he recovered

and continued, "Anyway, eventually the shouting ended and the man left, leaving a woman clad entirely in black. You know, from her head to her toes, like a nun, but covering her face, too."

"You mean a niqab?" I asked.

"Yeah, that. She turned to face me and told me to get out of her lap. Not lab, lap. All of her covered except her eyes and they were furious. But I couldn't stop staring at her eyes. She had eyes like yours – huge and dark and deep enough to drown in. It took me a minute to understand what she said because she had me absolutely mesmerised, but when I did, I burst out laughing. The wrong thing to do, I learned because she absolutely let rip. Your mother's voice was amazing. She abandoned English, or at least that's what it sounded like, but the message was clear. I was intruding and I needed to leave and …by the time this tiny, veiled woman was done shouting at me in Farsi, I felt like I was this high." He held up his finger and thumb, barely an inch apart. "I backed away from her, hands up in surrender, and called my boss. I told him there was a crazy woman in my lab who looked like she wanted to kill me and could he please find another facility if he wanted me to survive to finish this analysis. I heard the door close before I ended the call and she must have left, because she wasn't in the lab when I looked around again. Before she came back, I raced around the room, packing everything up in preparation for a move.

"The call never came. Every day I'd have to unpack more of it, and every day she ignored me. I could hear her on the other side of the lab, but whenever I looked at her, she'd either glare at me or turn her back. She never left –

didn't even break for lunch.

"And then one day, I heard her come in and then this weird sound, like when you whip a tablecloth off the table. So I turned around and she'd taken off that ghastly habit-thing. And underneath she was dressed…normally. Well, she still had a scarf over her hair and she had a long skirt and long sleeves and…it was odd. The only skin she revealed was her face, but it seemed like so much more. And she was beautiful, so beautiful…I don't know if I've ever told you, but you look just like her."

No, he'd never said it, but I'd seen the strange sadness in his eyes when he looked at me sometimes. It was the same look he'd always gotten whenever I'd asked questions about my mother. I knew. I nodded, not wanting to interrupt the flow of his tale.

"I couldn't stop staring at her and she got that same hard look in her eyes I knew from the day I'd met her. She told me if I was going to look at her like the other men did, then she'd put her niqab back on and never take it off again. She asked me if I'd never seen a woman's face before where I was from. I apologised and told her I couldn't stop staring because she was so beautiful. Then I introduced myself and apologised again for invading her lab, telling her I'd leave as soon as my company found me somewhere else or I finished testing all the samples. She told me her name was Fatima and not to be afraid because she didn't really want to kill me. I was so embarrassed, but then she smiled and…I think I fell in love with her then and there. A bit stupid really, like something in a book. Falling in love with someone because they told you they didn't want to kill you."

Nathan. Nathan had said something similar – that he'd never wanted to hurt me. Not that I'd fallen in love with him at the time, given the circumstances, but it was the first glimmer of trust that had led me to love him later. Of course, he'd thrown that back in my face when he'd chosen his career over me, but he'd made his choices and he was the one who had to live with them. I wondered if he ever regretted letting me go.

"Sweetheart? Do you think I'm crazy? Or have you heard enough?"

I shook my head, both to clear it and to answer him. "No, please, I want to hear it. And we all have our crazy moments. Love's supposed to make you at least a little bit crazy." I looked up to find him staring at me. "What?"

"You sound like you have personal experience. Do I get to meet him?"

I couldn't help it. I laughed. "Dad, I'm twenty-three and I'm not completely innocent any more, but I would tell you if there were someone in my life I needed you to meet."

He squinted at me. "Who was it? Was it that creepy Jason, Jo's brother? You know, I heard on the news that he got arrested in Sydney for having an orgy in a convertible. Him and three girls. You weren't one of them, were you?"

I gave a most unladylike snort. "Shit, no. Even the thought of Jason naked makes me lose my appetite. Why don't you tell me about you and…Mum, instead?" I couldn't remember if I'd ever called her that. I didn't know what I'd called her if I'd even been able to talk.

"Oh look, here comes dinner," Dad said, smiling at the waitress as she served our order.

Choking down the desire to ask a million more

questions, I concentrated on finishing my food so Dad would tell me more. Why had he decided to unburden himself now, of all nights? A chill crept over me as I feared the worst.

THREE

Dad gulped the last of his beer and ordered a third. I nursed my glass of water and shook my head at the waiter's enquiry. I didn't want any more alcohol. Even if I wasn't driving, I had to work tomorrow and a hangover wouldn't help me concentrate.

"If you don't want to hear it, you don't have to. You can go home. I'll get the concierge to call you a cab." Dad's voice broke into my reverie.

"No. I need to hear this. Please, continue," I replied.

"Well, from that day, whenever I left the lab to get a coffee or some food, I invited her to come with me and when she wouldn't, I offered to bring something back for her. She'd just smile, shake her head and go back to work. We did talk a little occasionally – like when we were waiting for the spectrometer or washing up the used lab equipment – but that's it. She didn't wear her veil in the lab any more, either. Every day I'd ask her out to coffee or lunch and every day she refused, but she looked wistful, like she wanted to. So I kept asking, long after I should have stopped.

"One evening, she left without saying good night – she always said good night – and I wondered what I'd done to annoy her. I figured my persistence might have pissed her off. Feeling a bit sad, I promised myself I'd back off the next day, but I'd go home early that day and have a drink from my small stash of illegal alcohol.

"I stepped out of the lab and ran straight into her. Well, into a short woman dressed all in black, but I knew it was her, even if I could only see her eyes. I apologised, feeling even worse, but she laughed and pulled me into the office across the corridor. She told me it was finally Eid, at the end of the fasting month of Ramadan, and she wanted to celebrate it with me, too, so she'd brought me some traditional sweets. And from under that dress she pulled out a dish full of…well, heaps of things, all covered in powdered sugar. More than two people could eat, I'm sure, but I tried. God, they were sweet. And then she explained to me that every day I'd tempted her with food and coffee when she wasn't allowed either of them, but tomorrow she could and if I asked her, she'd love to join me for coffee or lunch. She said they weren't supposed to even think about sex when they were fasting for Ramadan. And one thing led to another and…she kissed me. I was shocked. I mean, it wasn't as if she'd ripped our clothes off and had her way with me on the desk…well, at least not that night, but – "

"Dad!" Even with my eyes squeezed shut, my vivid imagination was showing me pictures I didn't want to see.

"I don't want to hear about you and Mum having sex in public in the Middle East! I can't believe you didn't get arrested!"

"Shh, the waiter's looking at me like he's going to come over or call security or something. I thought you wanted to know how I fell in love with your mother."

I swallowed. "I do, but not...not in graphic detail. I don't even read that sort of stuff in books."

He stared. "There's graphic sex in books now? And you're reading them?"

I wanted to laugh and tell him I had, just to see the shock on his face, but I doubted even he'd believe me. "Yes, there are a lot of books that are more open about these things now, but most of them involve bondage and tying women up who supposedly enjoy that sort of thing. I avoid them like the plague. So unless you'd like to discuss forced castration for convicted rapists and perpetrators of violent crimes against women, I think we should go back to Mum."

Dad choked on his beer, but he pounded on his chest until he recovered. "Ah. Okay. You know I'm sorry I couldn't be there for you five years ago, when all that happened. It was like losing her all over again and I couldn't...I couldn't..." He looked like he was going to cry.

"I know," I interjected. "There wasn't anything you could do, Dad. I had police and anti-terrorist teams looking out for me until they moved me into witness protection." Yes, my father was a coward about grief and loss and we both knew it. No one was perfect. It's not like I didn't have some serious phobias, too. He made time for the good stuff – graduations and award ceremonies and maybe even one day my wedding, if I ever got close enough to a guy to consider such a crazy thing – but when I was sick or in trouble, he'd be on the other side of the world, unable to cope with the possibility of losing me. I'd had appendicitis when I was ten and he didn't visit the hospital once. Jo's mum had had to drive me home and stay there until Dad came home from work, late that night. I wondered whether he'd have come home for my funeral if I hadn't survived the kidnapping. I guess I'd never know. I took a deep breath. "How did you guys ever decide to get married? I mean, I didn't think people dated over there the way they do here."

He took a deep draught of his beer. "Violence was increasing and there was talk of war. My boss rang me one day and said they were evacuating all their field personnel, but the office staff could stay for the moment. There were only the two of us left. He said he'd call again if things changed, but to be ready to leave on short notice.

"Fatima and I had been talking about politics, but if it came to evacuating, she'd go with her family and I'd go to the UK or Australia, depending on where the company sent me. They had the prospect of a new gas field opening up in Australia and plenty of exploration for me to do, but that meant leaving Fatima and maybe never seeing her again.

"When I got off that phone, knowing she'd heard every word, I just looked at her without knowing what else to say. So she hesitated for maybe a few seconds before she asked me to marry her and take her with me. She was willing to leave behind her family and friends and everything she'd ever known to be my wife. She wanted to live in a country where she didn't have to wear a niqab to stop men from staring at her like she was a piece of meat.

"And I agreed. I was so in love with her, but I hadn't really dared to hope that we could. The difference in culture and religion and everything…but I met her family the next day, and she told me her father had agreed to it, though the grumpy look on his face said that he wasn't happy about it. And within a week we were married – Fatima was my wife. She moved into my tiny company apartment near the university and things were good for a couple of months. I filled out all the paperwork for her Australian visa and citizenship and we waited. Before we even had a reply from the Australian embassy, we knew she was pregnant with you. I called the embassy every day, asking about her application until they evacuated, too. And then I knew it was only a matter of time before I'd have to leave. I could take her as far as Dubai, but she didn't have a visa to enter Australia, so she'd have to wait alone in Dubai until I could return for her with her visa. Alone and pregnant in a foreign country…I hated to do it, but we agreed she'd be safer with her family. They'd protect her and take her with them if they left.

"So the last time I saw her, she had her hand on her belly, over you, her eyes filled with tears that she was too strong to let fall, and she kissed me goodbye in her father's house, because it was illegal to even kiss in public there, so she couldn't do it in the airport. And the taxi drove me away."

He drained his beer, hiding the tears he was shedding behind the glass.

"War broke out a month later and I was reassigned to an Aussie project in Torres Strait. When I got home, her visa documentation was waiting for me and a crumpled letter with an ultrasound photograph, saying we were having a girl – it had arrived only a few days before. I tried to call her, but there was no answer at her family's house – their number was disconnected. It took months before I even knew that they'd left the country, but I didn't know where they'd gone. By that time, I'd filled out citizenship papers for you, too, and I filed them on your due date, saying it was your birthday. I had to choose your name before I'd even met you, without Fatima…I missed her so much. It took me almost two years before I finally tracked down her family in Saudi Arabia and another six months before I could contact them to ask for her. No one would tell me anything about her or you and I'm not sure anyone's English was good enough to, even if they'd wanted to.

"I had your citizenship certificates in my hand luggage when I boarded the plane. I was going to bring my girls home. Yet when I entered their house, and looked into her father – your grandfather's eyes, I already knew. My beautiful, wonderful wife of only two months was dead. When I asked about you, he tried to say the same thing, that you were dead, and I almost believed him, but one of the women brought a screaming toddler into the room who ran straight to him. Right away, he softened as he picked up the tiny girl, kissed her grazed knee, and wiped away her tears. It was like I wasn't even there – he was holding a child who mattered more than anyone else. And then she turned to look at me with Fatima's eyes and I knew who you were. I argued with him for two days – bloody impossible, seeing as his English was terrible – that you were my daughter, an Australian citizen, and you'd be coming home with me."

He sighed and lifted his beer, as if hoping the dregs would become a fresh pint before his eyes, but they didn't. The glass clunked back to the table. "You didn't understand a word of English. A woman I didn't know gave me a bag of clothes and toys that you seemed to recognise and that's all you had. The flight home was hell. My heart had died with Fatima and I had no idea what to do with a child, least of all one with her eyes, the part of her I knew best."

"Do you even know how she died?" I asked, stunned that he'd offered so little explanation. All these years, I'd waited to learn something, but it seemed like he didn't know, either.

"For many years, no. I wanted to, but all my Farsi was good for was making Fatima laugh as I made mistakes. I couldn't speak Farsi and her family didn't speak English. Or at least, that's what I thought. A few months ago, I learned that I was wrong." He rose from his chair and waved his credit card. A waiter hurried over to take the payment and we left, Dad tucking his wallet back into his pocket as we walked. "If I'm going to tell you the rest, I need something stronger than beer. Let's go to the bar and hope they have cask strength whisky."

FOUR

I sipped a lemon, lime and bitters as Dad nursed his whisky. I'd rarely seen him drink at home – he'd consumed more alcohol tonight than I'd seen him drink in a year. Once again, he'd picked an isolated corner table as if he was afraid of being overheard. Yet he sat in silence for several minutes.

"What happened a few months ago?" I prompted when impatience got the better of me.

"I was in Dubai for a couple of days before my flight to Sana'a, having coffee, minding my own business, when three men approached my table. The thinner, better-dressed of the three sat down across from me, while the other two flanked him, like bodyguards. And those two were armed. So instead of asking what they were doing at my table, I got up to leave and the seated man said, 'Stay, Malcolm Lockyer.'" He laughed nervously. "He had two blokes with guns, so I stayed.

"But then he said, 'You were Fatima's husband, weren't you?' The last thing I expected him to say. Twenty years of never hearing her name and here was this scary bloke speaking perfect English, who mentions her. And she was all he wanted to talk about.

"He explained that he was her cousin and when Fatima's family fled to Saudi Arabia, she stayed with his parents. She was his favourite cousin, even though he was a bit younger than her, because she wanted to get out and see the world, too. He'd been shocked to see her heavily pregnant – he hadn't even known she was married. Because he was home between finishing school and going to university in France, he spent all his time with her. And she told him stories about this crazy Englishman who thought she was going to kill him, but who loved her and wanted to take her to Australia to live with him. Her and her little girl – you. He said he'd never seen her so happy. And she made him promise to visit her in Australia on his holidays from university.

"The baby wasn't due until after he left for France, but Fatima went into premature labour and you were born a month early. August, not September. He said how much she adored you – couldn't look at you without smiling. She wouldn't allow her father to hire a nanny to help her care for you. She wanted to do everything herself because in Australia, she wouldn't have servants and she'd need to know. Fatima had her life all mapped out with me and I didn't even know.

"Then he went to university and everything was fine, until he received an early morning phone call from his father, telling him that Fatima had died. He jumped on the next plane home and made it just in time for the funeral. He demanded to know why her husband and daughter weren't there. Not even her own father stood by the graveside to see her buried. He swore that he would make those who'd killed her regret their actions in both this life and the next." Dad sniffled though not a single tear fell, and he drank again. "When he reached home, he found the house in an uproar. His uncle, Fatima's father, was shouting at his own father about trust and family and obligation and treachery, but it was clear that he was leaving. He said he approached Fatima's father to offer his condolences and was told that he was the only one in his family to be sorry for her passing.

"When he couldn't get much more information out of either man, he sought out his sister, who seemed to be avoiding all the arguing. She had her own problems, he found – she'd been promised in marriage to someone only a week before and she was angry at being sold, as she called it. When he asked about Fatima, she told him she'd been very sad about her husband's rejection for some time, so she'd killed herself. His sister had been the one who found her."

For the first time in my life, I watched my father burst into tears. "She killed herself because I didn't find her soon enough."

Roles reversed, but I didn't care. I hugged him, trying to soothe a grieving widower whose grief I could never comprehend, for I'd never lost my own world and believed myself responsible.

Some time later, I coaxed Dad into finishing his whisky

and I helped him upstairs to his hotel room. As he hiccupped, he related the final tidbits of his meeting with my mother's cousin. "He said her father died earlier this year and he'd been named as heir and executor of the will. Under Islamic law, it had to be a man, and Fatima had no brothers, only younger sisters. In her father's effects were some photographs of Fatima that he thought I'd like to have. He wanted to visit me in Australia and bring them with him. Visit us, so he could see you again."

Dad dropped his keycard twice before I took pity on him and unlocked the door with my steady hands.

"And what did you say?" I asked, dying to know before I left.

"Whatever he wanted," Dad replied, laughing shakily. "I'd have agreed to whatever he wanted, because he had two bodyguards ready to shoot me if I didn't."

I bade him goodnight and headed downstairs for a taxi. The whole ride home, Dad's words were swirling through my head. My mother's death was suicide and her cousin had sworn vengeance – her scary cousin, who brought heavily armed bodyguards with him to have coffee – and he wanted to meet me. None of it made any sense. All I knew was that my life was about to get a whole lot more interesting.

FIVE

"Seriously, what the hell is this, mate?"

Navid swallowed his huge mouthful of pie. "What do you mean?"

"This!" I shook the letter at him. "Is ASIO trying to buy my silence or what?"

Navid took the letter, held it at arm's length and squinted at it. Looked like he needed reading glasses. Was he really getting that old? He passed the paper back to me. "It's not a bad sum for not telling a story you're not going to talk about anyway. I'd take it and book a nice holiday with it if I were single like you. You could spend a month touring in the US or Europe for that, including flights."

"But I can't take a holiday if you need me as a witness in the inquiry. Have they finally set a date yet? It's weird, getting offered money for silence before the hearings. Is this because there'll be press coverage on the inquiry into that bastard Mott? And they want to make sure we won't talk to the press?"

Navid stared at something in the distance. "No, no one's set a date for the inquiry."

"So why now?" I persisted. "Why are they throwing money at me? It's Caitlin they have to worry about, and this is nowhere near as much money as the TV stations or magazines offer. I don't see her agreeing to take ten grand to keep quiet. Not when she can get a hundred times that for an exclusive."

Navid coughed. "I think they'll be offering her a lot more than that. After all, she's the one who almost died."

"So it's not just hush money? It's compensation for damages suffered and…all the other shit it says in the letter? What about my sister? What about Alanna? Did she get a posthumous payout, too? And a hypocritical letter saying the department deeply regrets her kidnapping, rape, torture and death, but here's some money to make it feel better? Shit, if Caitlin's letter says that, expect fireworks." My heart ached at just the sound of her name. I'd give anything to see her explode. I'd know she was alive and okay, wherever she was.

He lowered his voice. "If they can find her. There's a rumour in the department that all the documents in her file are gone. Papers, digital, recordings of statements… everything, just gone. And the details of her witness protection arrangements, too, so that means she's disappeared."

I stared at him in shock, silence money forgotten. "You don't know where she is? She could be dead or hurt or God knows what! You have to find her! She'll need to give evidence at the inquiry, too. I mean, she nearly died because of him." And I'd get to see her if she came for the inquiry, even if I had to camp outside the building. I'd know she was alive and okay, even if only for a moment. "Ask him where she is. He'll know."

"She was never going to be part of the inquiry. She didn't have any contact with him beforehand and her statements will be enough, or they would have been, if we could find them. All we have are the enraged emails from the hospital, which they were only too happy to give me. Mott forced them to go against hospital policy, allowing you to share a room with Caitlin. Said it was a matter of national security, for her safety…he said he'd have any hospital staff who objected arrested for assisting a known terrorist. I can't believe I didn't realise then that he was corrupt. Now, I don't even know if there'll be an inquiry at all." He sighed and lobbed his empty pie bag into the nearest bin.

I stopped dead. "What do you mean, no inquiry? I get paid off to shut up while that dickhead gets off scot-free? Fuck that."

Navid sighed again. "The justice system isn't geared toward punishing dead people."

"Yeah, which leaves Mott, seeing as everyone else is dead. Wait, hang on…are you saying he's dead, too?" My mouth hung open. "Who killed him? Whoever did it's a legend and I owe him a carton of beer. I've wanted to do it for years!"

Navid coughed out a laugh. "Then you owe Mott a carton of beer, because the official report says he killed himself. With an ornamental dagger, no less. Bit melodramatic, if you ask me."

I found myself shaking my head. "That can't be right. Mott was a mean bastard. He'd never do the world a favour and off himself. And if he did, he'd take people with him or at least set someone up for his murder so he could laugh all the way to hell. Who do you suspect?"

Navid shrugged. "Well, how many people hated him? It could be anyone."

Caitlin was good with a knife, I thought idly, not willing to believe it was her. If anyone deserved to be on the point of her blade, it was him. His negligence…his indifference to what she might suffer had almost gotten her killed.

"Look, I got to get back to work. They've got Michael and me looking for her. One girl in twenty million people, if she's even still in the country. The guys in Canberra want this whole affair over and done with as quickly as possible, so we got pulled off other projects to look for a girl who doesn't want to be found." He laughed but sobered quickly. "Hey, she never mentioned anything to you, did she? About where she was headed, or the new name she'd be using? I remember the day Mott told her about the arrangements. She was really pissed off about them. Wish I'd asked her then."

I shook my head. "If she'd told me anything, I'd have given in and started hunting for her long before now. I'd change my name and go into hiding, too, if I had to." His words started to sink in. "Hang on. She never met Mott. He visited her in hospital when she was unconscious, but never afterwards. I'd never have let that bastard anywhere near her!"

He wouldn't meet my eyes. "She spoke to me privately

when you weren't around, requesting a meeting with your superior. I made the arrangements and I drove her to the office and home again for both meetings. She spotted some inconsistencies in what he said, and told me she suspected he was corrupt. I dismissed it at first, figuring she was just a teenage kid with an overactive imagination, but some of the things she said rang some pretty loud alarm bells. Then I started to see him make mistakes, too. It took me four years to get enough evidence together to warrant an inquiry, and now he's dead, so we'll never know why he did it, or what else he knew." He laughed quietly. "I wonder if she knew. I'd love to ask her now."

I hesitated, then ploughed ahead anyway. "If you find her, can you tell me? I just want to know that she's okay. It's killing me, not knowing."

He shook his head and wouldn't meet my eyes. "Nathan, you know I can't do that. She's in witness protection for a reason, even if the official five years are up and she can let up on the secrecy now. She's not the sort to go splashing her photo on every social media channel she can find just because she can." He inhaled sharply, considering. "I'll tell you what. If we do find her and I get a chance to speak to her, I'll tell her that you wanted to know she was okay, and that you'd love to talk to her, but only if that's what she wants. It's not like you offered to go into hiding with her."

"I would have if she'd asked me, or even wanted me," I whispered, more to myself than to him.

He acted as if he hadn't heard. "See you later, mate."

"Yeah, see you." I sighed, looking at the papers clenched in my hand. "Hey, if I come back to the office with you, can you witness these? Not like I'm going to tell anyone, anyway. Maybe the money will come in useful. My wing mirror's fallen off again and we need a new letterbox."

He laughed. "You never change, do you? I bet you've never told your sister it's you crashing into the mailbox every other week, either."

Shit, no. I wasn't telling Chris that. She'd get me labelled as an unsafe driver and try to get my licence revoked. I'd be cooped up at home with her forever and at the mercy of public transport with all the nutjobs on the train to and from work. And she thought I was crazy. Commuters were worse.

SIX

"I know something you won't miss about Melbourne," Jo said as she peered through the window.

The packing tape made a tortured sound as I used it to seal another box. "What? The ever-changing weather?" I scrawled BOOKS across the top of the box with my marker, then decided to label the sides, too.

"No. The commute to uni. Squeezed into a packed train carriage with all those crazed commuters, forcing yourself not to freak out at the sheer number of strangers touching you…I've seen your face on the train. It's like you're trying not to scream."

I smiled wanly. Trying not to stab someone, actually. Five years and my skin still crawled if anyone touched me. Maybe I should have become a nun, not a doctor. No, I wouldn't be allowed to carry a knife everywhere if I were a nun. Plus, there was the matter of having killed people…"I'll be able to walk to work now. I told you that apartment next to the hospital was a good investment."

She stuck her tongue out. "I'm an accountant, not an investment adviser. But I still think you should've rented it out this year, before you moved in. Six months' rent is a lot of money to throw away…"

Jo had wanted to be a vet, but she hadn't scored high enough in her final exams to get into the course, so she chose accounting instead. Who'd have guessed she could be more passionate about numbers than she was about puppies and kittens?

It wasn't about the money. It was about having my own space that no one else had lived in or done things in. A place without a past so I could create my own future there. Of course, I picked Perth. After so much time away, I wanted to go home. With a new name, a new career and a whole new life…but it was home. Someone else's afterlife…haunting the place where I'd nearly died. It was fitting. Every time I looked at St Elsie's Hospital next door, I'd remember my time there as a patient and hopefully have more sympathy for my patients. Or go to pieces and be admitted to the psychiatric ward.

No, I told myself. I was prepared to go back and face any demons that I hadn't slaughtered in the past. Given they were probably on their last legs after their last encounter with me, it'd be an act of mercy to put them out of their misery. Euthanasia, even, though that wasn't legal in Western Australia.

A blurry hand waved before my eyes. "Hello? Are you even listening to me?"

I shook my head. "Sorry, Jo. I should have been."

"I hope you introduce me to him soon, because any man who can make you daydream that deeply has to be drool-worthy. I want to know his name, his bank balance and how many times in a night."

"How many...?" My eyes widened as her hands eloquently described fast-paced sex. "None, Jo. If I'd slept with a man, I'd have told you."

She sighed: the deep sort that said her heart ached for me. "It's been five years. No one can go that long without wanting sex. I know you got hurt, but you said you'd slept with that sleazy guy in Perth, which means you're hardly afraid of intimacy if you let him touch you. Now, I know you're not pining away for him, so why haven't you even flirted with anyone else?"

Because I didn't want anyone to touch me. And when the man who'd saved your life several times over, risked his own life and his sanity, plus killed for you and stayed at your side until you recovered, thought he wasn't good enough for you, you begin to believe that no one will be. Why would I settle for a one-night stand with someone who wouldn't kill for me?

Six years ago, I'd have told Jo all of this, but now I couldn't. After what happened, some stories were best left untold. And I'm not sure she'd look at me the same way if she knew about the people I'd killed, Even if they did deserve it.

"I haven't met the right one," I replied curtly. "I'm looking for a hero who's not just Prince Charming."

Jo grinned. "A knight in shining armour with awe-inspiring sword skills?" Her hands described the size and nature of his sword.

"A knight, perhaps, but with dented armour and maybe scorch marks up the side, to show he's taken on an army and he'd walk through fire for me. A sword with a few nicks in it, so I know it's not just for show. And later, when we're alone, he'd take it all off and he'd make me feel like I was his whole world."

She burst out laughing. "So, you're after Sir Perfect with experience? Men like that don't exist. You might get some of it, but not everything. Just as long as you don't settle for some sleazy bastard who fools you into thinking he's perfect, I guess."

Not perfect. Just…a man who'd do what Nathan had for me. And more. A man who wouldn't leave me to pursue a pipe dream. Yeah, a man who didn't exist.

I heard the buzzing of the postman's motorbike and glanced out the window. He was just leaving our mailboxes. I jumped to my feet, swiping a hand across my face to hide the tears I hadn't managed to stop. "I'll go empty the letterbox. Be right back."

I kept my eyes on the path beneath my feet, desperately trying to control my streaming eyes. Five years was enough to know a man didn't want me. It's not like he'd have trouble finding me — his agency had hidden me, after all. And they hunted terrorists, for God's sake. They'd track me down in a day.

In between the inevitable junk mail, there was one official-looking letter addressed to me. I tore it open. Well, speak of the devil. It wasn't from Nathan, but it was from ASIO.

I set the letter aside to look at later, when Jo had left. I didn't want to have to explain more than she could handle.

"So why are you leaving for Sydney a week early? What are you going to do until the concert?" Jo asked, stacking up her finished boxes. They were taller than me.

I shrugged. "Does it matter? Go to Taronga Zoo a few times. Do all the meet-the-animals experiences, freak out at the emus walking around that are taller than I am, and check out the harbour views when I get tired of walking. Eat seafood at that restaurant in Darling Harbour we went to last time. I don't know. Just…be a tourist on holiday, I guess. For the first time in a while."

She pulled herself up to sit on the edge of the dining table. "Promise me one thing." She paused for a response, but I wasn't doing it until I had more details. "Promise me you'll go to a pub at least once and buy a drink. Give yourself a chance to meet people."

I laughed and shook my head. "Hell no. After the lab on date rape drugs in pharmacology, I'm not sure I'll ever drink in a pub again. So many of them are odourless and tasteless and colourless and virtually undetectable. Some of them don't even show up in your blood afterwards. And so many of them to remember. One was blue, one tasted like soap or salt, one turned a drink cloudy… It's enough to make me drink from a hip flask through sheer paranoia!"

She shrugged. "Fine. Don't then. But you will have a glass of champagne with me in the VIP lounge at the Opera House before the concert. I won't let you get out of that."

I smiled. "Of course. I wouldn't miss it. I've never been to a concert at the Sydney Opera House and it's meant to be spectacular."

"Don't you wish you'd let the removalists pack for you? It feels like we've been doing this forever, but only half your house is packed up," she moaned, looking around.

I grabbed the stack of newspaper on the dining table and dumped it on the kitchen counter. "Back to work, then. I'll wrap the glasses if you get the rest of my books, then we can go out for dinner."

"Deal."

SEVEN

Better today than tomorrow, I told myself after Jo left. What were the chances of them finding me the day before I left this house for good?

I breathed deeply as the phone rang, my eyes fixed on the letter though I'd memorised the words on it by now.

"Hello, Australian Security and..."

"Hello, my name is...Caitlin Lockyer," I said, wincing as I said the unfamiliar name aloud. It had been a long time since anyone had called me by my real name. "I received a letter today about an ex gratia payment and I'd like to discuss it."

I wanted to ask if it was a joke. There were a lot of zeroes after the dollar sign in this letter and it seemed too good to be true.

No amount of money could pay for my pain, but it sure could help to make me feel better about it afterwards.

"Yes, Ms Lockyer. I'll put you through to Legal now…one moment, please."

The phone rang again. I tapped my fingers in time to the tune in my head, a remnant of last night's rehearsal.

"Hello, Mike Lawler speaking," a pleasant male voice answered.

I took another deep breath. "Hi, my name is Caitlin Lockyer and I received a letter from your office."

"Ah, Miss Lockyer. If you're concerned about the delay, I assure you our office did everything in their power to locate you, but the witness protection records were corrupted and we were unable to find information about your current name or address for quite some time. The delay was factored in when we calculated the sum in your letter." He cleared his throat.

"So this isn't a joke?" I asked weakly. The sum he referred to was more than I'd received for my TV interview. It was more than people got when they were sent to jail for crimes they didn't commit. Wrongful imprisonment and more besides. They'd set a price on rape. My skin crawled at the very thought.

"I assure you, ASIO's budget doesn't allow for jokes this expensive. After this incident, we'll be lucky if Treasury allows us a stationery budget before next year. We almost had a fight break out between two office girls over the last ream of printer paper." He coughed out what sounded like a laugh. "We'll be lucky if the government doesn't decide to cut their losses and privatise us next. But that's not your concern. Yours is to read through the offer and the conditions attached to it. If the offer meets with your approval, you need to sign it in the presence of a witness, get them to sign it, and send it back to us."

I waited in silence for him to say more, but he didn't. After maybe half a minute, I chose to speak. "If this offer is genuine, then I do have some questions before I sign."

"Ask away," Mike said.

I hesitated. "This…media clause. The one that says I can't discuss past events with the media. You know that, in my line of work, media contact is inevitable."

"But not as Caitlin Lockyer. Under your new name, any and all events that involve your new persona are excluded. It's detailed in the conditions down in…ah…fifteen…no, sixteen point three…" I heard him flick through pages – this old-school lawyer still preferred paper copy to electronic.

I flipped to that section in my own papers and read it with some relief. "Then I'll have no issues signing it. I do have one more question, though." I paused, debating whether I should bother. But I wanted to know so much.

"Ask away," Mike said again.

"The…other…parties involved in this…incident. Were any other offers or payments made to other people for this?" I couldn't bring myself to say Nathan's name. His rejection still hurt, even five years later. He'd saved my life, set me well on the way to recovery, dedicated months of time to my wellbeing…and then walked away from my offer of more.

"Miss Lockyer, due to the sensitive nature of this matter, I can't disclose information about any other offers or payments made in relation to yours." He sounded like he wanted to say more.

"So there are other offers?" I pressed, crossing my

fingers.

A heavy sigh blew into his phone. "Yes. One other offer was made."

"How much was it for? Did he accept it?" I burst out, dying to know. If I deserved compensation for what happened to me, so did Nathan. Duped by his boss and forced to do horrible things…

"Miss Lockyer, I can't discuss the terms of someone else's offer or payment. He's not similarly constrained – I suggest you ask him." Mike cleared his throat. "Was there anything else?"

Disappointment welled up like a sprinkler in my chest. I couldn't ask Nathan – he hadn't spoken to me for five years. "No," I mumbled.

"Then, if the offer meets with your approval, sign the paperwork, have it witnessed and send it to the address detailed in your offer letter. Payment will be processed and you'll receive your cheque in a few weeks."

We both said polite goodbyes and I hung up.

I slumped to the kitchen table, wanting to cry or beat my head on its surface. I needed to discuss the offer with Nathan before I accepted it – needed to know he'd been compensated enough for the hell we'd been through. Nothing could pay for my pain – and his was greater than mine.

EIGHT

Writing this shit down helped Caitlin, so I guess it can't be that bad. I don't want to leave it anywhere Chris can find it, though, so I figured if I emailed it to you and deleted it off my computer, she'd never see it. And if you've found a way to check your email in the afterlife. . . I miss you, Alanna. Every damn day.

Tonight I went to the morgue again. I was looking for you — I knew I was there to identify you. It smelled like formalin, just like the dissection labs at uni, and the cadavers seemed to be the only other people there. There was no one else — just me. No police or staff in scrubs. Sometimes they're there and sometimes they aren't. No idea why. But this time was different again.

Until I got to the coolers where your body was stored. There must've been half a dozen of them crowded around you on an examination table, all wearing scrubs and not saying anything. Just staring and doing things to your body and you were fighting them and screaming. The smallest one had a knife between your legs and she was making incisions. They didn't bleed, of course, because from your blue skin I could tell you were dead, but you were still screaming. She was spelling out my name on your thigh - and I moved to get a better look and I realised she'd already written Chris's name on your other leg. Carved into your skin just like Caitlin.

There was another body on the other examination table - two tables, two bodies, but the other one was covered and ignored. And then it sat up and shoved the plastic sheet off and it was Caitlin. Her skin was as pale and bluish as yours, but her eyes had hell in them and she lifted up a gun. She shot the people around you, one by one, and they fell on the floor, blood oozing from the head shots. And then she slid off the table and walked over to you. She whispered something and touched your face and you reached up and touched hers for just a moment before your arm flopped back on the table and you were dead again.

I must have said something because she turned to stare straight at me. And she lifted her weapon, aimed it at me, and I woke up.

I bet there's dream interpreters who'd tell me all sorts of things about what it might mean. That you're dead and that Caitlin would kill the people who hurt you. That maybe she's dead, too, and she's out to kill me. Or maybe I don't eat enough bran. Or dairy. Or something.

I know what it means, though. It means I'm probably going crazy and not going to get any more sleep tonight unless I take some pills to knock myself out. So that's what I'll do.

NINE

I sat staring at my phone for a full fifteen minutes before I dared to make the call. For five years, I'd been good and not called anyone in Perth, but those conditions had lifted now the five-year mark had passed.

What'd happened to me? Had I gone so soft I didn't even have the guts to make a single phone call?

It's not like we'd ended on bad terms. I'd kissed him goodbye, tongue and all. He'd even said he loved me, though actions spoke louder than words in this case because he hadn't loved me enough to come with me.

I hadn't truly needed him any more, and he knew that, but he could have checked in on me once in a while. Just to make sure...

Mentally, I shook myself. Maybe he had checked in on me, covertly and carefully so I'd never known he was there. After all, he'd probably had formal anti-terrorist agent training now. Maybe he was pulling Bond-girl types who were far superior to some scarred victim, a reminder of his first, near-failure of a mission.

But I wasn't just a scarred victim. I'd taken out two of them by myself with no help from him, then gone on to make deals with people to ensure I had a financial safety net in case my mental health fell apart and I couldn't work or study. A house. Investment properties across the country. And now I was a doctor with a job. I didn't need the money the government was offering me to shut up. But I did need to know why. Surely Nathan, working for ASIO and all, would be able to explain the motivations behind the enormous bribe being pushed in my direction?

I hit the call button.

A snippy recorded voice told me the number was disconnected and that I should check it before dialling again.

Shit. Well, there went his mobile number. Maybe Nathan had had to change it after some dangerous terrorist had gotten a hold of his old one and tried to use it to stalk him through the phone's GPS. Or he'd had to switch to a more covert number that no one had. Or maybe...

Maybe I was reading too much into it.

I decided to call his house instead. He might not still live there, but it'd been his parents' investment property, so it was a start. Maybe his sister still lived there.

It rang and rang and no one answered. So much for needing courage.

For three days, I kept calling, losing count of the number of times I tried and no one answered. No answering machine, no recorded message, nothing. So when

I stood in my empty house with my suitcases by my side, it took almost no thought at all to dial his number one last time. It's not as if anyone would answer.

One trill. Two. On five, I'd hang up and give up.

"Hello?" a female voice demanded.

Or not.

"Chris?" I replied, crossing my fingers.

"Yeah. Who's this?" If anything, her voice sounded suspicious. Well, that wasn't surprising. The people who'd kidnapped me had threatened to hurt her, too. She was probably as paranoid about strangers as I was.

I took a deep breath. "My name is Caitlin. Is your brother home?"

"No, he's not."

"Can you ask Nathan to call me, then, please? My number is —"

"No. I won't."

Silence. What do you say to that?

"Then can you tell me when he will be home, so I can call again later?" I tried.

"No. I don't know when he'll be home and he won't talk to you when he is. He won't even remember your name, Katie. He never does. Once he's fucked a girl, he's got what he wanted from you and he'll forget your name because he doesn't care. And no, you're not different. All girls are the same to him. He only wanted you for one thing. Deal with it, Katie, and if you don't like it, don't fuck guys you don't know."

I forced myself to stay calm. Nathan had evidently gone back to his sleazy ways once I was out of the picture and it wasn't any of my business who he slept with. James Bond, indeed. "My name isn't Katie and I'd like to discuss financial matters with Nathan. It's kind of urgent."

"If you're pregnant, take it to the Family Court. And make sure you get a paternity test. Nathan may forget your name, but he never forgets contraception. He wouldn't get some slut like you pregnant, so go back to your low-life boyfriend and tell him to pay for his own problems. You won't get a cent out of my brother for your bastard kid."

I couldn't seem to close my mouth. Who said things like that to someone they didn't know? And with such viciousness in her tone, like she really hated me when she had no idea who I was?

Numbly, I tried to respond, but she took another breath and let rip with more vitriol than I thought one person could contain. She inferred that I had sexually transmissible diseases; called me a slut, a slag, a hoe and a skank; suggested that my mother was all of these things and my father was a paedophile with a penchant for incest. Then she started on her hopes for my imaginary child.

With shaking fingers, I terminated the call. It had lasted just under six minutes and I don't think even the bitch who'd tried to kill me had insulted me quite so much.

I remembered the fierce girl who'd wanted to protect me and her brother when I met her five years ago and tried to match her to the foul-mouthed harpy who'd spewed obscenities into my burning ear. What had happened to her in the intervening five years to turn her so bitter? Had some of my tormentors survived after all, only to target her?

A thought niggled through my shock. Nathan still lived with his sister. Did that mean she'd had to deal with his increasing post traumatic stress disorder for the last five years as he struggled to do a job that only made his mental state deteriorate?

If I wanted answers, a phone call was worse than useless. I'd need to show up in person and hope Nathan was home. Because whatever his sister said, I knew he'd never forget me, even if he wanted to. But first I had a concert to attend in Sydney. And I intended to have a blast.

TEN

"All passengers travelling on the Qantas flight to Perth, please proceed to Gate 21 for boarding."

The voice over the speakers jolted me out of my doze. The concert had been so brilliant I could barely sleep last night, and now I was paying for it, but I'm sure part of it was my excitement at finally going home.

Of course, I'd think of Nathan, given the phone call to his sister still preyed on my mind. Slut, hoe, whore…I should've told her that I'd never slept with her brother. Though I would have if we'd been together longer. I wondered if he'd changed much in the intervening time. It had been five years since I'd last seen him, after all. But if he was still pulling girls for one-night stands and his sister was fielding his calls, I suspected his body was still as chiselled as I remembered it. Who knew? Maybe more, given his tactical training and all. As for the mind within that buff body, I vacillated between the troubled, traumatised man I'd known and the well-adjusted, highly trained operative he'd probably become. Surely that training included how to deal with death, killing and witnessing all manner of horrible things. He could probably teach me a thing or two about coping with my fear of physical intimacy with anyone. Maybe he'd be willing to do that naked…

I shook my head in an attempt to dislodge the explicit thoughts and stared at the clouds massing in the skies over the tarmac. It was definitely autumn, with a storm brewing to remind us that winter wasn't far away. From Melbourne's mad weather to Sydney storms, I'd had enough of the east coast's weird weather. What would it be like not to have four seasons in the same day, like I'd had in Melbourne? Or storms that wreaked havoc on the whole city, like they did here in Sydney? Perth had always seemed to have the best weather.

How would Perth have changed in five years?

I tried not to think how much I'd changed in that time, but I knew I had. Would I want to be back home, despite the differences? Or would I be better off doing my internship on the east coast? I could have chosen somewhere on the Gold Coast, near the beach. Except they got cyclones and floods and…no.

I sat in my assigned window seat and buckled the seatbelt. It was time to go home.

ELEVEN

"Miss? Everything is unpacked and put away as requested. Including the computer set up in the study. We're a full service removalist and if there's anything else we can do —" he presented me with a business card "— don't hesitate to call us for anything."

I surveyed my immaculate apartment, profoundly glad that I'd hired someone else to turn it into something that resembled a home. After Jo and I had done all the interminable packing, I was thoroughly sick of the whole moving process, so I'd called them to ask for the extra service. After all, I could afford it, even without the huge government payout. That reminded me — I still hadn't signed the paperwork. I needed to try contacting Nathan again. But he could wait until tomorrow.

Right now, I wanted coffee. Time zones messing with me — it was daylight here in Perth, but it'd be dark and dinnertime in Sydney and Melbourne. A little bit of caffeine should help me stay awake for a few more hours. I plodded to the kitchen and was delighted to find the kettle plugged in and on the bench, waiting for me. I filled it with water from the tap and clicked it on before searching for the rest of what I needed for my caffeine hit. Mugs were in the cupboard over the kettle and there was a fresh carton of milk in the fridge – a nice touch, I thought as I mentally thanked my conscientious removalists – but there didn't seem to be any coffee. Not even a sachet of two-years-past-the-use-by-date decaf in my brand new kitchen. I turned the kettle off mid-boil and headed for the study to check when my online grocery order was due to be delivered. And to make sure I'd ordered coffee.

My computer seemed unusually slow today, as I scrolled through the pile of junk mail that'd accumulated while I ignored my email in Sydney. Buy this, ON SALE, check out our new…all got deleted. Something odd had managed to dodge my spam filter, I noticed, my cursor hovering over the one from DoctorLove1986 at a generic email address. The subject line was my misspelled name.

Oh, this should be good, I thought, figuring I'd open it. Would it be a Nigerian prince professing his undying love, an expert physician telling me I needed a penis enlargement or just some dating site desperate for more people to join their paid service?

When I read the first line, my jaw dropped.

TWELVE

I'd never have done it if it weren't for you. I wanted you back. I wanted answers. And I wanted vengeance.

She'd slipped me a business card saying she could give me what I wanted. She said she knew who'd hurt you and she could help me.

I couldn't help it. I called her, wanting it to be true and she told me. . . she said she could help me get close enough to take a knife and carve my name into their skin, just as they'd done to you. God help me, it was like she was offering me everything I wanted, because the thought of killing your kidnappers and carving them up, the visceral, primitive pleasure of exacting my revenge with nothing but a knife in my hand. . . shit, you did the cadaver labs with me. You know I'm good with a scalpel when I'm not distracted by the female med students.

She said she didn't want to say much over the phone, so could we meet somewhere in person? She named a bar and a time and I was happy to agree. I didn't care if they found me - I wanted them to.

I was so stupid.

I texted my boss, telling him I'd made contact and was going to try and find out more from the girl. No reply.

I went. I ordered a beer and waited. I didn't even know what she looked like, so when this stunning little brunette came up to me and full-on kissed me, I was surprised. Hey, you know me, though - I ran with it, even when she grabbed my arse. She didn't taste of alcohol, either - mint, maybe, like she'd just brushed her teeth or had one of those super-strong breath mints. Funny the things you remember.

She introduced herself as Laura, the woman I was waiting for, and she offered to buy me a drink. So I gulped down the rest of my beer - and it tasted a bit like soap, like the detergent hadn't been washed out of the glass properly. I didn't think anything of it at the time, and the beer she brought back tasted fine, so we got to talking.

She didn't say much, for all she wanted to talk. She asked me all sorts of personal questions - what kind of women I liked and what I was like in bed. Hey, she's not the first woman to come on to me in a bar and I found it kind of hot. Okay, very hot. She was hot.

You're not even here and I can feel you glaring at me. I get turned on by dominant women, okay? Or I used to. And ones who are confident about showing their bodies, and she was. . . well, hot.

I got sick of talking about me, so I pushed

her about you. Asked her what she knew and whether she could really tell me who did it. Who hurt you.

She said yes, she did know and she could lead me to them. For a price.

I'd have sold my soul for you, I swear, so everything I owned wasn't too high a price. I would've paid it.

But when she reached under the table and grabbed my dick through my pants, she gave me the shock of my life. She said all she wanted was a night with me. All night. . . doing whatever she wanted. Shit, the way her fingers knew what they were doing, I wasn't going to refuse. It was cheap to me - one hot night for all my vengeful dreams to come true.

I finished up my drink, grabbed her hand and took her to my car. You know, I think the dregs of the second beer tasted like soap, too, now I think about it. Anyway, at the car, I asked her where to, but she just kept looking at the car like she was impressed. And then she lifted that tight little dress over her head, opened the back door and stood there in nothing but her high heels and told me to lie down on the back seat of my car. The chick didn't have any underwear - so hot.

As soon as I was down, she didn't waste any time. She climbed into the car, shut the door behind her and sat on my face. She started giving orders, but I didn't pay much attention. When a naked girl sits on your face, it's pretty self-explanatory when you know what you're doing.

I know, I know. You don't want to hear this. You never did.

But it's the last thing I remember. This girl's pussy in my face and then. . . nothing.

I mean, it was dark in the car and all, but not dark enough for me not to notice whether I was conscious or not.

I woke up with my head against something hard and it wasn't dark anymore. My mouth tasted like I'd been licking a furry cat, not some girl who'd had every hair waxed off, and my head was pounding.

And then some nasty bloke said, "Good morning, sunshine." Real close.

Fuck, that did it. I woke up fast. Passing out while giving a girl head was bad enough, but with some bloke around? I like my virginal arse just like it is, thanks. There. I bet you're surprised at that. I bet you thought I'd do anything in bed, but my arse is sacred. I have standards, you know.

Anyway, the sunshine bloke. My eyes snapped open and I was sitting in the back seat of my own car, my head up against the window as we drove down the freeway. I still had my clothes on – even my wallet and phone in my back pocket.

But I had a hangover from hell after just two beers. That meant someone must have spiked my drink, I figured. No way I would've passed out with no memory without drugs. I remember there are all sorts of drugs you can slip into a drink and some of them are damn near undetectable – just a slight difference in taste or colour, but in a pint of beer with a pair of perfect tits in front of me, and I wasn't going to notice much else.

"Oi, sunshine. The lady says you don't even give good head. Passed out before she was finished with you. What kind of man can't please his woman?"

I glared at the guy but even that made my

head hurt and I had to close my eyes. The headache was blinding. Whatever drugs they used on me, I hope they're banned.

"Are you sure you didn't get the sister instead?" He sniggered. "What was her name? Alanna?"

"Alanna's the dead one," the woman said. Laura. She was the one driving. "If you mean the one who's still alive, his little sister, that's Chris. No, this one has a dick. Bit small, but I still found it."

"I wanted the little sister. What am I supposed to do with a bloke? I like women," the bloke whined.

"No!" My shout hurt my ears, but I didn't care. "Leave my sister alone!"

"Aww, that's not what she said. She begged for it. Never had a decent cock before and she'll never have better now. I don't bang dead girls."

God, I was slow. Maybe it was the drugs making me stupid. She'd promised to bring me to the man who killed you and she had. Was this the prick who did it? I wish I could've asked you.

I wanted to kill him there and then, but I needed to know for sure. "Did you kill my sister?"

"Nope," he drawled. "Helped dump her body on the beach, though." He lit a cigarette, sucked on it and blew a cloud of smoke out the window. "Is your little sister as much fun to fuck as the other one? I mean, you fucked 'em both, right?"

I leaped forward to punch his lights out, but it was like I'd been tied to the seat - I went nowhere. I glanced down and realised it was a seatbelt. I fumbled for the button to release it. It didn't matter if he could lead me to the others - I wanted to kill him here and now.

"If you do what you're told, there's no need for anyone else to get hurt. Right, Nathan? If you cooperate, your little sister will be safe." Laura glanced in the rear view mirror and her eyes met mine for a moment before hers were back on the road. It was like a warning - she'd keep up her end of the deal if I kept up mine. And Chris would be safe.

I nodded.

The bloke sniggered again and said he was going to call me Chris anyway, just in case.

She told him to be quiet, and parked the car. We were on the Terrace, in front of a tiny old church surrounded by high rises. She said something about picking up a friend, but I wasn't listening. I was trying to work out whether to get out of the car and run or whether I should stick around to do what I was here for. I reached for the door handle, hoping they didn't see me, and clicked the lever to open it, but the bloody door wouldn't open. I yanked on it again, not caring if they saw or heard, but the door still wouldn't open. I was child-locked into the back seat of my own car. At least I had my phone. I could call someone.

I whipped it out and noticed my boss had messaged me last night while I was still unconscious, probably. He told me to stay with the contact, to cooperate and use condoms, like he'd expected me to sleep with her. I let go of the door. That left vengeance as the only item on the table. No backing down now.

"Who's the best looking woman here?" the bloke said suddenly. He pointed with his cigarette, out his open window. "I say that

one's an eight, maybe eight and a half out of
ten."

I glanced at the tall blonde he must have
been looking at. She was an eight, but not my
type.

"C'mon, pick one!" he growled and he clicked
the safety off my gun as he pointed it at me.
My weapon, the one that was normally locked in
the glove box.

I glanced around and pointed at an Asian
girl in a miniskirt. "That one's a nine."

He responded, but I didn't hear the words.
I'd found the perfect ten and she was crossing
the road toward us.

I could see hundreds of commuters and people
handing out flyers, him and his smoke curling
out the window, and then nothing but her. She
pushed her sunglasses back onto her face, but
her eyes had seemed to stare right back at me,
as if she could see me through the tinted
windows. Huge, dark, soulful eyes that I wanted
to swim in. She was little, but not a kid. I
can't say how I knew. It was just the way she
carried herself. The way she walked, moved, her
expression. . . I mean, she was wearing a t-
shirt and jeans. She could've been a teenager,
and I found out later that she was, seventeen
going on eighteen, but she didn't act it. She
walked across the street like she owned it.
Like it was her own personal dance floor.

I heard the car door open and didn't care. I
just wanted to watch her as she rounded the car
to the footpath beside it. And she stopped.
Someone opened the door on the other side from
me and I saw her lean in. My heart leaped when
I wondered if she wanted to speak to me. And
why.

I was face to face with her and she smiled.

My heart stopped and I think my brain did, too. Miss Ten-Out-of-Ten beaming at me like I was her hero, before it all went wrong.

She hit her. Laura hit her and the smile was gone when Miss Ten landed in my lap. Her sunglasses were gone and those huge eyes begged me for help. I grabbed the door handle - the useless, child-locked door handle - and yanked, but I couldn't get out. I was trapped in the back of my own car with her and I heard Laura gunning the engine, pulling my car out into traffic. Leaving just a sparking cigarette butt behind as we drove off.

The girl was gasping for breath, not screaming, but the windows closed before she tried to. And when she did, it wasn't with raw panic like she was scared. Shit, she screamed insults and orders. She was furious and in my lap. You would have laughed at me. I was terrified of this girl half my size.

And then she gave me hope. Instead of diving for me, she attacked the bloke in the passenger seat. I wanted to tell her to get the gun, but he moved too fast. He hit her.

You know I've never seen a woman punched before? Oh, I've seen them in the ED at the hospital, after domestic violence and stuff, so I know it happens, but I've never seen a bloke cowardly enough to hit a woman. And he just didn't care. Punched her right in the face and she landed back on me.

I could feel her shaking. She was hurting and terrified and she didn't even whimper. Nope, no tears either. It was like this tiny girl was steel all the way through. She was perfect and I was in love.

And then the big bloke shoved a rag over her face and tried to smother her with it. He was twisted right round in his seat, pushing her down against me as he knocked her out with chloroform, the way we did rats in the labs at uni. I tried to push him away from her, to help her, but his words stopped me dead.

"It's her or your sister. Your choice," the bloke told me.

I didn't know her. I didn't know what she'd done, or not done, and I couldn't handle losing Chris, too. Not after losing you. And there was my lifeline, Laura, the woman who'd promised me vengeance. Surely she'd help her, just like she was helping me.

Then it was too late. She stopped fighting and went limp. He held the sweet-smelling rag over her face for another minute, just in case, but she wasn't moving. Down rolled the window and he lit another cigarette, the smoke streaming away as we headed down the freeway again.

I'm not entirely a bastard, I swear. I didn't trust Laura completely, so I grabbed my phone and texted my boss again. I couldn't just cooperate with kidnapping. I told him what had happened and asked for help. Backup to help me save this girl.

He sent me the same orders back. Told me to cooperate with them until he contacted me.

And I did. It was all my fault. I know now that she was the one who drugged me and trusting her was a mistake from the beginning. Shit, trusting anyone in this mess was a mistake. And that poor girl, the perfect ten, will hate me for the rest of her life because I didn't save her from them.

It's my fault they chose her. My perfect ten was enough to condemn her to torture and rape and almost death because they made me pick their victim. And I picked her.

I wanted to be her hero - everything she wanted. Instead, I was the villain's sidekick, not even important enough for her to know my real name.

Can you ever forgive me for being so stupid?

THIRTEEN

There was no signature at the bottom, but I knew it was from Nathan. How'd he get my email address and why was he suddenly sending me his traumatic memories?

I checked it again. No, he hadn't sent it to me at all. He'd sent it to an email address I didn't recognise. What the hell? And there was a whole series of them, dating back over the last few weeks — all of them unopened, with the same subject line.

I lowered the lid and it wasn't silver like mine — this one was pink. This wasn't my laptop. But I did recognise it. This had belonged to Nathan's sister, Alanna. He'd written the email to her, and in the last few days, too. But Alanna was dead — or that's what I'd thought. Had she been hidden in witness protection, too? If she had, then she'd surely responded to this email or one of the ones before it. Or was someone else using her account now?

I scanned the list of sent ones and figured the top one was as good a place to start as any, even if it had been sent six years ago. Well, the email subject was:

```
Nathan is a whore
```

I couldn't resist. I opened it to read the rest.

```
Do you think Nathan will ever manage to
stick with a girl for more than a night? I'm
seriously starting to worry about him. At the
rate he's going, he'll sleep through the entire
med student body before he graduates. I hope he
doesn't get anyone pregnant.
    I've tried talking to him, but he just
laughs and says I'm his idea of the perfect
woman, but twincest is just gross, so until he
finds my double, he'll have as much fun as
possible.
    Careers day today. Nathan was supposed to
help out with handing out flyers and stuff, but
he never turned up. I gave a presentation to
all the high school students about how great it
is to study to be a doctor, but I wondered if
most of them knew just how much hard work would
be involved. Some of them looked like they were
in it for the money or because their parents
told them they had to.
    There was this one girl, though. . . she
looked about twelve years old until she opened
her mouth. It turned out she was only a few
months shy of graduating high school and she
had her heart set on medicine. Something about
her intensity and the way she spoke. . . it
reminded me of me, before I started studying.
Kind of starry eyed and all, but like she had
the steel to keep going even when things seemed
```

impossible. She had this one line. . . about how she could save someone's life and that would make all the years of study worth it. I wish I could have summed things up so well - actually, I used the line in my presentation. It just sounded so good. . .

As I watched her in the audience, I wondered what would happen if Nathan actually turned up for once and saw her. Or if he met her at uni. She looked like exactly the type of girl he goes for - hell, the opposite of me in looks as she was small and dark. And she had these huge eyes that just kind of drew me in. Really pretty, too.

Wishful thinking, I guess. Wishing that Nathan would treat women as more than an evening's entertainment. What'll happen when he meets a girl with the guts to tell him to go to hell instead of giving in to him?

I swear he's scratched his car again. There's red paint on the letter box, like he scraped it along the side. If you. . .

I jabbed at the mouse to close the email. I didn't need to scroll down to the signature to know this email was written by his sister Alanna. I could see her face, beaming at me beside Nathan's as they stood on a Rottnest boat on the computer's desktop background. I stared at the happy picture of her with Nathan, my heart twisting and breaking at the thought of what had happened to her, then to him. Tears blurred my vision as I changed the computer settings to take the heartrending picture of happiness away, leaving only the blue default background.

The funny part was that I remembered that day at uni. How could I forget the day I met her?

FOURTEEN

My friends had gone to lots of different sessions and looked at everything. They didn't think they had much chance of getting into medicine and the presentation was at the same time as one in Fine Arts that included a live demonstration they all wanted to see, so in the end I'd been the only one to go to the session on studying to be a doctor. I knew this was what I wanted and in a matter of months I would start medical school, or an acceptable pre-med alternative until I applied for graduate medicine.

I felt self-conscious as I walked into the empty lecture theatre, smoothing my wool school uniform skirt over my stockings and wishing I could wear something warmer in winter. It was dark in there, with most of the light coming through the open doorway at the bottom, near the projector screens at the front. I walked down the stairs slowly, trying to decide where I should sit.

I chose a seat three rows from the front, right in the middle. I sank into it, dropping the obligatory showbag full of brochures and cheap plastic pens covered in logos onto the floor beside me. I settled down to wait the remaining time before this presentation was due to start.

Almost as soon as I sat down, a tall, fair girl came in through the bottom door. She headed to the lectern and flicked a sequence of switches, bringing the projector screens to life. She watched them nervously, glancing at her watch and then returning her gaze to the screens, her back to me.

She pulled up the presentation, called, "Why Study Medicine With Me?" before she turned around. She looked up, closed her eyes, and started to speak.

She delivered the entire presentation very quickly, moving the slides in perfect sequence, all with her eyes closed.

I wondered why she would start so early and run through it so quickly, especially when I was the only prospective student in the audience, but I was too shy and uncertain to say anything.

When she finished, she returned to the first slide and took a deep breath, her eyes on the screen.

Next, she walked deliberately over to the bank of light switches by the door and flicked them all on. The dim lecture theatre blazed with light that made me blink at the sudden change.

Her chin held high, her back very straight, she marched back to the lectern and took another deep breath, this time facing the empty lecture theatre. As she started to exhale, her eyes met mine and her breath left her in a sudden rush.

"Oh hell," she blurted out. "How long have you been sitting there?"

I didn't know what to say. "Not very long," I squeaked out.

Despite my vague reply, she seemed to grasp the situation better than I had. Her expression cycled from surprise to embarrassment to hilarity before I even understood what was funny.

Laughing, she responded, "Well, I doubt you'll sit through my presentation again, when you just got the nervous version in five minutes instead of the slow version in twenty!"

She stepped onto the first row of seats. In two strides, she stood in the row below me, her eyes level with mine.

"I'm Alanna Miller, a final year student." She smiled, holding her hand out to shake mine.

I remembered my manners and shook her hand, telling her, "I'm Caitlin." I didn't know what else to say.

She tilted her head slightly to one side, her smile shrewd now. "So, why are you here a full fifteen minutes before you need to be?"

"I want to study medicine." The words were out of my mouth before I'd realised I was going to share any personal information with this friendly stranger.

"Not everyone gets in and even then, not everyone finishes. You have to get top results in Year Twelve. Then you have to keep working really hard all the way through the course and after it. It takes a long time and it's a hell of a commitment." She looked wistful. "If you fail a single unit, you have to retake the entire year of units, so it takes even longer. Why would you volunteer for that?"

Most of this wasn't news to me, but I was surprised by her honesty. Wasn't she supposed to be advertising the course? She looked like she was laughing inside while her expression was serious.

I took a deep breath before trying to voice the words I'd told myself countless times, but never spoken aloud. "One day I could save someone's life and that will make it all worth it."

She laughed again, nodding knowingly. "You sound like me, before I started. I bet I'll see you at all the med school parties next year."

Having been unusually open, I felt brave enough to ask her a personal question. "But if you're in your final year, won't you be an intern next year? Why would you go to parties with the students after you finish?"

She bit her lip briefly before she spoke. "My brother had to repeat a year, so he'll drag me to all of them. He says he has a better chance of picking up if girls know he has his sister with him." She looked me up and down, as if trying to guess my dress size. "You're really pretty. He's definitely going to be interested in you."

Wonderful. There were himbos at med school, too. But this one would be at least five years older than me, so he probably wouldn't bother with me. "What advice can you give me about him?"

"Tell him to take a hike or you'll kill him if he so much as touches you!" She lowered her voice considerably. "My brother is the king of the one-night stand and his reputation precedes him. I can't imagine why most girls bother with him unless that one night is really amazing. I've seen him on the pull – he's the most charming man you could meet, talking some girl into coming home with him, but by the next morning she's gone and he's forgotten her name. The day he drives a girl home or even makes breakfast for her, I think I'd die of shock."

I shrugged. He didn't sound like anyone I'd bother with. "What's his name and what does he look like?"

"He's my twin, so he's a bit taller than me, but his hair's the same colour." She looked mischievous. "I'll introduce you to him at the first party I see you at next year. I want to see Nathan's face when he meets you!" She gave me one last conspiratorial grin as she took a flying leap over the bottom row of seats to the front of the lecture theatre.

She turned to face the half-full lecture theatre with a professional smile and proceeded to tell everyone else why they'd want to study medicine with her.

And at the time, I'd listened, spellbound, without a second thought for her charming brother.

FIFTEEN

An irritating buzz dragged me out of my memories. I rose and found the intercom unit. "Yes?" I asked tersely.

"My name is Craig and I have a Woolworths Online delivery for Miss –"

"Yes, that's me. I'll open the gate for you. Mine's the one up the top at the north end."

"Uh, which way's north?"

I sighed. It wasn't his fault he didn't know – I wouldn't know either if it hadn't been a selling point of the apartment. "Can you see the one on the top floor with the door open and an arm waving out of it?"

"No…oh, wait, yeah, I can."

"That's me. I hope you have a trolley that can handle three flights of stairs, because your service said door to door delivery."

"Yes, miss, it can. It's in the special instructions for this order. I'll be right up with your groceries."

Thank God for online food shopping. If only it'd been available when I first reached home from hospital all those years ago – but if it had, I might never have left the house once I got home. I might still be a prisoner in my own home, terrified to go out and seize the life the world had waiting for me.

"Miss? I'm going to need to see some ID. There's alcohol in this order and I can't deliver it unless I know you're over eighteen."

I laughed and dug out my freshly-minted WA driver's licence – complete with my new title.

"Doctor? You look too young to be a doctor." He squinted at me as if he thought it might help to make me look older.

"That's what my patients say, too. I'll take that as a compliment because I feel about twice my age after the day I've had. I hope there's lime and soda in there to go with the vodka." I peered into the nearest crate, but it only contained boxes, no bottles.

He checked the printout in his hand. "Yes, lime cordial and sparkling water. Everything just as you ordered, doctor." He nodded at the darkness behind me. "Where do you want this?"

I pointed. "The kitchen bench, please."

The immaculate marble countertop soon vanished under an avalanche of plastic bags and Craig stacked the empty crates with a loud crack before bumping the trolley down the stairs.

I closed and locked the door behind him, then proceeded to put my purchases away. Maybe cooking dinner would take my mind off the haunting memories of the Millers.

Or maybe it would just make me want to delve deeper into the past of Alanna's life and Nathan's nightmares.

SIXTEEN

After dinner, I gave in and read another one of Nathan's emails to his sister, tears dripping down my face as I knew for certain that Nathan needed help.

Sometimes I dream about the day I kidnapped Caitlin. It always starts in the car, with her unconscious weight on me. Sometimes I can smell the chloroform and I've lost count of the number of times I had to watch him dose her with it, pinning her against me as she struggled.

I've tried talking to her and apologising for what I knew would happen, but the drugged girl never acknowledges me. Maybe because she never did in reality.

They made me pat her down and check her for weapons. She didn't even react when I slipped my hand into her pocket, she was that deeply asleep. I'd gone through her handbag when they weren't looking, admiring the triumphant look on her driver's licence photograph. She must have passed her driving test on her first attempt, I remember thinking. Caitlin Alana Lockyer.

I'd been wrong – they were watching me. He grabbed the wallet and licence from me and tossed it out of the window, where it bounced into the bushes by the side of the highway. He demanded her phone, too, which I handed over to watch it fly over the bonnet of the car to the road. If we didn't smash it, one of the cars behind us probably did. Her bag had other stuff in it and I recognised the Swiss Card. Alanna had owned something similar. I managed to sneak it out of her bag before he took that from me, too, not knowing about the package of blades and tools hidden beneath Caitlin's comatose cheek. I slipped it into my pocket, figuring it might come in handy. I never thought she'd try to stab me with it.

The clearest part is when the car stops. He tries to take her off me, but he can't, so he tells me to bring her. It's always the seatbelt holding her in the car, not me, as it was then, but I know I have to stay with her. I won't hurt her.

I click the seatbelts free of both of us and lift her out of the car. Then, it was the weirdest feeling, having a sleeping woman in my arms. Now, it's comforting, because of how many times I carried her. Bush surrounded us, low scrub and the smell of salt on the breeze. It's funny what you remember. I hadn't paid much attention to where we were going, but I remember the smell and the twisted trees. I followed him down an overgrown track, deeper into the scrub, until he rounded a corner and disappeared.

The black hole just yawned in front of me — concrete steps leading down into the dark. He shouted at me to hurry up with the girl and I did, ducking my head even though I didn't need to. Sometimes, just that ominous darkness swallowing us is enough to wake me up, because the moment I carried her into that bunker, it was over. Any hope I had was ripped away.

But sometimes I can't wake up from the nightmare and I fall deeper, my hesitant steps carrying her into her prison, where she'll know torture and terror and eventually dance with death. My fault.

The rope burns my hands as I bind her legs, then her arms with it while faint light trickles through the horizontal slit of a window. Wide enough to slip a letter through but not wider than my hand. And too high up to reach. I get up to leave and tell him I've done as he ordered and tied the poor girl up, but the open doorway isn't open any more. It's blocked by a heavy fire door, and there's no handle on this side. Just a metal plate riveted in place. I bang on the door for a bit and shout, but I get no answer, so I figure I'm as much a prisoner as she is.

After a while, there's a shower of sand from the window and a laughing voice tells me he's lost the key and he'll let me out when he finds it. In the meantime, why don't I break the girl in while I'm waiting?

I was stupid enough to ask what he meant. His response is crude and graphic and I hope to God she never heard it. I remember kicking the rocks around, clearing the floor so there was space for us both to lie down, though I wasn't going to do what he said. I just wanted to sleep off my hangover.

I stuck that Swiss Card in her pocket, figuring if they tied me up, too, then at least it'd be easier to get to that way. I never thought she'd be the one using it.

Then the window light started to fade as rocks and bricks were shoved into the gap until all I saw was black and we were buried alive, in a bloody dark bunker in the middle of nowhere. That's usually when I wake up, my heart racing as I gasp for breath. And take sleeping pills, because there's no way I'll sleep again after that.

But some nights, it's not enough. Sometimes, that dream morphs into the night I found her, bleeding out on the floor and I can't get her out because the door's locked. Those are the nights I wake up shouting. And the nights when no matter how many pills I take, sleep avoids me. Like tonight. But I'll try just a couple more and hope it'll be enough.

SEVENTEEN

After working from dawn 'til dusk all week, I was ready to go home to bed, but I couldn't miss the doctors' sundowner, where all us shiny-faced interns got to meet the cynical senior doctors we'd be working with for the next year. Having done most of my course on the other side of the country, I'd expected to know no one, but I'd already spotted two familiar faces. If only they hadn't known me as a patient…I crossed my fingers that they wouldn't remember me. Surely they'd both had plenty of patients in the last five years who were far more memorable than I was.

"Now this is a lovely surprise." The Irish burr almost made me choke on my wine, but I recovered and managed to smile as I turned to face the doctor who'd supervised my first year prac. And been my doctor after Nathan dragged my dying body into hospital.

"It's been a long time, Dr Lannon," I replied, taking another sip so I wouldn't have to say anything else.

"That it has. You're the first year who stole my parking spot, aren't you?" Dr Lannon grinned at my look of horror. "I'm the Director of Emergency Medicine now, and no one else has ever dared to do it. I'm sorry, but I've forgotten your name, and staring intently at the name badge on your chest will probably get me accused of sexual harassment. Can you remind me instead?"

I laughed. My identity was still secret – he'd only know my new name. I unpinned the badge and raised it to his eye level, suddenly feeling very short compared to the tall, Irish doctor. Aside from some additional lines around his eyes, he didn't seem to have changed a bit. "You can tell your wife you were a perfect gentleman. How is Althea?" His wife had been my physiotherapist – the woman who'd managed to help me walk again. I owed both of them a lot for my recovery.

A shadow seemed to pass across his expression, but he hitched his smile back up as if it had never happened. "Oh, fine, fine."

No, something wasn't fine, but I didn't want to pry. The last thing I wanted to do was get one of the senior doctors offside – and the director of the area I wanted to specialise in, no less. Who'd have guessed that all the trauma I'd been through would make me choose emergency medicine as a career path? Not me five years ago, that's for sure. I held up my empty wineglass and used my need for another drink as an excuse to walk away.

"Ohhh, you managed to get tickets? How? I heard they sold out in like the first day and they aren't doing extra shows. They're going for like five hundred dollars on eBay now…"

"My sister works in the ticket office in the city. I gave her the money and she bought them for me. I've never heard Chaya play live – they never come to Perth. I heard the concert at the Sydney Opera House last week was awesome. I hope the Perth one's as good."

"I can't afford either of them. My uni books this semester cost over six hundred dollars. Maybe if I'm lucky I'll get the Blu-ray for Christmas…or it'll be on TV when the tour's over. Besides, I'll probably be working that night. I need to do extra shifts to pay for my uni books."

One of the catering staff broke off her conversation to ask, "What can I get you?"

I set my wineglass down. "Do you have anything without alcohol? My body thinks I'm still on Sydney time and if I drink any more, I'm scared I'll fall asleep."

The girl grinned and poured me a soft drink. "You're the only doctor here who isn't drinking, then. Even Dr Lannon's getting into the whisky tonight and he never drinks."

I glanced at the doctor, only now noticing the drink in his hand. Even as I watched, he set the empty glass on a table and left the room. His smile had definitely vanished. Please, don't let me be the one who said something that pissed him off, I prayed. Could this evening get any worse?

"I heard you'd dropped out," a female voice said.

I whirled, hoping they weren't talking to me. This time, I faced the dark-haired doctor I didn't want to speak to. "Me?"

She nodded and peered at my name badge, then seemed

crestfallen. "Oh. I thought you were someone else. A patient."

I managed a smile. "A patient who was a med student, but dropped out before she finished? Nope, definitely not me. As you can see, I've finished my degree and I got a job here, too. What did the patient do to make you remember her?" Maybe if she told me, I'd know whether or not to avoid her.

She shrugged. "Oh, it was a really nasty case. Sexual assault, but she refused to admit it was rape. She wouldn't take counselling past the first session, either. I was an intern like you then, so no one listened to me, but I remembered it because when she was discharged, I felt like there was more we should have done. Like I failed her, because she wasn't right in the head when she left."

Memories clicked and I tried not to wince. She'd delivered a blistering lecture on how I wouldn't recover until I came to terms with my mental condition. At the time, my mind had been full of thoughts of vengeance, not my mental wellbeing as I had no idea whether I'd survive long enough to need sanity. I was glad for the dim lighting in the room – with the normal bright hospital lights, she'd spot the faint scars on my wrists. I resolved to wear long sleeves if I was working in the same ward as she was.

I made small talk with her for a few more minutes until I could politely leave. I'd had enough of this party and I'd promised to meet Dad for dinner at his place.

As I approached my car, I scanned the parking lot almost automatically. It had become a habit. The security guard stood beside the ticket machine for the visitor parking, his radio hissing on his hip as he peered at the perpetually broken machine. If I broke into the Porsche beside my modest car, he wouldn't hear the window smash. Movement to my right caught my eye – in the shadows I could just make out the shape of a man standing behind the fire hydrant.

That's the fifth time this week, I thought uneasily. Why was this man lurking in the shadows of a hospital parking lot every night? Maybe I should speak to security about him.

The jingle of metal hitting the ground dragged my attention back to the security guard as he started swearing loudly. The ticket machine continued to spew coins at his feet. He wouldn't notice if an intern was attacked by a strange mystery man, either, I realised, my eyes darting to the fire hydrant. But the shadowy man had vanished. I didn't hallucinate, nor believe in ghosts, which meant I hadn't imagined him. He'd been real so the risk of danger from him was real, too. And the broken ticket machine could be a coincidence, but staying safe meant assuming nothing was a coincidence.

I jerked the car door open and pulled it shut behind me, securing the locks again with the touch of a button. Frequent glances in the rear-vision mirror relieved me of the worry that anyone was following me, so I headed for the freeway and Dad's place.

Dinner with Dad couldn't be anywhere near as stressful as drinks with doctors.

EIGHTEEN

It was strange seeing Dad's furniture in a different house, all laid out and lived in, for he'd been here for five years. As long as I'd been in Melbourne – neither of us could live in his old house any more.

Despite moving from south to north of the river, he'd still chosen a restored cottage with all the walls painted in the same boring shade of beige. Without me around to tell him otherwise, he'd bought all matching beige curtains, too, so the place would've looked blank inside if it weren't for the pictures on the walls. Artwork, mostly, except for the photos. And most of those were of me. My graduation photo took pride of place over the ornately tiled fireplace, too pretty to have hosted a fire in its present state, but beside it was a picture I'd never seen before. It looked like me holding a baby and smiling, something that would never happen this side of hell freezing over.

"I told you that you look just like her." Dad stood at my side, nodding at the impossible picture.

I peered at the baby's scrunched-up face as realisation dawned. "No wonder I don't remember this photo being taken. So you saw Mum's cousin and he gave you this?"

He nodded. "A whole box of them. I'll show you later if you like. He was very disappointed that you couldn't be there, so he asked me to give you a letter and plead that you'd contact him so he could meet you. He said something about a family debt that needed to be repaid, but he'd only discuss it with you, as Fatima's daughter." He dug the letter out of a drawer and handed it to me. "Please do it. It wasn't like Dubai – he didn't have any bodyguards with him. I don't think they could get Australian visas."

No, goons for hire from Saudi Arabia probably appeared on several lists of people who weren't allowed into Australia. Thank God for that. It didn't mean he couldn't afford to hire some Australian muscle here to intimidate or even stalk people. There were plenty of perfectly legitimate security firms in Perth who provided staff for surveillance – and at a surprisingly affordable price, too, I'd found when I first looked at getting additional security for my place earlier in the week. Just getting quotes – I wasn't quite paranoid enough to feel the need for a personal bodyguard. Yet.

I fingered the sealed envelope, wondering if my mother's cousin had hired the shadowy man to keep an eye on me. And why. Maybe his letter would shed a little light on my stalker.

"I got back late from work, so I just started dinner. You don't mind if it takes another half hour before we eat, do you?"

I assured him I didn't mind as I sank into the sofa with the strange letter.

Dear Kiana

I understand that you took a different name in Australia, but this is the name my cousin Fatima gave you and the name I hold in my heart, for you are family.

And because you are family, I owe you a debt. More than one, in fact.

First, there is the matter of Fatima's dowry and your own. Her father, your grandfather, loved both of you very much and set aside a small sum of money for her, which on her death he held in trust for you. As the executor of his estate, following his death earlier this year, I believe he would wish you to have this as a small token in memory of him. Tell me how you would like the money transferred to you and I will arrange it.

Secondly, there is the matter of some property in Australia. He originally purchased it as a wedding gift for Fatima and her new husband, but as she never reached Australia, the gift never changed hands. Instead, it was leased and the rent held in trust for you. I have enclosed a copy of the deed for this property and the relevant forms to change the name of the owner to whatever name you are known by now. You can forward the signed papers to the conveyancer whose details appear on the documents and they'll make the necessary arrangements. If you wish to inspect the property before taking possession of it, I have included the name of the property manager who arranged and terminated the last lease. The property is presently unoccupied. Contact her and she will provide the keys to the house.

Thirdly, there are the tragic circumstances surrounding your mother's death. I offer you my belated condolences on the loss of your mother and I beg to be allowed to convey these to you in person.

The remainder of the letter was a list of his contact details in several different countries, as well as his name.

Mohsen Rezaei

I shrugged. I didn't recognise his name, so I took a closer look at the other papers in the letter. A business card for a Perth conveyancing company was stapled to an official-looking form, which I set aside, and the deed to a property at 100 Osprey Bay Drive, Osprey Bay. A quick check told me that it was on the coast, just past Busselton. I only thought there was a resort in Osprey Bay – no houses. Well, evidently there was one and it belonged to me.

As if I needed more property. It was probably an old, run-down place that was twenty years behind on maintenance. But if it wasn't…a beach house in Busselton would be a wonderful place for a break, when I found the time.

I decided to make arrangements for an inspection and a much-needed holiday down south. Heaven knew I needed it. And if the stalker followed me, I'd know I wasn't simply paranoid. If he tried anything, he'd soon discover that I wasn't the defenceless little girl I'd been five years ago. And I'd be armed.

NINETEEN

As the sun rose, I stumbled home from my night shift, wanting nothing but sleep. Yet when I walked in, I detoured to check my email – no, Alanna's email – to see if Nathan had written anything else. Sure enough, he had:

I remember the shouting clearest, though not the words because I tuned out. He was so furious he was spitting and every third word was fuck or fucking. He referred to a fucking knife a lot, too. It wasn't until he pulled out my gun that I started to pay attention.

I stared into that narrow muzzle and the words rang in my head.

"You're going to fuck her and I'm going to watch and if I don't like what I see, I'm going to drag your fucking sister in and show you how you fuck a feral little bitch into submission. And then I'm going to shoot you."

I said I'd do it. God help me, I said I would. I couldn't let Chris get hurt. He grabbed the collar of my shirt, stuck the gun against my neck and hustled me to the bunker.

While I stumbled along, I concocted a plan. I'd persuade him to leave us alone or at least keep quiet, and I'd seduce her. Not rape - it wouldn't be rape if she agreed to sleep with me. If that didn't work, then I'd tell her the whole sordid tale and beg. And if she still wouldn't agree, I had my sleeping pills in my pocket and I'd find a way to persuade her to take them. And then. . . and then. . . Oh God, I couldn't. I knew I couldn't do it.

I don't remember what I said, but by the time we reached the door of her prison, he'd agreed to let me go in alone. But he was right outside the door.

The moment I saw her, I knew it wouldn't work. She hated me for what I'd already done to her and she'd happily kill me herself before she'd cooperate with me, let alone sleep with me. The sleeping pills in my pocket were our only hope. I just had to get her to take them.

I told her they were headache pills. In the dim light, it wasn't like she could tell the difference. She took them and backed away from me as if she knew I wanted to hurt her. I didn't want to hurt her. I wanted to sleep with her. I wanted to spend all night giving this girl pleasure like she'd never known until those dark eyes didn't burn with hatred any more. And she'd never let me do it.

I wanted to tell her not to take the pills. I wanted to ask her to rage at me while I made love to her, because if I didn't, they'd hurt her and I couldn't stand it. I'd never hurt her. Never.

With a jerk of her hand, the pills vanished into her mouth. She tilted her head back to gulp down the bottle of water and it was too late. She glared at me as if she could read my thoughts, daring me to come closer so she could try to stab me again. Yeah, she'd tried that once. She missed, though. Pity. It might've saved her some pain if she'd killed me. And I wouldn't have had to stand there and betray her.

I watched them take effect. Her eyelids dropped slowly, as if gaining weight until they were too heavy to hold up. I'd given her my normal dose, so it should send her right to sleep. She wouldn't remember a thing – lucky.

Maybe I didn't have to, then. With him not watching, I could take her clothes off, put a condom on, jerk off and he'd never be the wiser. I'd just say I'd worn her out and that's why she was sleeping.

It felt like she fought the drugs forever before she finally toppled over sideways, sprawling on the mattress like a drunk. Right. I had to get her clothes off before he came in and then manage the fastest wank in the history of mankind. Well, at least I'd have my fantasy in front of me to think about as I beat off.

I felt around in the dark for her and found denim. She moved under my hand, but I squinted until I could see the faint outline of her body, dark against the mattress beneath her. First, the jeans.

She screamed and fought me. It was like she hadn't taken the sleeping pills at all, she just went crazy, like she was on different drugs entirely.

I heard him laugh outside and I got desperate, yanking on her clothes more roughly than I wanted to. If he walked in, I had to make it look like I'd done what he asked. That meant the jeans had to come off. In a whisper, I tried to explain it to her. That there was a man outside with a gun, ready to kill us both and my family, too, if I didn't do this.

She begged me to stop and it almost broke me. The screaming and insults I could take because I deserved them, but when she begged, I was ready to give in.

"Give me the bitch's clothes," he shouted through the door and I saw it open a crack. "I bet she wet herself in fear. Don't forget her wet undies."

I forced myself to think of patients in my practical placements for uni. She was just another unconscious girl in the ED, drunk and passed out, who I needed to get into a hospital gown to send her to x-ray to check for fractures. I added her underwear to the small pile of clothes and handed them to him without a word.

He said something about watching as he just stood there in the doorway. Oh God, faking it wouldn't work. I was going to have to do it. At least she'd be asleep so she wouldn't remember it. As I unzipped my pants, I prayed I wouldn't hurt her.

"Please," she whispered. Oh God, she wasn't asleep. No. I couldn't do it. Her fear turned me into a limp noodle with all the stiffness of a wet strand of seaweed. I couldn't.

I must have said it aloud because he threw her clothes on the ground and came striding in, unbuckling his belt. If I couldn't do it, he was going to rape her before my eyes. And it'd be my fault, because I gave her the sleeping pills that had left her helpless, before I took her clothes and the only weapon she had to defend herself.

I crumbled and told him I'd do it, but not with him watching. He laughed and mocked me, but it didn't matter as long as he left. This time, he did, but he locked the door behind him. Leaving me alone with her. I listened for the scrape of footsteps outside, to see if he was leaving or eavesdropping on us. A rock clattered across the concrete and his swearing sounded distant. Then I heard the pound of feet retreating up the steps. If he wasn't listening, I wouldn't have to.

But there was the matter of the used condoms. . . I'd wait until she was asleep before I jerked off, or I'd give her the wrong idea.

I glanced at the mattress to see if the pills had knocked her out yet and she was gone.

Oh God. Had he taken her? Had she found a way out and he'd caught her, locking me in here alone? Or was she still in here? She could hurt herself if she fell and she'd taken a heavy dose of sedatives. She'd be clumsy as a drunk in the dark and with the rubble on the floor. . .

I swept the room with my torch, trying to find her. And when I did, I froze. She had one arm across her breasts, but the other was curled into a fist and the curves silhouetted behind them. . . oh God. Ten. A perfect fucking ten. If she didn't put some clothes on, I was going to beg and we'd both die.

I struggled out of my jumper, unable to get the image of her perfect naked body out of my head, and that's when she tackled me. The torch smashed somewhere and my fingers brushed against beautiful skin before she darted away into the darkness.

I heard her body slam against the door repeatedly – the only timber in the room – until it sank in that we were locked in here together and there was no escape.

That's the real fucked-up part of it. I was ordered into that room and locked in with her so that I'd rape her, but I couldn't do it, yet I wanted to. I know I wanted to and I couldn't bring myself to touch her because she hated me. My nightmares go further. I always end up giving in and she screams and fights me until I realise I've killed her, but I'm sure I didn't. I'm sure I didn't hurt her.

I should never have given in to temptation later. Now I know what it's like to feel her body, naked against mine, writhing in the bits of bliss I managed to bring her, my traitorous mind twists the memory into my dreams. I think. Did I do it and deliberately try to forget hurting her? I couldn't hurt her. I couldn't.

But the nightmares are so real. . .

And then I take more pills to make them go away, but they always come back. I swear it can't get worse, but it's not getting better, either.

Angrily, I shut down the laptop. He'd never hurt me. He hadn't wanted to and he hadn't done it. And if he'd forgotten, then I needed to remind him. But first…I needed to get to bed before I fell asleep at the desk. Bloody night shifts.

TWENTY

Jo looked far too cheerful for this hour of the morning. In fact, everyone looked far too cheerful. When you've worked in the Emergency Department for five night shifts in a row, 10 am is officially an ungodly hour. I needed a whole pot of coffee and another one, too, or I was going to face-plant on the table and snore into next week.

"How's work at the hospital? Getting used to people calling you doctor yet?"

I tried to focus my bleary gaze on her face, but gave up. Insufficient caffeine, sleep and…something else. Mental acuity, maybe.

"I hate ED and I don't ever want to work in one again. I think I want to specialise as a doctor who deals with sleeping disorders. Or an anaesthetist." I drank deeply and clunked the cup back to the table. A mug, not a tiny teacup.

"That bad, huh?"

I nodded. "You don't know the half of it. It's the last week of the school holidays."

"Lots of kids getting sick and breaking bones? I'm not sure I could handle dealing with a child who's hurt and doesn't understand. And their panicking parents..." Jo's eyes widened in horror. "Give me numbers any day. They don't cry."

"Oh, I deal with numbers, too. Two hundred kilometres per hour – that's how fast the souped-up V8 was going when the seventeen-year-old drunken idiot driving slammed it into a traffic light, slicing his car in two. Three of his passengers were wearing seatbelts – he and one of them weren't. Only two of the passengers survived. Or a hundred and eighty – the speed a motorcyclist was doing when he came off his bike on the freeway before three cars hit him. He's in ICU and we're not sure if he'll wake up. Or two hundred and twelve stitches – that's a total, on five different people who decided to have a brawl with broken bottles in Fremantle last night. Every single one of them was underage. Or six – the number of vomit bags a fifteen-year-old girl used before I had to pump her stomach for alcohol poisoning." I sighed. "And zero, the number of hours of sleep I've had in the last twenty-four hours."

Jo patted my hand sympathetically. "It sounds awful. I shouldn't have asked to meet you for coffee, but I was dying to see you, so I didn't think. I should let you get home so you can sleep."

I shook my head. "I'm not sleeping well at home, either. I think I have a stalker. He only comes out at night, though."

She bit her lip, as if she was trying to keep the words

inside her mouth.

"Just spit it out, Jo," I said tiredly.

Jo cast her eyes down. "Well, you are back in Perth and this is where he lives, isn't it?" My blank look seemed to be enough to persuade her to explain. "The sleazy stalker who wouldn't leave you alone when you were in hospital. Nathan. Nathan something. Nathan Miller."

"He wasn't a stalker. He was there to protect me," I insisted.

She lifted her gaze, but she still didn't seem to want to meet my eyes. "I know you liked him well enough, but I thought he was creepy. I didn't feel comfortable around him. Perhaps he's stalking you again here." She held her hand up to silence my protest. "Not necessarily in a bad way. Maybe in a good way. Maybe he's keeping an eye out for you." She didn't look like she believed her own story.

Again, I shook my head. "Nathan wouldn't skulk around. He'd show himself and tell me he's trying to protect me, because he knows how I'd react if I felt I was in danger. He wouldn't want to scare me by staying in the shadows and not showing his face."

She sighed. "You haven't seen him in five years. He might have changed a lot in that time. I mean, we have. I'm now considered an enchantress with all things number-related; you're Fiona Stanley Hospital's newest miracle-working angel, sorry, doctor. Maybe he's become the creepy sleazebag he was always meant to be. Have you seen him yet?"

"What? The stalker? No, I said he hadn't showed his face. I don't know what he looks like. Just that I get the feeling I'm being watched a lot. Especially at night."

Concern filled her eyes. "No, though I think you should call Trevor and tell him about the stalker. I meant Mr Sleazy. Have you seen him yet?"

No, but after his sister called me a whore, I've been dragging my feet instead of calling him or going to his house. I pressed my lips together and shook my head.

"Are you going to?"

After reading the emails he'd been sending to his dead sister, how could I not? If only to clear up his cloudy memories and tell him he'd never hurt me. Definitely never raped me, nor had he wanted to.

"Please don't." Jo's words took me by surprise and she seemed to realise this, so she continued, "You're so much better now. Not a shadow of yourself like you were five years ago. You have enough on your plate with moving back and your new job at the hospital. You don't need him messing your life up again."

I opened my mouth to tell her it wasn't his fault my life had been messed up by meeting him, but I snapped it shut again. I couldn't say a word without incriminating Nathan and myself.

She sighed. "I can see you're exhausted. Look, we should catch up again when you're not falling asleep on your feet. Are you still okay to pick up Jason from the airport tomorrow?"

I nodded.

Jo grinned. "Thank you so much. Then I can go shopping for something new to wear to the concert. Living in Melbourne, you'd think I'd have thought of it then, but no, I had to forget until I arrived in Perth. Come join me if you can. It wouldn't hurt for you to wear something new, too."

I smiled noncommittally as we rose, hugged and I plodded home.

No matter what Jo said, I would go and see Nathan eventually. He needed to talk about his nightmares to someone and I was the only person who knew what had really happened in the dark. On my next day off, I resolved, falling face-first onto my bed. I had no intention of getting up again until I had to go back to work.

TWENTY ONE

I grabbed my bag and trotted down the ward. I'd allowed plenty of time, but I hadn't counted on my shift going overtime by more than two hours. ED had been hectic, but the general surgery ward had its own drawbacks – not to mention a spate of winter colds and flu that had kept them short-staffed all week. Now I had to make it to the car and fight peak hour traffic to get to the airport on time. I quickened my pace.

"Ooh, hang on!"

The voice was a moment too late – I slipped on the wet floor and nearly face-planted on the carpet at the end. The voice's owner thrust a sizeable hand in front of my face.

"Let me help you up, doctor."

Forcing myself not to shudder at the prospect of being touched by a stranger, albeit a very helpful one that I worked with, I managed to rise without his assistance. I summoned a smile instead. "Thank you —" I glanced at his name badge "– Peter."

He grinned. "Can't have you hurting yourself on your way to save someone's life."

I tried not to laugh. "I'm on my way out. My shift's over. Time for me to leave the lifesaving to someone else for a few hours."

"My shift ends in ten minutes. Want to get coffee?" he asked eagerly.

I forced myself to keep a smile on my face, despite the desire to run, screaming. He was a good-looking bloke and he didn't need my issues to shadow his ego. "No, thank you. I'm picking up my friend from the airport. He's flying in for a concert next week and he'll be waiting for me."

"Oh, you mean Chaya?" Peter seemed to grow even more eager than I'd believed possible. "The only time they play Perth and it's their farewell tour. Where's he flying in from? I heard the Sydney concert at the Opera House was awesome. Why'd he bother coming here?"

I smothered my laughter by clearing my throat. "It'd be pretty hard for there to be a concert without him. He's in the band."

"Ohhh." He nodded. "You mean you'll get to go backstage and everything? Why doesn't he just get a limo to pick him up from the airport? With the money Chaya make, surely he can afford it."

He would, if I dallied any longer, and I needed to speak to him before he lost himself in the fangirls of Perth. "He's…my partner. And I've missed him," I admitted. It had to be the first time in my life I'd missed Jason, but it was the truth.

"Oh." His face fell. "I guess you can't have that coffee, then."

I nodded. "Enjoy your evening, though!" I set off again, waiting for barely a split second before I decided it'd be faster to take the stairs than wait for the lift. I pounded down the steps, wishing I could agree to something as simple as coffee with someone. Anyone. But I still couldn't stand anyone touching me. Sure, I touched my patients, but that was different. I was as cold and unattainable as the clouds scudding across the sky this morning. Besides, what sort of doctor would I be if I fell in love or even lust with one of my patients?

I squeezed between the red Mini and one of the Porsches in the doctors' car park to get to my less flashy car. I probably had the money for a Porsche, but, like the owner of the Mini, I preferred to invest it elsewhere instead. Plus, a flashy car would make me stand out and I'd spent years perfecting the art of blending in.

Pulling out of the parking lot, I nodded to the security guard and sped on my way. I floored the accelerator down the highway to the airport, hoping Jason's flight had been delayed or that my run would be smooth. I was ten minutes from the airport when I saw the orange flashing lights — road works along the highway, with the snail-crawl speed limits that were put in place to protect the road crew. The road crew looked like they'd knocked off for the day, but they hadn't changed the signs to let us go faster. Gritting my teeth and gripping the steering wheel, I crept along in my car, wondering if I'd get to the airport faster if I walked.

When I stormed into the terminal, I was fifteen minutes late and fuming. Keeping my fingers crossed, I checked the arrivals board, only to find that Jason's flight had been twenty minutes early. He was probably halfway to a hotel by now, thinking up ways to make me feel guilty for forgetting him. As if my job and my patients didn't matter.

I pulled out my phone and called him, scanning the seats at the terminal in the faint hope that he'd have waited for me. Fat chance.

Behind me, the first few bars of Chaya's *Necessary Evil* sounded as a mobile ringtone. I whirled and Jason winked. I ended the call before it had started and shoved my phone into my pocket.

His happy smile wasn't directed at me, but at the air hostess sitting across from him, sipping her coffee through a perfect, red-lipsticked mouth. He said something to her and she erupted in a fountain of giggles. I wondered if she'd given him her phone number yet – or if he'd decided to enrol her in the mile high club during the flight from Melbourne. Neither would have surprised me.

"Brooke, this is Angel," Jason drawled loudly. "Brooke's the air hostess who gave me the most amazing service on the flight. Absolutely first class."

A blowjob so good he wanted another one, I translated in my head.

Brooke blushed, giggled and did her best to look like an appealing manga character. I gave her a bland smile in response.

"She volunteered to help crew a flight to Kalgoorlie when one of their flight crew got stuck in a car accident in the roadworks on the highway, so I offered to buy her a coffee while she was on her break between flights," Jason continued. "You should really come to the concert, Brooke.

I know someone backstage who'd love to see you again." His eyes dropped to his pants.

"I think you should offer to take her to dinner properly before the concert," I said brightly. "But my bathroom's off limits, Jason." After catching him in my shower, squeezed between no less than three naked girls in Sydney, I'd offered to castrate him if I caught him in my room again.

He laughed off my implied threat and rose with Brooke. He murmured something that included the word 'pleasure' and kissed her hand for several seconds before releasing it. She giggled again and made the signal for him to call her before she strode off to the departure gates like a catwalk model.

"C'mon, I'm not carrying your luggage and parking here is more expensive than health care," I grumbled, wishing Jason would tear his eyes away from the girl's perky bum. She had legs like jet streams, so the skirt that would have looked modest on me almost revealed her underwear with every step.

When she'd vanished through security, Jason shouldered his backpack and pulled the handle out of his suitcase, looking expectant. I led the way to my car.

The moment the car doors closed, he was off. "She has the most incredible mouth. What I'd give to have those long legs wrapped around me…"

I jerked to a halt at the traffic lights. "She gave you a blowjob in the galley and you were interrupted before you could bang her on the bench." He spluttered, but no words came out. "I'm right, aren't I? Normal people use the toilets for privacy."

"But there's no excitement in that. The thrill of being

caught just heightens the…the…"

"Thrill?" I finished. "Here's something. No orgies until after the concerts. I'm not saying no fooling around, but if you're even one minute late, I'll slice your percentage of the take in half for the show."

"You can't do that! These shows will pay the last instalment for my private resort up north! You can't mess with my retirement plan," he protested. "All that stuff's set out in signed contracts!"

"Want to bet?" I asked grimly. "The only signed contract says what the band gets. Up until now, we've agreed to split that evenly. Piss me off one more time and I'll do it, I swear."

"All right." A lengthy pause was followed by, "All the concerts? We have two shows in Perth. You mean I can't let off a little steam in between the two?"

I swallowed. Sexually frustrated Jason was almost as hard to deal with as oversexed Jason. "As long as you're on time for the second show, I don't care what you do after the first. But if you turn up looking wasted, I will insist on a drug test. You play somewhat sober or not at all."

He cheered like a little boy, then dropped his voice. "You know, I wouldn't need all the other women to satisfy me if I had you. Just you. I wouldn't even look at another girl if I had you."

"Good thing for all the other women that you don't, then, isn't it? Imagine how disappointed they'd all be if you settled for some dull doctor," I responded, tuning out of the conversation as I had to run the gauntlet of merging in Perth without getting flattened. Why would Perth drivers never learn how to merge two lanes of traffic?

TWENTY TWO

When I'd finally managed to extricate myself from Jason's hotel room so I could settle down with a quiet dinner at home, my attention strayed from the inane TV cooking show to Nathan's haunting emails. I flipped through them until I found an early one I hadn't read yet:

I have nightmares about ambulances now and I've found myself freezing when I hear a siren. That's because the trip in an ambulance to take Caitlin to hospital really was a nightmare. I hadn't slept in weeks - I'd had sleeping pills with me, but I gave them all to Caitlin. That was the problem that night - I'd given her sleeping pills to knock her out, not knowing how badly injured she was. Add hypothermia and getting shot - both of us, not just her - and I'd made so many stupid decisions that night that it's a wonder she survived it.

And me, drifting in and out of consciousness, staring at her as her face turned into yours and back to her own deathly pale one. That's not just in the dreams — that's what I saw the day it happened. Not sleeping does that to you. Hallucinations and stuff. But maybe it was just my mind making up pictures that weren't as bad as the reality.

She'd lost so much blood it wasn't hard to see a corpse instead of the living, breathing girl I desperately wanted to survive. I was useless. Pressing a wad of gauze to my own gunshot wound, unable to help her.

It's the first time I realised you were right. Bombing out in first year and having to take a year longer to do my degree, going to pieces when you went missing instead of taking my exams, dropping out when you died because I couldn't face a cadaver after seeing yours in the morgue after the autopsy. . . I wanted to go back, but the first whiff of formalin as I walked past the dissection labs and I was done. If I'd finished my degree when you were supposed to, I'd have been an intern doctor by the time I met Caitlin. I'd have been qualified to help her, not nearly kill her. Now I'll be a security guard for the rest of my life because I'll never be able to go back to uni.

But that was just the start of my fuck-ups. I should've finished my degree. I should've saved you from them. I should've smashed the window of my own car and dragged Caitlin out of there before they could hurt her. I should've saved her sooner or never left her side. It's not like I slept at all.

And the most colossal fuck-up of all was realising that I loved her — the girl I'd nearly killed and I'd had to watch bleeding out on the street as she took the bullet that was meant for me. I was supposed to be saving her life and instead she nearly died saving my worthless hide. I should've died then and there. She didn't need me. Strongest woman I've ever met – yes, even stronger than you were, and that's saying something. But she survived when you didn't, so she had to be.

I failed her as much as I did you. Maybe that's why you're always accusing me in my dreams. I know I deserve it. I deserved to die for the things I did. The others did and it felt good to shoot them. I never thought I'd be able to kill someone, but when it's about saving someone you love or vengeance for someone you've lost, all that goes to hell and you pull the trigger and just enjoy it. I should feel like a murderer, but I'm not sure the men I killed were even human any more. Oh, they might've looked it, but in their heads, they were worse than animals. What they did to you. What they did to Caitlin. And maybe they turned me into some sort of animal, too.

I hope I'm never in an ambulance again. I think I'd go raving mad, imagining I'm in there with you and Caitlin and utterly useless. It's probably better just to put me down like some rabid dog. Do they really foam at the mouth? I mean, the list of symptoms say they do, but I've never seen a recorded case in Australia. Maybe I'm the first.

Shit, I'm rambling. If anyone reads this, they'd cart me off to the funny farm right away. Probably for the best. I wonder if they have straightjackets still? Just as long as they don't take me in an ambulance.

God, I think I am crazy. Can't sleep and ambulances scare me. Maybe some more sleeping

pills will help. They can't make the mess in my
head any worse.

The day after tomorrow, I resolved. I'd use my day off
to go and see him. If he needed my help, after all he did for
me, I couldn't deny him. And if he didn't…at least I'd know
he was okay.

TWENTY THREE

"Doctor to 207! Doctor to 207!" The carrying call echoed down the ward as my pager purred on my hip.

I set my steaming coffee down with a sigh and headed to answer the summons. An intern doctor's job never ends.

Three patients and my second marriage proposal for the day later, I batted the soap dispenser to disinfect my hands so I could finish my coffee. Hopefully, before I fell asleep on my feet.

I waved the water off and wiped my hands, tossing the paper towel in the bin as I passed. I snatched up my mug, striding as fast as I could to the handover room, where I might be able to grab two minutes to drink my coffee.

My hopes for peace shattered when I saw I shared the room with the next shift of nurses. They huddled around the recorded handover, narrated by this shift's nurse manager. A few glanced up at me as I entered, but they were intent on the dull story of the day.

Welcome to a general surgery ward, I thought as I carefully sipped my coffee in the faint hope that it was still hot.

"…206 suffers from dementia, if found wandering the ward, please escort her back to her room. Mr Foster, the amputee in 208, is diabetic and not permitted additional sugar, doctor's orders. He's tried to bribe two orderlies to buy him chocolate from the gift shop. Room 210 is only seventeen; motor vehicle accident; multiple fractures and parents are in attendance…"

I took another slurp of my lukewarm coffee, hoping it could still keep me awake through the last hour of my shift. One more hour and I'd have four days off – heaven, surely. I'd spend the first one sleeping and the second one looking for Nathan. The email he'd sent two night ago told me he was getting worse.

The clustered nurses scribbled notes quickly as their patients came up in the droning, recorded voice.

The nurse manager's voice rose, sounded hurried. "Patient in Room 214 is not assigned to one nurse – Room 214 is to be included in all rounds this shift, once the patient is transferred from ED. Arrived by ambulance at noon and due for transfer once stabilised. Suicide watch patient, frequent checks as time permits. Unconscious at start of shift; when patient regains consciousness, notify Dr Hogan immediately. Patient name is…" The shuffling of papers punctuated her pause. "Nathan Miller."

My empty mug shattered as it hit the floor.

TWENTY FOUR

Voices talked without cease, waking me up when all I wanted to do was sleep.

Go away. I didn't open my mouth to say it, nor open my eyes to see who it was.

"I just found him asleep." Chris hiccupped, or perhaps it was a dry sob. She sure didn't sound happy. "Then I saw the empty box of sleeping pills next to his bed. I don't know how many he took, but it was a new box last week..." She sounded like she was crying.

"Has he been down or depressed lately?" asked a female voice I didn't know.

"A little, for quite a while. I know he's had trouble sleeping since our sister died..." Chris sniffled.

If you'd seen what they did to her, you'd have nightmares too. What they did to Alanna. What they did to Caitlin...

I drifted back into dreams, none of them pleasant.

TWENTY FIVE

"Have you had your tea break, yet?" This voice I only heard in dreams now, but I'd never heard it say this before. Wonderful. Hallucinations.

"No, but Dr Hogan wanted someone to stay with this patient as much as possible, because he'll wake up soon and she wanted to be notified as soon as he's awake," an unfamiliar male voice mumbled.

The dream voice sounded like she was smiling. "I'll stay with him for a bit and cover for you. I'm done with my patient list, but I'm still here for another half hour."

Mumbling and flustered, he protested weakly, "Oh, no, Dr Miller, I couldn't..."

Dr Miller. That would have been me or Alanna by now if I'd kept studying. If she'd lived. This had to be a dream and it would only end badly.

I felt the heat of someone reaching over me and heard

the huff of breath as she stood back on her feet before she reached over me again. The fabric of her shirt brushed my nose and I caught a slight whiff of her perfume. I tried to hold my breath so I didn't sneeze.

"If you open your eyes now, you'll have the best view of my breasts anyone in this place has ever had," the dream voice told me archly. "I know you're waking up, Nathan."

If I opened my eyes, I'd see that it wasn't her and I'd just imagined a voice like hers. But if I didn't, the dream would turn darker and more disturbing until I was forced to wake up.

Groggily, I blinked at an expanse of blue shirt. I focussed on the name badge pinned to it. *Dr Alana Miller*, I read. Different spelling. Alanna was dead. I knew she was dead and it wasn't her voice I was hearing.

"Oh shit."

The room went dark as a flat piece of plastic smacked into my face and stayed there.

Gentle hands lifted it away and patted my face. Her big, dark eyes, filled with concern, were all I could focus on. "Oh, Nathan, I'm sorry. It was clipped to the top of the bed head and I thought I could reach it, but it slipped…" She bit her lip. "I know you're not really one of my patients but I had to know. If you'd really…really tried to kill yourself." Her beautiful eyes filled with tears.

I opened my mouth to speak, but nothing came out. My mouth was too dry to even clear my throat.

"Oh! Let me get you a drink." As she walked over to the sink and poured a cup of water from the tap, she had lost none of her grace, but her dancing step was brisk and businesslike, more a march than the ballet I remembered.

As my fingers closed around the cup, I realised that she was just as real as the plastic in my hand. She was alive. After so long, wondering and worrying… Five years. How much had she changed?

I took a gulp of water and attempted to clear my throat. "You're alive. I tried to find you, but it was like you'd disappeared, or died," I rasped, taking another big mouthful of water. "What are you doing here?"

"I went over to Melbourne to study. I wanted to come home to do my internship." She hesitated as if she wanted to add something else, but she didn't say it, looking down at her shirt instead. I followed her gaze to her name badge.

"You're not Alanna Miller," I said. "You look nothing like her. You didn't even spell it the same."

She looked uncomfortable. "I know. It's just that I had to change my name and this is the name ASIO gave me. Alana is my middle name and it seemed…appropriate, somehow."

I wanted to throw the cup of water in her face and tell her it was NOT appropriate to name herself after my dead sister, but I'd drunk it all. I slid out of the hospital bed and lurched over to the sink to refill it, shrugging off her offer of assistance. I was dizzy by the time I made it back to bed and too glad to hit the pillows to throw the hard-won cup of water at anyone.

"I tried calling your house, but for ages no one was home. One day Chris answered the phone and she told me that you probably wouldn't remember me and I shouldn't waste my time. I didn't call again." Her voice was low and sad. "I've been back here for only a few weeks and I hadn't worked up the courage to try to contact you again. I imagined you were happy and living your life again. I didn't think you'd appreciate someone you barely remember wanting to catch up. Then I came into work today and your name came up at handover. They said it was a possible suicide attempt and I couldn't stand not knowing. I couldn't believe that you would try to kill yourself." Her voice choked up with tears. "Nathan, why did you take so many sleeping pills?"

"So I could sleep," I told her. "I wanted the bad dreams to go away and let me sleep."

"You still have nightmares?" she asked in a low voice.

"Who told you about them? Was it Chris? Did she tell you to stay away?" I demanded.

Caitlin looked almost guilty. "No, Nathan. You had them in hospital and when we slept together. A couple of times you woke me up with your thrashing around or when you pulled me into a bone-crushing hug. I remember one night I was scared you'd break my ribs, you were so determined not to let me go."

My mouth opened and wouldn't close. "I hurt you? Oh shit, I'm so sorry. You should've said something. If I'd known, I'd have slept by myself, somewhere where my nightmares couldn't hurt you."

She pressed her lips together, as if she was trying to hold words in. "What are your nightmares about?" she asked timidly.

"Mostly about you." I regretted the words even as I said them, downing the water so I didn't have to look at her. That lasted about a second – I couldn't keep my eyes off her. It'd been so long and I wanted to drink her in, not cold tap water.

She looked stricken. "But it's been more than five years since you've seen me. Chris said you wouldn't even remember me." She sat down heavily in the chair beside the bed. "What did I do to you that still gives you nightmares now?" Her voice shook slightly and her hands tightened on the mattress beside me, her knuckles as white as the sheet she clutched. She looked down at her hands instead of me.

Not wanting to answer, I followed her gaze to her hands. The faintest scar remained across her wrists and all bar one finger had healed straight. I found myself telling her without deciding I wanted to. "Your hands were covered in blood and your fingers were...broken." My fingers traced the impossible lines her fingers had been bent into. "There was so much blood. Sometimes, you were screaming at the pain and other times, you're dead, but I couldn't stop them. I couldn't do anything about it." I closed my eyes and the images were there, the ones I could never escape from. "I dream about what you looked like lying on the beach, when I thought you were dead, what you looked like in the ambulance, when I realised what I'd let them do to you. I dream about you lying cold and dead like Alanna was in the morgue, with the same broken fingers, the same...oh God, the same injuries." I opened my eyes to make the images go away, but I couldn't look at her. I stared at her hands, trying not to see the blood in my memories.

Her voice was hesitant but curious. "In your file, it says your nightmares are of her. Did you have to identify the body after it was found?"

Wordlessly, I nodded. "She was so cold and so...damaged. I couldn't believe anyone could willingly hurt someone like that. And then when I saw you in the ambulance...I realised I'd let them do it to you and I hadn't stopped them. Sometimes the dreams start with her, but then it's you."

I heard her gasp. "You gave me your sleeping pills. You stayed with me, night after night, and you didn't sleep. You were having the nightmares then and trying to protect Chris and me from what they did to her...Oh hell." She took a deep breath. "You let me tell you what they did, you wrote it all down."

"I just tried to help you," I mumbled, embarrassed.

She appeared to be fighting to say something – or not say it. When she finally opened her mouth again, it seemed to take a huge effort. "When...when I slept with you –" she blushed furiously, but continued,"– I remember you did sleep, sometimes. I mean, you weren't up all night...oh hell..." For all the innuendo in her words, there was no invitation in them. No, that door was firmly shut.

"There were some nights we didn't get much sleep," I acknowledged with a smile, wanting both to remember and forget those amazing nights I'd spent with her. I remembered them in my dreams, the ones that had started out well, but they always ended with blood, screaming and death.

My comment flustered her even more. "I meant that some nights, just by being there, maybe I helped you sleep. I wondered if it might help you if I stayed. One night, after all the nights you were there for me, is the least I can do."

I wanted to say no. I wanted to tell her to stay far away from me and all the trouble that came with me. I wanted to tell her everything and apologise for still breathing. But more than all of that, I didn't want this dream to end.

"Please stay," I said.

TWENTY SIX

"Oh shit. Dr Miller!" an unfamiliar voice hissed. "Dr Miller!"

I opened my eyes to see an orderly pacing around my bed, hissing for Dr Miller. I looked around for the elusive Dr Miller, before realising he meant Caitlin. She still sat on the chair beside the bed, but her head rested on her arms on my pillow as she slept soundly.

"Shhh, don't wake her," I told the orderly.

He wrung his hands. "But she'll get in trouble if Dr Hogan sees her here asleep and she's on her way."

"Then let me," I said softly. "Caitlin, angel. It's Nathan. Wake up, angel."

I reached out and stroked her hair lightly. It was softer than I remembered and much longer, too. "Caitlin, wake up, it's Nathan." I took her hand in both of mine and squeezed her fingers gently. "Wake up, angel."

Her face lit with an incredible smile, the like of which I never thought I'd see again outside of dreams. "Nathan?" she murmured, her eyes still closed.

"Right here, angel." I told her. "You've fallen asleep at work, so you have to wake up now."

"Hmmmm?" She blinked, sitting up slowly. Her hands flew to her shirt. "Oh shit – I didn't mean to fall asleep!"

"Thank you for staying." I told her. "It looks like I – no, we – got a good night's sleep."

She smiled, a little embarrassed, and opened her mouth to say something, but didn't get a chance.

"Ah, you're awake." The voice was unfamiliar and so was the woman it came from. "You're in hospital, Nathan, and I'm Dr Hogan. Do you remember what happened?"

All of it. What they did to Alanna, what they did to Caitlin, the end of my contract because my job was done. Years of doing nothing but security shifts. Wondering what had happened to Caitlin, dreading that she was dead and one of them had survived to go after her. Years of nightmares and sleep deprivation. Waking up here and finding out she was alive.

I cleared my throat. "I couldn't sleep, so I took some sleeping pills. When they didn't work, I took some more. I woke up in the middle of the night and couldn't get back to sleep, so I took some more. Then I woke up and she was here." I smiled at Caitlin.

The smile she returned was brittle and didn't reach her eyes. She looked worried.

Dr Hogan gave a perfunctory smile, her eyes flicking from Caitlin to me. "Your sister was worried about you when you didn't wake up and she found the empty pill bottle. She called an ambulance, which brought you in here." Because she thought you'd tried to kill yourself, was what she didn't say.

Caitlin's fingers twined around mine, squeezing my hand. Dr Hogan's eyes settled on our joined hands and she looked disapproving. Annoyed, I replied, "If I want help sleeping, I take Temaze. If I'd wanted to kill myself, I'd have done something else that would have worked. I took a lot of Temaze because I really, really wanted to sleep and it looks like it worked because now I feel really well rested. Thank you for your help. I'm sorry my sister worries so much she called for an ambulance. Are there any problems I should know about, or should I be thinking about being discharged?"

She looked distracted. "No, it seems like you've had almost no side effects from your overdose, except for a lot of sleep that you clearly needed. If nothing else comes up, I'll probably discharge you today." She turned to Caitlin. "Dr Miller, could I have a word with you outside, please?"

Caitlin nodded mutely and followed her out.

I strained to hear what they were saying.

The orderly finished cleaning the bathroom and started to tidy up the room. "So you know Dr Miller?" he said finally.

"She and I are old friends," I replied tersely, trying to hear the conversation outside.

"...Nathan Miller isn't my patient, but he is an old friend of mine. There's nothing unprofessional about visiting a friend in hospital. I have a few days off, I'm not even rostered on today..."

The orderly switched the vacuum cleaner on.

"So what do you know about Dr Miller?" I asked him, over the noise.

"She's an intern from over east. She left her rock star boyfriend over there and decided to come back here to do her internship. She won't mix work and her social life, though — completely professional, no matter what." He looked carefully at me and grinned. "Pity, isn't it?"

"...that patient's head is a mess. Everyone he sees says he should get some psychiatric help, but he won't do it. The guy has vivid nightmares so bad he's afraid to go back to sleep, but not about things he imagines — he dreams of horrible things he's seen. He saw his sister's tortured dead body and not long after that he found another girl's tortured body on a beach. I'm asking you to stay out of his head."

"Yeah," I replied, distracted.

Caitlin said something in a low voice that I couldn't catch. My heart leaped at Dr Hogan's reply.

"Then try to persuade him to get some help. If you really are his friend, maybe he'll listen to you. If he's in here again, I will hold you responsible."

I could hear footsteps going away down the corridor, but I couldn't tell whose they were.

The orderly switched the vacuum cleaner off and called, "See you later," as he headed out of the room.

Caitlin came back in, her face clouded with annoyance.

"What did you do to her to make her dislike you so much?" I asked her.

Caitlin looked suspiciously at the doorway, but Dr Hogan didn't appear. "Nothing. She's just very protective of her patients, that's all. I remind her of a patient she had a long time ago who lied about what had happened to her and compromised the level of care she could give that patient. The same patient she thinks you found left on a beach to die, so she doesn't want me anywhere near you."

"She told you that?"

"She told me some of it when she was an intern, but that was years ago." She looked angry at the memory. "She gave me a lecture on how I couldn't recover properly unless I had psychological help, which meant telling someone everything. She likes you a lot more now than she did then." Her face cleared as she looked at me. "She'll arrange your discharge papers and you could be out of here in an hour or so." She hesitated a moment. "If you like, I could give you a lift home. My car's still in the doctors' car park."

"What do you drive?" I asked her, suddenly interested.

"A little Peugeot," she said quietly, "A white one."

TWENTY SEVEN

Caitlin's car looked almost new, a pristine white hatchback that contrasted strongly to Alanna's battered old convertible. I threw my bag in the boot and slammed it shut, almost missing Caitlin's wince at the force I exerted on her car. Virginal car, I guessed, looking at the number plate. She can't have had it for more than a few weeks.

"So is the car a virgin? Never been touched by a man?" I asked as I slid into the passenger seat.

The Caitlin I used to know would have blushed and had difficulty answering. The confident woman beside me replied, "Oh no, I insisted she get started early. I had a team of two men detail her, polishing and rubbing every surface, before she was mine, and the same guys service her interior every fortnight. I can't stand that chemical new car smell."

My jaw dropped. Two men at the same time? Was she saying she'd…surely not Caitlin. How much had she changed in the last five years? "So you've been with other men while you were away?" I wanted to bite my tongue, but it was too late – the words were out.

Dark eyes drew me into their fathomless depths as somewhere on the surface, Caitlin x-rayed my soul. I couldn't look away.

"Do you really think it's any of your business, whether I've slept with one man or even hundreds? If you'd wanted to be a part of my life while I was in witness protection, then you should have come with me." She reversed smoothly out of the bay, curving into the lane and accelerating toward the car park exit. "Do you still live in the house you shared with your sister before?"

My mouth was already open to protest that I'd never been offered witness protection, but the thought of going home to Chris's shrieking fury made me close it again. "Yeah, I still live there, but I'm not really in a hurry to get home. My sister freaked out when she found me asleep, so she'll want to take her frustration out on me by screaming a lot when I get home. Maybe…maybe I could take you for coffee somewhere so we can catch up?" I glanced at my watch to make sure it was an acceptable coffee time. 10 am was normal for most people, right?

"The closest place for coffee would be my place," she said, her eyes firmly fixed on the road. "It's one of the few luxuries I allowed myself over in Melbourne, and there was no way I was leaving my expensive coffee machine over there when I left. I might even have a packet of Tim Tams left, seeing as I can't remember eating the ones I bought last week." Her hands tightened on the steering wheel. "You know what? Stay for the whole day if you want. It's my first day off in ages and I have nothing planned. It'd be fun to catch up properly."

I didn't need to summon a grin to my face – it appeared all by itself. "I'd love to."

I expected her to head for where she'd lived before – her father's house – but she turned left at the traffic lights instead of right, pulling into the street behind the hospital. I'd thought the place was a parking lot, but as we approached it, I realised that parking only took up the lower levels of the building. The upper levels had windows and balconies. Caitlin parked in a numbered bay and then led the way on foot to a hidden courtyard. Open to the sky above, trees stretched up past the second storey landing.

"Wow," I said softly, staring up at the soaring branches. "I had no idea any of this was here. It looks like a parking lot from the street. These trees must grow pretty fast."

Caitlin laughed. "The place is called Fiona's Forest Apartments. The landscapers sourced full-grown trees for the courtyard – it was in the plans, as the place wasn't built yet when I bought it last year. Some of them are fruit trees, too. Mulberry, lemon, pomegranate, mango..." Caitlin pointed as she named them.

I followed her up two flights of stairs, then lost count of the rest until, panting, we reached the top level of the apartment block. I wondered at my breathlessness. Hadn't I been doing enough cardio at the gym? Or had I been laid up in a hospital bed too long? I needed to get back to the gym and on the treadmill. Or go for a run tonight.

I stared at Caitlin, her face flushed from exertion, but her eyes sparkling with excitement. If the teenager I'd first met was my perfect ten, this woman was easily an eleven.

Maybe a twelve. The girl of my dreams…

Definitely a long run. I'd need an hour of pounding the pavement to get these stirring thoughts out of my mind. Maybe even two.

"I'll have to ask you to forgive me," Caitlin said as she turned the key in the lock, "but most of my furniture stayed in the townhouse in Melbourne, so I don't have much here. Well, I have all my stuff, my books and the kitchen stuff, but I haven't had time to do much furniture shopping. Only the stuff I ordered to be delivered when I arrived. I keep telling myself I'll get around to it when I get some time off, but today's the first day I've had off since…well, since I started, I think. I have four days off now, so hopefully I'll get that problem sorted over the next few days."

She swung the door open and I followed her in, trying not to look surprised at how bare the place was. A tiny sofa stood in a sea of timber flooring, next to a side table that might fit a plate and a glass on it, provided the plate wasn't too big. A folding table with two plastic chairs looked out of place in the spacious dining alcove beside the galley kitchen.

"Who's the second chair for?" I nodded at the table.

Caitlin studied the grain of the timber floor, tracing the pattern with her toe. "For a guest. You're the first one I've brought here."

I whistled. "I'm honoured. So my arse will be the first one to grace your chair?"

She coughed. "Well, no, not really. I think I've sat in both chairs, so my bum's been there first." A pause. "I should get you that coffee. How do you take it?"

"Do you have any decaf?" I asked automatically.

She turned horrified eyes on me. "Oh shit, I forgot. You don't drink coffee."

"I do," I admitted. "I try to avoid caffeine because I have enough trouble sleeping, is all. But you know that now you've seen my medical records." I wanted to be angry about it, but I couldn't. Caitlin deserved to know the truth about me – every sordid detail. I just didn't have the guts to tell her.

She blushed. "Not last night."

"No, not last night." I exhaled slowly. "I never thought I'd get to sleep with you like that again. It was wonderful."

Caitlin laughed. She didn't seem to want to stop.

I went over the words again in my head. "Shit. I didn't mean…"

She reached for my hands. "I know what you meant. For some reason, I'm your security blanket – the one thing you need in bed with you so you can sleep. I've been called worse things."

I shook my head. "Not a blanket. A teddy bear, maybe. One I want to hold tight to and never let go."

I reached out for her slowly, my fingers sliding lightly along the sides of her waist until my hands rested on her back. Part of me needed to give her every chance to back away and let me know what I feared most – that in putting her through hell, I'd burned away any chance I had with the girl she'd been. The rest of me was begging her: Please let me kiss you. Even just the once, so I can remember it.

TWENTY EIGHT

My eyes locked on hers, vigilant for any change of expression that would be a precursor to the word *no*. She gazed back at me, a small smile on her face, until my lips met hers and she closed her eyes as I kissed her lightly.

I pulled away a little, expecting her to break out of my hold, but she stood still, opening her eyes slowly. She let out a fresh peal of laughter, her eyes meeting mine again.

"You always did touch me like a china doll you were afraid would shatter." She put her hands on my shoulders and pressed her body against mine as she stretched up onto her toes. "You won't break me, Nathan," she whispered into my ear. Her hands moved mine so that I held her tighter.

I closed my eyes, wanting to savour the moment, but the memory came unbidden. "I did break you, once. I broke your fingers. On the beach." End it, she'd said, her hands on the gun as she held it to her head. Her eyes filled with despair and defeat as she tried to pull the trigger herself when I wouldn't. The audible snap of bones breaking as I wrenched the gun away from her and her wail as I turned away from her, turned on Mike who'd done this to her, done this to Alanna... How could a girl with all her fingers broken fire a gun? She couldn't shoot anyone, especially herself. So I did what she needed me to do. End it.

"Re-broke them." Her voice was soft. When I didn't open my eyes, she took my face in her hands, pulling me down to her level. "Look at me, Nathan. You re-broke fingers that weren't healing properly. You wouldn't have been able to break them unless they were as badly healed as they were, and it was only a matter of time before a doctor would have had to do it anyway. You also saved my life. You saved me from more pain." Her eyes bored into mine.

"I broke your fingers so I could kill Mike." I kept my voice low. "Then I blamed it on you."

Her voice was equally low as her eyes didn't leave mine. "If I could have killed him, I would have tried. I probably would have failed, too. You saved my life. You saved me from more pain."

"I still hurt you," I mumbled.

She smiled then. "Actually, you didn't. I was so cold I didn't feel much of anything. I didn't know I'd been shot until you told me. I still remember seeing that cop pull a gun on you and I couldn't run fast enough to reach you before he shot you. Who else would have taken a bullet for me?" Her smile turned wistful. "There's so much I want to forget from that time, but then I remember all the things you did to help me. Always, my memories of that time come back to you."

"This is crazy," I said hoarsely. "Talking about what happened to you as if it's nothing but a normal memory. I'd do anything for you to forgive me. It's been five years since you left me outside that church and every day I've wished I'd never let you go."

Her hands slid under my shirt, kneading the muscles along my back. "Of course I forgive you. You did what you had to in order to save your sister."

I shook my head. "No, not all of it. Letting you go when I should've...should've..."

Caitlin pulled my shirt over my head and dropped it on the floor. "There is one thing you could do for me. Something I've wanted for a long time," she breathed before her lips fused to mine.

Oh God, kissing her brought back memories. And burned new ones into my lips, my tongue and my head. No other girl could compare.

"Anything," I gasped. "I'd do anything for you, angel."

"Come with me." Still kissing me, she walked me further into her apartment. I couldn't look at anything but her eyes burning with...desire? Or had I imagined it?

She broke the kiss, took a step back and started to undress.

I glanced around, realising that she'd brought us to the bedroom. Her bedroom. She wanted to...she really wanted to...but what if I hurt her?

"Ow!" she said suddenly, sucking her finger.

"What happened?" I asked, immediately concerned. All these years and my heart still jumped into my throat at the thought that she'd been hurt.

She sounded embarrassed. "Nothing. I just stabbed myself with my name badge and now my finger's bleeding." Turning to face the mirror, she pried the badge from her shirt and threw it on the dressing table. Next, she attempted to undo her shirt buttons with her free hand, swearing under her breath.

I stepped forward to stand behind her. "Here, let me help." I reached around her to undo the buttons for her. As I leaned down, I pressed my lips to the back of her neck. She shivered suddenly and I noticed goosebumps on her arms. "Are you cold?" I asked with concern.

"No," she answered breathlessly. "Actually, I feel a little hot."

I kissed her neck again, feeling the warmth of her skin under my lips. The last button slid out of its snug home and I pulled her shirt down, baring her back. So smooth. Almost no sign of the blood, the ulcers, the cuts, the bruises, the dressings – just a few faint scars on her now smooth skin. I unhooked her bra, letting the straps slide over her shoulders as I moved my lips in a line of kisses down her spine, to the waistband of her pants. I didn't want to stop, but this was Caitlin. I couldn't keep going without her consent. I needed to hear it to know I wasn't making a mistake. "Angel," I began, not sure how to ask. How did you ask a girl you almost raped whether she'd permit you to worship her like she deserved?

Her pants slid down to her ankles and she kicked them away, leaving me staring at a pair of bright pink knickers emblazoned with the words KISS MY ASS.

I touched my lips to one cotton-covered cheek, then the other, before Caitlin shoved her knickers over her hips to fall at her feet, too.

Naked. She was naked before me and for the first time in my life, I had no idea what to do. But I could think of a hundred things I wanted to do. Then she turned, her eyes burning with desire as she looked down at me. My hands hovered over her hips, wanting to touch her and terrified I'd do something wrong all at the same time.

Frozen for a moment, we stared at each other. The only sound was her rapid breathing, racing mine.

"Nathan, I want to feel you inside me. Here." She seized my hand and plunged it between her legs. So wet and ready for me. I wiggled my fingers and she moaned, "Yes."

I backed her up against the dresser, then lifted her onto the top so her back was pressed against the mirror. Brushes, combs and bottles scattered everywhere, so I swept them onto the floor as I spread her legs. My angel. Glistening. For me.

I buried my face between her thighs, tonguing her until she bucked beneath my hands. "Do you want me to stop?" I asked breathlessly, kissing her thigh. I would. I swore I would, if she said so.

Her half-closed eyes widened, drinking me in. I didn't know what I was looking at. Anguish? Passion?

"Nathan, if I want you to stop, I'll say so. Right now, I want you inside me."

She pressed her hands to the back of my head, tilting her hips toward me.

When my lips were still inches away from her, I pushed my finger slowly inside her, taking her by surprise.

"More," she gasped and I gave it to her. Another sliding finger and a swirl of my tongue. "Oh God, more, Nathan, please!"

I took my time, savouring every stroke, every moan, every shiver of pleasure as I coaxed her to her peak. When she screamed my name, I plunged my fingers in to the hilt so I could feel her body quaking around me. I waited until she stilled before I withdrew my dripping fingers so I could taste her essence. God, so sweet. How could I have forgotten how good she tasted? Would she let me go again? Or had we done too much already?

Caitlin lay panting against the fogged up mirror, her breasts heaving with every blissful breath. Yet she kept her legs wide open, as if inviting me inside once more. Cautiously, I pressed my lips against her inner thigh.

I began, "Angel, would you like to –"

Her eyes snapped open. "Your turn." She slid off the dresser and hauled me to my feet, fastening her lips to mine. Pressing her body against me, her hands fumbled with my pants. She growled when she couldn't unfasten them, trying to drag them down, but they wouldn't budge.

God, I wanted her, but… "Angel, we can't. I can't."

"I'm not a child any more and I know what I want, Nathan. I want to return the favour in full. Help me get these pants off."

"I don't have any condoms," I said weakly. Lied, actually. There were several in my wallet and a couple more in my phone case.

She snorted. "We don't need them. My implant will stop pregnancy and I don't have any diseases to give you." She paused, alarmed. "You don't have anything, do you? Something you picked up from the hundreds of girls you've been with while I've been away?"

Maybe I should've said yes. After all, I'd already lied once. Instead, I shook my head. "Nope, I'm clean. But we still can't."

"Why the hell not?" Her eyes filled with fear and she groped for her shirt. She pulled it on, holding it closed with her folded arms as she huddled on the bed. "Oh God, you don't want me."

I sat beside her. "I want you, angel. I always have. I'll help you fog up every mirror and window in your house just like that." I waved at the dressing table. "But don't ask me for more than that. This morning I woke up in hospital. I haven't seen you for five years. Until this morning, I thought you were dead. It's a lot to take in." True excuses, but none of them was the real reason. That was one shameful secret I intended to keep to myself.

TWENTY NINE

I felt Nathan get up, but I couldn't bring myself to watch him leave. God, what was wrong with me? Nathan had been discharged from hospital just over an hour ago, and I knew better than anyone how unwell he was. Yet I'd jumped him as desperately as a drunken fangirl might attack the object of her obsession. I'd seen girls do it to Jason all the time.

And yet…it was as if we'd never been apart. He played my body better than I played the piano and the music was rapturous, to say the least. How had I forgotten that? I never forgot anything, but in all my fear of being touched by strangers, somehow I'd hidden the memory of his more than welcome touch. So five years of pent-up lust had exploded in a damaged man's face when he deserved better from me. Dr Hogan was right – I should stay the hell away from Nathan so he could sort his head out. I only messed things up more.

I gathered my clothes up from the floor – yesterday's clothes, I realised, and they certainly smelled like it. I needed fresh clothes and a shower. Then coffee and breakfast and maybe sorting out my furniture problems. Nathan's well-hidden shock at my pitiful attempt at furnishing the place was an unspoken reprimand. I'd picked out the bedroom suite online with the sofa to match, but I'd kept the sofa in the lounge to make it look less bare.

Not for the first time, I regretted leaving all my furniture in Melbourne, but I'd taken great care furnishing that townhouse. The restored building had deserved the antiques or antique style reproductions I'd filled it with, none of which belonged in this modern place. But that didn't mean I didn't miss them. Hell, the old daybed in the spare bedroom had been perfect for playing guitar when I'd wanted to lose myself in my music. Shit, I hadn't played in weeks – I needed to fix that, and soon. Right. New furniture today, delivered today or tomorrow.

I took a quick shower and picked my clothes out carefully. I needed to look my age, as shop attendants tended to ignore scruffy teenagers unless they suspected me of shoplifting. Though how I'd manage to steal a sofa was beyond me. I laughed as I pulled on a winter dress, hoping to pair it with some high boots to keep me warm. It might not be Melbourne, but Perth still got near-freezing temperatures in winter. Maybe I should get a couple of throw rugs for the lounge room, too, for snuggling under if I managed to watch some TV. And dining chairs with cloth seats. The plastic ones were cold on my backside in the mornings.

I'd need the house plans, I decided. I didn't want to repeat the nightmare of that oak dining table that had turned out to be all of thirty centimetres too long for the townhouse's dining alcove. For six months, I'd endured the stupid thing sticking out into the lounge so I bumped into it far too often, until I managed to find a smaller, more appropriate replacement for the monstrosity that I'd sold at auction for a tidy profit. It made me feel better about not using it for firewood, anyway.

I crossed to the spare bedroom, where I kept all my important documents in the desk drawer. I carried the folder to the poor excuse for a dining table and flipped through the pages until I reached the stack of plans I'd copied. I grabbed two and noticed the unsigned ex gratia paperwork sitting underneath it. Shit. I should've asked Nathan about that instead of begging for sex. He might still be here if I had. All this time trying to speak to him, before destiny threw him into my lap and I wasted time by spreading my legs instead.

"Fuck!" I slammed my first on the plastic table.

"What? Are you okay?" Nathan sat up on the couch, giving me the shock of my life. "I know I probably should have left, seeing as I refused your generous offer and all, but it seemed a bit rude to just walk out without saying goodbye. And now…God, you look beautiful."

I couldn't help it – I laughed. Destiny had given me a second chance and I wasn't going to throw this one away. I'd behave myself this time. "You always were good at compliments, even when I was spotted yellow and purple with bruises."

Nathan paled and he blinked rapidly, clenching the sofa

arm so hard his knuckles turned white.

Post traumatic stress disorder. Injuries did to him what darkness did to me. Textbook pages fluttered in my head as I strode to his side and dropped to my knees. There was no hesitation as I wrapped my arms around him. His body shuddered, but he didn't push me away. "I'm sorry. I shouldn't have said that."

We probably looked ridiculous, him and I, with my arms barely meeting around his hard, muscled body. I can't say I didn't enjoy it, though. Nathan evidently spent a fair bit of time at the gym, working off his frustration. I burned to tell him that I knew about his nightmares and the emails he'd sent to Alanna, but I didn't dare. I'd caused enough trouble today. He needed to tell me about his nightmares on his own.

"Nathan," I began softly, "you know that if you want to speak to someone about your nightmares, you can talk to me. You don't need to hide anything from me because I was there. If I'd wanted to turn you in to the police, I'd have done it years ago. I promise I'll listen without judging. Without saying anything, if that's what you want."

I felt him shaking his head as he pulled away from me. "No, angel. I can't tell anyone about them. But thank you." He wiped his face with his hands and his eyes looked suspiciously red. So what if he'd shed tears? I'd cried on his shoulder often enough. It was more than fair that he got to do the same to me.

I rose, feeling even more awkward. "I guess I should take you home then, unless you still want that coffee. We'd have to head to a coffee shop for it, seeing as I'm fresh out of decaf." I frowned at the loveseat that was dwarfed by his body. "And then I'll have to get a proper sofa for this room because I think the only way we'd be able to both sit on that is with me on your lap. It looks like kids' furniture with your legs hanging over the side like that."

Nathan grinned. He still looked pale, but this smile reached his eyes. "How about I come with you? That way you can measure your new sofa against me to make sure it's big enough." He waved at the length of his body.

"You want to come furniture shopping with me?" Even as I said it, I didn't believe it.

He shrugged. "Sure. It beats going home to my sister. I have so many missed calls and texts from her that my phone battery's about to go flat. Well, after I sent her a quick message saying I'd been whisked off by a beautiful doctor and I'd be home when she's finished with me." He coughed. "And I can't see you carrying a new sofa up all those stairs by yourself. Plus, when you get sick of shopping I can buy you coffee." He gazed into my eyes and I felt a glimmering of hope. "My manners are a bit rusty, I think, doing things arse-about like I did today. There's been no one but you for me for the last five years, angel. Not a hundred women. Just one. And you don't know how much I've missed you."

My tummy flipped. Then it growled like I'd swallowed a dragon. Oops, I'd missed breakfast. That explained the strange sensations. "Sure," I responded with a smile.

THIRTY

After four shops of finding nothing but a pretty throw rug that wasn't even for sale, I was ready to head to IKEA and spend the next three days assembling my purchases. At least their rugs were for sale.

"One more," Nathan coaxed, pointing across the car park. "We haven't been in that one yet."

I hadn't noticed the furniture store squeezed between two baby shops. "Okay, one more. If they don't have anything, I'm going to IKEA."

Nathan shrugged. "I still owe you that coffee and I've heard theirs isn't bad. And I'd get to show you my handyman skills as I build your furniture for you. On second thought, let's skip this place and head straight to IKEA. I haven't had one of their cheap hot dogs in years."

I laughed and tugged on his arm. "After this shop, you're on."

We never made it to IKEA. Shop number five was perfect. When I mentioned my bamboo floors, one of the staff started pointing out matching options. The dining table, matching buffet, bar stools for the breakfast bar, coffee and side tables… "All I need now is a lounge suite," I said, scanning the shop.

The shop assistant pointed out two and three seater sofas, but I shook my head. I'd had that sort of old-fashioned style in Melbourne. For this place, I wanted modern. "Something long and connected that kinks around a corner with space for two of us," I said, then looked up at Nathan's laughter. "What?"

He jerked his head at a bright blue sofa that peeked out behind an enormous dining table. "Is that long and kinky enough for you, angel?"

Blushing, I swallowed back my retort as I strode across the carpet to the…shit. Kinky corner sofa. Well, I know I wouldn't be doing any kinky stuff on it. The slightest suggestion of bondage and I'd call the police. At least I knew Nathan would agree with me on that one.

Without a word, he stretched out along the generous three-seater, raising his eyebrows at me. He patted the blue suede beside him. "If you sat here, you could stretch your legs out that way and I could rest my head in your lap." He winked and I was stunned to see the shop assistant blush.

Shit, I'd forgotten about the sleazy comments he'd occasionally let slip. The charming man who'd even had some of the nurses blushing for him when I was in hospital. Then, it had scared me a little and reminded me of Jason. Now, I knew I could handle it. After all, he was all bark and no bite.

"C'mon angel, come try it out with me."

I laughed. "If you think it's comfy enough, that's all I need to know. I'll take that, too."

The shop assistant's eyes widened. I wondered if they worked on a commission basis here. If so, Wendy — at least, that's what her name badge read — was in for a nice bonus this month. We followed her to the counter, where she keyed my selections into the computer. "Now, will you need delivery for these?" she asked.

I nodded. Despite Nathan's valiant offer of assistance, there's no way in hell I'd ask anyone except an experienced removalist to shift my furniture up the stairs to my place. And even then, I'd offer them a bonus for the back-breaking job.

She called the warehouse and happily told me it could be delivered tomorrow morning, provided there were no stairs.

Nathan laughed.

I forced myself to keep a straight face. "There are stairs. I'm on the third floor."

Her smile died and she turned her back on me to continue her conversation with the warehouse scheduler, dropping her voice as if she didn't want me to hear it. When she finally faced me again, she said, "That'll cost extra. And you'll have to pay the removalists direct in cash."

I nodded at the numbers. That was normal. "Tell them I'll add a case of beer each from the liquor store up the road. I'll pay for Crown, but they can pick whatever they want up to the same value."

She looked shocked but grudgingly relayed the offer to her counterpart on the other end of the line. "The drivers are about to finish up for the day, but they've agreed to deliver yours this afternoon."

Now I smiled. "That sounds lovely." Worked every time.

THIRTY ONE

Caitlin ended the call and set her phone down on the kitchen bench. "They're downstairs. Can you give me a hand moving the loveseat into my bedroom?" She waved at the tiny sofa.

I burst out laughing. "That's seriously what this thing's called?" I lifted it easily. "Making love on this would be pretty cramped. One wrong move and you'd end up on the floor."

Caitlin pushed aside some of this morning's debris with her foot, blushing redder with every step. The moment we'd put the sofa down, she dropped to her knees to clean up the mess of bottles that we'd knocked off the dressing table. I glanced at the mirror. The fog had faded, but I could still see the faint outline of where her body had rested, the line of her thigh along the top of the dresser...

"I should probably wipe things down in here, too." Her

voice sounded faint. "Can you put the table and chairs on the balcony, where they'll be out of the way? I'll be out in a minute." She started rubbing a cloth in furious circles over the mirror, then swirling it across the dresser surface, too.

"Angel, I..." I swallowed. I wanted to apologise for rejecting her and tell her the real reason why. But I couldn't do it. So the coward in me said, "Sure," and I headed for the folding table.

An open folder of documents sat on top of it, which I moved to the bench before I returned the table to its flat storage state and carried it to her balcony. I dumped the stacked chairs beside it.

I picked up the folder. "Angel, where did you want me to put these?" I glanced at the papers. The top one was a letter from ASIO, identical to the ex gratia letter I'd received. How much had they offered Caitlin? Curiously, I shuffled through them to find out. "Fuck!" Three million dollars. More than she'd been given for the television interview. The money they'd offered me wouldn't have paid for her furniture purchases today. Well, it explained why she'd spent so much without blinking at the expense. Not if she had this much money to play with.

"What is it?"

The sound of her voice made me drop the folder guiltily. Papers flew everywhere. I sank to the floor after them, crawling on my hands and knees to collect the lot. I found the unsigned agreement that had been in the envelope with the offer letter. Three million dollars and she hadn't accepted it? Why the hell not? I shoved the page at her. "Why haven't you signed it yet?"

"I wanted to speak to you first. I wanted to know if

they'd made you an offer and whether you were going to accept it. I tried calling but I only got your sister and she said she wouldn't give you a message for me." She swallowed uncomfortably and I realised I'd asked about something that was none of my business. It was up to her if she wanted to accept compensation for what they'd done. She continued, "I wanted to know why. Why now, after the interview and five years have passed. What's changed?"

She didn't know about Mott. I knew Navid was lying. No way would Caitlin have met with him. It must have been something she said that had tipped him off, but purely accidentally. She hadn't known. Hell, I hadn't known until Navid told me. I only knew he was a bastard.

"One of the ASIO agents was accused of negligence," I admitted grudgingly.

She perked up. "You mean that dodgy bastard Mott? Is that what they're calling it? Throwing your life and mine away so he could have kinky sex with Laura? I hope she paid him for it. Not that I think he would've been worth much."

My mouth flew open in shock and I couldn't seem to close it. Shit, I couldn't even catch one of the cyclone of questions swirling through my head.

Someone knocked on the door and Caitlin dashed to answer it. Forty-five minutes later, after the removalists had left, grinning, as they anticipated their free cartons of beer, I slumped on the sofa. I still wasn't sure what to ask first.

Caitlin bounced onto the blue cushion beside me. "Mott? It really was Mott?"

I nodded.

"Shit, I hope they take their time on him in prison. He

deserves years of torture for what he let them do to me. But he likes that sort of stuff – at least that's what he said. Something about Laura being a wicked dominatrix. How long's his sentence?"

I opened my mouth, but nothing came out. I cleared my throat and tried again. "He won't get one. He killed himself a few weeks ago. Just before they sent the letters. That's why they sent them."

Caitlin closed her eyes. "How did he die?"

Looking at her screwed-up face, I wasn't sure if she wanted me to answer, but finally I did. "He stabbed himself with some weird knife. In the neck. Apparently it was really quick. Maybe he really didn't want to go to prison."

Caitlin's eyes snapped open. "Or he knew things no one wanted him to say in court." She inhaled sharply. "If he did kill himself, it's because he was offered a slower, more painful option. The question is whether he did it himself or if he hired someone else to do it. Because if he wants to silence everyone, I'm next."

"What do you mean you're next? You're suicidal, too?" I realised how bad that sounded, then added, "Suicidal like he was, I mean?" Not me. No matter what the doctors and my sister said, I wasn't ready to die yet.

"No. But I do have a stalker." She glanced out the window, where the sunset had turned the clouds pink. "I only see him at night, but I've seen him in the hospital car park and the one downstairs. It's like he's watching me, waiting for the order to…I don't know." Caitlin sighed, her shoulders sagging under the weight of her worries.

"Let me stay and watch, then," I suggested. "I'll keep an eye out for this stalker and if we do spot him, I'll tell you if

I recognise him. Maybe even speak to him to ask what he's doing here. ASIO might have you under surveillance because they're worried."

The tension eased in her expression. "It'd be…hell, it'd be such a relief just to know I'm not alone in the house. Stay as long as you want. I know I'll sleep easier with you here."

And I'd sleep easier knowing she's safe, I thought but didn't say.

"Well, good thing you got a new couch," I said brightly. "Beats that little, cramped thing you had before. A pillow and a blanket and I'm set for the night."

"I wouldn't make you sleep on the couch, Nathan, unless you really want to," she said gently. "There's a bed in the guest room." She nodded at a closed door beside the study.

No matter how much I wanted to, I wasn't sleeping with her, I inferred. Her grin widened as I watched, though, and I wondered. What would she say if I asked to sleep in her bed?

THIRTY TWO

Her sweet body was a gift I didn't want to relinquish, my arms wrapping around her protectively as she drew sobbing breaths to keep pace with her hammering heart. I wanted to tell her she'd be all right, that I'd keep her safe, but I knew I'd be lying. We weren't alone and he was watching. Listening. Waiting for me to stuff up so he could have her and hurt her and…

"Fuck her right here and now."

God, I wanted to. This beautiful girl with more fire in her little finger than all the other girls I'd slept with combined had in their entire being.

"Start with a kiss."

She tensed in my arms, ready to run or spit in my face, like she'd done to him. He deserved it, though. For what he'd done to her. For what he was forcing me to do to her.

"I'm not going to hurt you," I told her, trying to say it

quietly so he wouldn't hear. He'd make me hurt her, or Chris would die. I begged them both to forgive me – the girl in my arms and the sister who'd never know what I'd done to save her life.

Trying to ignore the killer watching me, I kissed Caitlin, exactly like I wanted our first kiss to be. Did I imagine her response? Her lips melted against mine, as if she wanted me as much as I wanted her.

Her body, squirming under mine on the mattress. Her voice saying no while her body said yes. And my body roaring its agreement.

No. No, she didn't want to be raped. She didn't want me and she was struggling to get away. Oh God, I'd almost raped the girl and I'd wanted to do it.

NO.

I jerked awake, my heart still racing from yet another fucked-up dream. I hadn't wanted to rape her. Shit, that's the first night I discovered impotence wasn't a myth. I'd had all the hardness of a limp noodle and I couldn't have done anything to her if I'd tried. That's why I pinned her to the mattress – to make it look like I could do it and hide the obvious truth that I couldn't. My own head was messing with my memories.

I reached for the pills beside my bed and they weren't there. The lamp had moved, too, I realised by the time I'd managed to find the bloody thing and click it on.

Oh shit. No, I'd moved. This wasn't my room or even the sterile hospital room I'd woken up in this morning – I was in Caitlin's guestroom, the one with the mosaic mirror that reflected my fractured mind. And I needed my sleeping pills to chase the bad dreams away.

I stumbled out of the room, heading for the bathroom. A quick glance told me there were no pills here, either, though I checked all the cabinets, just to make sure. No, nothing but some paracetamol and a whole heap of beauty products. Like Caitlin needed any of them.

Maybe she'd left them in the kitchen? Or beside the front door when we came in?

I prowled around the house, checking every spot I could think of in the living areas, but I came up blank. Without my pills, there'd be no more sleep for me tonight.

Caitlin would remember where she'd left them. Did I dare wake her up, though? Shit, I probably had already, stumbling around her house as I searched for the drugs I desperately needed. It's not like I wanted to take the whole bottle, I told myself, padding across the carpet to her room. I just wanted the recommended dose to put me back to sleep.

Her bedside lamp lit up the room when I swung the door open, so I could see her body cocooned in the quilt, but not her face. I stepped cautiously around the bed. "Angel," I began.

A sharp crack sounded and my muscles locked up like they were on fire. Then everything went black.

THIRTY THREE

Sunlight burned my eyelids, so I forced them open. How in hell had I ended up sleeping on the floor of what looked like Caitlin's bedroom? I had the same pillow and quilt from the guestroom and every muscle hurt like I'd been in a fight. No need to ask who won – it had to be the other guy. I groaned as I sat up and then flopped back down, wishing my head would just explode and put me out of my misery.

"Nathan?" Caitlin peeped around the door frame.

So much for keeping her safe last night. Her stalker had been in her room and I'd been no use whatsoever.

"Are you all right?" I asked, praying that she'd somehow managed to fight him off while I'd distracted him.

"I'm fine. I should be asking you that. I'm really sorry I tased you. I should have warned you that I sleep armed now, but I didn't expect you to come into my room while I was asleep..." She tailed off and seemed embarrassed.

No less mortified than me. I'd crept into her bedroom while she slept like some sort of stalker. I'm lucky she didn't have the knife she'd stabbed Simon with.

"Why were you in my room?"

"I couldn't find my pills and I needed them to get back to sleep," I admitted.

Caitlin edged into the room and perched on the bed. "You had another nightmare last night? Can you tell me about it?"

That I wanted to rape her? "No."

She shrugged. "No pills then. You tell me what's messing with your mind and stopping you from sleeping and maybe I'll let you have your sleeping pills again. One dose at a time."

I raised my head, wincing as pain ambushed me. "Well, your taser did the trick for me, I guess, so I don't need them again until tonight."

"Nathan..." she began, then seemed to change her mind. "Fine. If you're not ready to talk to me...fine. I should make you breakfast, though. To apologise for, well, running an electric current through your body until you passed out from the pain."

"When you put it like that, it'd better be the breakfast of champions," I grumbled, sitting up. "Shit!" I grabbed my head as the throbbing grew unbearable. "Oh God, I'll do anything. Just never use that thing on me again."

"I didn't mean to. I'm sorry. I'm not used to waking up and finding someone in my bedroom. And with this stalker..."

I recognised the way she turned away as an effort to hide her tears. Trying to ignore my headache, I clambered to my feet and wrapped my arms around her. "No, I'm sorry. It was stupid and I didn't think how much I might scare you. I should know better." I wet my lips. "Tonight I'll just lie awake instead and watch for your stalker. Safer for both of us."

I could feel her relaxing in my arms, so when she sighed and pulled away, I didn't try to stop her.

"Nathan, if you won't tell me your nightmares, there's another way to help get rid of them."

I stared at her. Nothing got rid of my nightmares. Except her.

She swallowed, then continued, "You change the endings. When you're awake, you do it, so that when your mind goes through the nightmare again in your sleep, it'll use the new ending instead. They call it imagery rehearsal therapy. It's real and it works for a lot of people."

I laughed and it sounded bitter to my ears. "Imagine a different ending? What, that you weren't abducted, hurt, tortured and almost killed? That my sister didn't die? That's not going to happen, angel. Did it work for you?"

"No. It didn't have to. I wrote every damn thing down and handed it to you, ASIO, the police…and they went away. Yours aren't and if you won't tell anyone about them then maybe you should try something different."

I sighed. "Angel, my nightmares are about the things that scare me most. Memories that make me feel every negative emotion I can name. I remember the agony of my heart breaking in two and knowing it was all my fault. You think a sugar-coated fairy tale that ends happily ever after is going to cut it with a bit of wishful thinking? You know better than anyone that life isn't a romance novel, angel.

The bloke who saved your life isn't a hero, he's just another villain who wishes he wasn't. But wishing doesn't make things true. Wishes are…wind. Nothing else."

Instead of giving up, she smiled. "That's what I said, too. If you want to forge a new ending to a powerful memory, you need to burn that new one into your brain like a brand. Not through wishful thinking. Action. Changing the ending. What's a hero's usual happy ending? Not in a fairy tale. Pick an action movie where the gritty hero shoots the terrorists and saves the day."

I snorted. "He gets the girl. Romance novels all over again, angel. Life isn't like that."

Her eyes held sympathy and sadness. "I'm offering, Nathan. Sleep with me for a night and when the nightmares wake you up, I'll help drive the bad memories out of your head. I'm a little rusty, but if you tell me what you like, we could try…"

"Sexual healing. You want me to use you as a prostitute so I'll feel better? No. You're better than that. Worth far more than that. I don't deserve you." I rubbed my neck as a pulse of pain intruded. "Besides, you'll probably just tase me again. And you'd be justified."

She squeezed my hand. "I'd put the taser away for the night. Just think about it, Nathan. That's all. I want to help you."

God, I wished I could tell her that even thinking about her body, writhing in passion with mine, would be enough to bring on nightmares, not end them. Because that's how the worst ones started. What began as the best dreams always ended badly. In blood, death and pain.

And the last thing I wanted was for her to let down her

guard and endanger herself for me. If that stalker managed to get in while I was sleeping like a baby, I wanted her armed and able to stun that bastard into oblivion.

THIRTY FOUR

Two am. Well, I'd managed half a night's sleep before the nightmares woke me. I stumbled to her kitchen, avoiding Caitlin's room, and poured myself a glass of milk. I itched to pour some alcohol into it, but I didn't know where she kept her brandy and maybe it was best that I didn't. If I were drunk, I'd give in and go into her bedroom and maybe do something we'd both regret. Or get tased again.

"Can't sleep or did a nightmare wake you?" Caitlin clicked on the light and I was mesmerised by the beautiful girl in a short, satin nightie. More beautiful than I remembered in my dreams, but that would probably change now I had this vision to remind me.

"First the second one, now the first," I said, gulping down the rest of my milk so I wouldn't have to say any more. "But if you'll tell me where you hid my sleeping pills..."

"There aren't any in the house. Your doctor refused to write a prescription and I agree with her. But I can write you one, and I will if I feel you're trying to use other means of ending your dependence on sleeping pills."

Her confession startled me. I didn't have anything to help me sleep? And she'd write a prescription, jeopardising her career if I just told her about my dreams?

"You're trying to bribe me with sex and drugs. Hardly ethical, doctor," I retorted, clunking my glass into the sink. I attempted to shove past her, but she braced her hands against the benches, blocking my way.

"I'm trying to help you and I'm beginning to think I'm the only one who can. You won't tell anyone else because it might land you in prison. I understand, I really do, hence why I'm willing to listen because I know what happened and I don't want you arrested, either. And I'm not just offering sex like it's a physio session or a prescription or some other service I provide to my patients. I wouldn't…I don't…" She dissolved into tears.

Shit, if there was one thing that broke my heart, it was Caitlin crying.

"You want to help me get over what happened to you? Great." I pointed at the ASIO offer letter. "Promise me you'll sign that. They let Mott terrorise us both and did nothing to stop him. Take them for every fucking cent they're willing to offer and then use it to go on holidays. To stay drunk or high or whatever it takes to numb the pain until the money runs out. Ruining people's lives. Stealing them from their loved ones and…and…" Fuck, I was going to cry, too. I really was losing it.

Caitlin's hand touched my back. I squeezed my eyes

shut, hoping I could crush the tears out of existence.

"I'll sign it if you witness it. But only if you promise to come on holiday with me. You need it. You know you do. Something to help you heal."

"If we sleep in separate rooms, then okay," I agreed and watched her sign away her silence. She'd given it to me for free, millions of dollars' worth, because she didn't believe I deserved to go to prison. My memories would punish me every day for the rest of my life no matter where I was. And I deserved it, no matter what she said.

She threw the signed papers on the table and we both sat there for a moment, not saying anything.

Caitlin broke the silence. Of course. She'd always been braver than me. "I'm going back to bed. You're welcome to sleep with me if you like."

Sleep. Ha. Being in bed with her would inspire my worst nightmares and I'd hurt her — she'd said as much before. When I had a nightmare, I hurt her without even being aware of my actions. I didn't dare share her bed, awake or asleep.

THIRTY FIVE

Three days I'd resisted her and it only got harder. No, I wouldn't tell her about my nightmares. No, I wouldn't sleep with her no matter how much I wanted to. Watching her sit in front of the dressing table only reminded me of my first morning here and how irresistible she was in the throes of passion. Perfect. Beautiful. Everything I wanted. And everything I couldn't have.

I had to go back to work or I'd go mad. I knew her time off was up – she'd said as much. Staying in her house without her would be weird, even more of an imposition than it was now, with her home. It was time to go back home and face Chris' wrath.

"Are you free this Friday or Saturday night?" she said, glancing at me before her eyes returned to her reflection as she rhythmically brushed her hair. A river of wine in the sunlight streaming through the window.

Just like the first time I saw Caitlin, her dancing step carrying her down the Terrace. Should have carried her far away from me and the darkness that pursued me.

"No, I'm working." I managed to say. I didn't want to tell her what my job was now. I did security work for a firm that did mostly big events. I'd been there a while and I was good at it – after my experience guarding Caitlin. I was the security supervisor for a couple of big concerts this weekend – no way I could back out of those. But one look at her made me want to.

"Never mind, then." She shrugged. "Maybe we could meet up another night, when you're not working."

Yes, please. And at the same time, no.

THIRTY SIX

I usually didn't pay much attention to the band or the music when I was working. There were too many other things to occupy my mind. Like why Otto hadn't turned up for work this week and he wasn't answering his phone, either. He wouldn't be the first – shit, not even the tenth – guy to decide that security wasn't for him and not even bother to give notice. The welfare office sent unemployed guys on a short course in security and my boss, Dennis, was a sucker for hiring them. If they looked intimidating enough, even the few weeks' work he'd get out of them was good enough for him. Most new staff didn't stay long.

Not to say all of them were bad – actually, some of them made decent security guards and they wanted the job. There were always a few who were so inured to welfare handouts that they couldn't stick with any job for long, but Otto hadn't struck me as one of those. He was a good, solid

161

bloke to position outside the band's exit door, because he looked scary enough to deter all but the most crazed fan. No, he was like most of the new security guards we hired – just there to collect a paycheck to pay their bills. If another job came up that paid better or had better hours, they'd be gone and replaced with new ones who felt the same way. There were a few who were more experienced, who knew what to look for in order to stop trouble before it started. Then there were the ones who started trouble all on their own.

Without him here tonight, exit duty fell to me. Wonderful. Especially as last night's concert had demonstrated that this band's fangirls were the crazy, screaming variety I liked least.

I moved around a lot, checking that everyone was where they were supposed to be, wanting to be nearby in case trouble did start.

I found myself humming along with the music and I realised it was familiar. This was an Australian band – I'd heard them a fair bit on the radio and even liked a few of their songs. Maybe I'd bought one of their albums. If I hadn't, I should.

That made a nice change – working with background music I liked. I had a vague feeling that I'd fallen asleep to their music before – a remarkable feat in itself – but that wasn't going to happen now, while I was working. I focussed on the crowd, catching myself humming or singing the words under my breath more than once.

The band finished their final set. The stage went dark and people started to head outside. As the Arena cleared, I left it to the rest of my team and headed for the backstage entrance. When the band left, I'd need as many staff there as I could get.

As I waited, I thought of Caitlin. I wondered if she would have wanted to go to this concert. What would it have been like to have been two in the crowd, instead of outside of it, watching for trouble? Would she have enjoyed it? I couldn't remember this band being around when I knew her before, when I might have asked her if she liked them.

Out of the corner of my eye, I saw a small shape in the clear space beside the back entrance, wearing a dark sweater and jeans. For a second, I thought it was her, but the girl darted between two other security guards and into the small crowd of fans waiting for the band and I lost sight of her. Sensing trouble, I followed and grabbed the girl's arm before she could get any further away and pulled her back to the light at the entrance. "Hey, wait a minute. What were you doing there?" I boomed in a loud voice I only used for work.

A heavy hand came down on my shoulder. "Let her go." This voice was soft with the implied threat of violence. Like a razor sharp knife in a tissue paper sheath.

I turned to see the face that matched the voice and recognised the band's security consultant. Someone had told me this guy was an ex-US Marine. He was American, certainly, and he'd demonstrated he knew how to protect people better than I did, when we'd discussed security arrangements before the start of the concert. So what was this girl and why…

I realised I wasn't holding her anymore, my hands up near my shoulders to show they held nothing. She didn't run back into the crowd as I'd expected; she stayed standing next to me.

The security consultant's gaze dropped from my face to hers. Small, warm fingers slid up my chest, under my jacket and under his hand. I inhaled sharply and closed my eyes as the memory hit. Her hands, sliding around me as I held her on that benighted beach. A beach full of police officers, who all wanted to help her, and she clung to me. She'd been scared and cold, clinging to me for the warmth I could give her to stave off hypothermia. Cold arms and hands and...

It's cold tonight – how come her hands were so warm?

Warm fingers effortlessly pried off the vice on my shoulder. I didn't need to look at her face, nor hear her voice. I knew it was Caitlin. It was her fingers on top of my left shoulder and her palm resting against the scar that was all that remained of where I'd been shot. I didn't need to look at her, but I sure as hell wanted to. She was close enough to touch, her shirt brushing against my work jacket, so that I could feel the heat of her body through my shirt. I ached to touch her, to wrap my arms around her and not let her go, but I didn't dare do it.

"It's all right, Trevor." She smiled at him, the rueful smile I'd seen endlessly in dreams. "I was going to ask if Nathan could see me safely home tonight."

A chance comment, only just remembered. Her rock star boyfriend. I felt my stomach plunge down to my feet and hit the concrete paving.

I noticed the drip of liquid on the pavement and followed the path of it up to the source. Her hair was wet, the end of her braid dripping as if she'd just gotten out of the shower and she'd been in too much of a hurry to take the time to dry it properly. Why did she take the time for a shower after the concert, yet not have time to dry herself?

A shout behind me heralded the kind of trouble I expected. The male singer who headed the band had appeared and the scantily dressed, heavily made up girls clustered near the entrance surged toward him. Yet Trevor the security consultant stood by and didn't budge. I itched to do the job I was here to do, but Caitlin's fingers lingered on my shoulder and I was loath to move away from her. All three of us stood and watched as the girls crowded around him, hiding him from view for a moment before he emerged, now with a girl on each arm, headed toward a dark limousine parked nearby.

Caitlin lifted her chin. "You'd best make sure Jason gets to the limo without too many of them along. That thing only seats eight and he's already invited way too many people to his private after party." She winked at Trevor. "Then you get an early night. I know Josie's waiting for you in a hotel room somewhere nearby."

Trevor jerked his head toward me. "You trust him?" His eyes were on Caitlin, as if I wasn't there.

Caitlin's face lit up with a smile. Her eyes met mine as she replied, "With my life."

Trevor hurried off toward the singer, who I realised I recognised as Caitlin's green friend, the one who visited her in hospital so many years ago.

"You're dating him?" I asked her incredulously, as she calmly watched him take off with half a dozen girls who were certainly after more than just his autograph.

Her eyes narrowed. "Have the orderlies been spreading stories again? I told one of them I had to leave early to meet my friend, who'd just flown in for a concert this week."

"How can you be a doctor and date him? He loses his lunch at the first sight of blood!" I wailed.

"That doesn't stop him being my business partner. He sings better than I do and he definitely gets the fans more excited than I ever could, but he'd have nothing to sing about if I hadn't written all his music. His bass guitar work can't carry the melody and he wouldn't have a recording contract without me." She laughed quietly, sounding harder and more businesslike. "I probably should have asked for more than him, given that I do more work, but I don't really need more, and when he makes his flamboyant exit, I get to slip out unseen." She eyed me thoughtfully. "Or I would, if you hadn't been here."

"I'm sorry," I responded automatically. I was — sorry that I'd messed up her plans, sorry that she had to find out I was nothing but a hired security guard like this, and sorry that she needed a security detail after the events of five years ago.

"Don't be. I missed you tonight and I intended to call you when I got home. Now I won't have to. Come home with me tonight?" She looked way too eager.

"Sure." The word was out of my mouth before my brain knew what it was saying. "Um, I have to stick around until we empty the place and lock up, though. It might take an hour." She wouldn't want to wait that long for me. Not when she had rock stars and groupies and God only knew who else to take care of her.

She shrugged. "I don't mind. I'll be up for a while. I'm always pretty buzzed for hours after a show. I always thought musicians needed drugs to get high, but when you've got thousands of people screaming your name…or at least the name of the band, no drug can compare to that high. I'll miss it now this tour's over." She swung her arms, raring to go. "So, what do you want me to do? Patrol the place with you? I promise not to harass the band."

If she walked by my side, I'd have eyes for nothing else. Someone could set fire to the Arena and I wouldn't notice a damn thing. And I'd be worried that something might happen to her if she were out here on her own…or even waiting in her car. "No," I began slowly, "I think you'd be better off waiting for me in the security office. It's where all the surveillance feeds go, so you can watch me on the dozen or so screens in there, and it's secure, so you'll be safe there until I can leave."

She grinned. "Sure. I'll keep an eye on things for you."

THIRTY SEVEN

Nathan swung his arms wider as we walked through the deserted Arena as if he was trying to make himself look bigger and scarier. Whenever we encountered someone else, he stiffened and looked at them suspiciously while moving just that bit closer to me.

I found myself smiling at the protective display, knowing it wasn't necessary. No one recognised me. No one ever did. Five years of working in one of Australia's most popular bands and no one looked twice at me. The spotlight was on Jason both onstage and off – we'd made sure of that from the beginning. So without my dramatic, dark clothes and makeup, I was just another groupie or teenage fan to most people. Hell, they didn't even know my name. So much for a rock star life. The money was nice, though. And walking onto that stage, knowing that they were cheering for the band I'd built, from writing the songs and securing a deal, to locking Jason in his hotel room on tour so I knew he'd be there come concert time.

He'd only disappeared once. It was after we'd opened for another band, but we were playing our own show two nights later in a much more intimate club. I'd insisted on a meeting the afternoon before the concert just so we could take a look around the venue, and he hadn't turned up. Two hours later, Trevor produced him, wearing a pair of handcuffs, a black vinyl g-string and not much else. That's the day Trevor became my permanent security chief…at Jason's expense.

Well, that was one thing I wouldn't miss – worrying about whether he'd turn up trashed to a concert or not at all. I was done babysitting grown men who should know better. Well…

I stole a glance at Nathan. He wasn't exactly capable of taking care of himself, either, but that wasn't through being irresponsible. He had an excuse and I owed him a debt. If I took care of Nathan, it wasn't babysitting at all, but repaying a favour that was long overdue. Just as long as I didn't have to deal with finding him twined around several naked women. I wanted him twined around me and only me. If he didn't want that, well, then he could go find someone else who was more to his taste.

I surveyed the long line of framed posters advertising upcoming shows. "Ooh, Blue Phoenix! They're doing an Aussie tour? It's been a while since their last one."

Nathan halted. "Who?"

I laughed. "Blue Phoenix. They're really big in the US, but they're actually a UK band. Jason's a big fan and he persuaded me to agree to open for them at some of their east coast shows. I liked their music well enough, but what I didn't know is that their concert after parties are legendary. Jason thought he was in heaven. When he finds out, he'll beg me to stage a comeback so we can tour with them. I'll go to the concert with you if you want. They are good."

"Never heard of them. But if they party like your sleazy singer, I'll probably be working that concert. Me and every other security guard they can pull on shift for that." Nathan swiped his pass card over a scanner and punched a code into the keypad, then shouldered open the unmarked door beside it. "We're here. You should be safe in the office. Don't open the door for anyone."

I assured him I wouldn't.

Nathan lingered for a moment, then caught sight of something on one of the monitors over my shoulder and unclipped the radio from his belt. "I'll be back as soon as I can," he promised, lifting the radio to his lips as the security door thudded shut behind him, leaving me alone with the security monitors.

I sank onto a stool in front of the screens and sighed.

Despite my feigned excitement in front of Nathan, the prospect of an hour in the security office was boring as all hell, but I figured it was worth the wait. Spending the rest of my evening with Nathan was definitely better than sitting at home by myself, as I had after so many other concerts on the east coast.

And I'd rarely been into the security office for such a big facility. I tried to ignore the screens, but they quickly sucked me in.

Drunk fans staggered through the foyer as the merchandise people packed up. The road crew smoked home-made cigarettes outside one of the roller doors, rolling more on the loading dock. I wondered idly if it was tobacco or something else. I'd never bothered to ask.

An unfamiliar man in a uniform like Nathan's marched along the corridor outside, then paused at the door. I heard the keypad beep and the grinding of the electronic lock before the door swung open and I was face to face with a man I didn't know.

"Who are you? You're not supposed to be here. Get out," he ordered, striding forward.

I smiled politely. "Nathan told me to stay here." I deliberately slowed my breathing, trying to stave off panic.

"Nathan Miller? Bullshit. He's the one who said he'd castrate the first bloke who brought unauthorised personnel into a restricted area, because this band's security chief is one mean bastard. They say he was a marine in Afghanistan. I'm not losing my balls for some teenage fangirl. OUT!" He reached for the baton on his belt.

I stared at him. Trevor had evidently made quite an impression. But that baton had better stay where it was or this man's genitals were the least of his worries. "No, I'll be staying right here, thank you."

"No, you won't. If you don't get out on your own, I'm authorised to remove you. Forcibly if necessary." He curled his fingers into fists, flexing his arm muscles. They were probably impressive by most people's standards. "I'm sure you don't want that. Best if you just do as you're told, okay, sweetheart?"

"It's best if you don't touch me," I replied carefully, eyeing his hands. Surely he couldn't be that stupid.

Both arms stretched for me.

Evidently he was.
His fingertips touched my shoulder.
And my night went to hell.

THIRTY EIGHT

I left the police with the two would-be prize fighters, who'd decided to start a punch-up outside the side entrance. I couldn't get any sense out of the drunks and it was better if they sobered up in the cells for the night, where they couldn't hurt anyone else. What I'd give for a job that didn't involve breaking up brawls. Every damn concert had one. Even the Wiggles one – two mothers screeching at each other, manicured claws out as they pulled each other's hair, while their toddlers threw tantrums on the grass. I'd had enough for one night and the foyer was empty. I intended to lock up, go home and leave the place to the two night shift guys, though I hadn't seen them in over an hour.

Irritated that I couldn't even raise Steve or Jerry on the radio, I strode back to the control room to see if I could find them on the security cameras. If they were holed up backstage with a couple of fangirls, there'd be hell to pay.

I swung the door open and stopped dead. "What the fuck happened here?"

Jerry scooted along the floor, twisting so he could see me. His handcuffs jingled as he sat up. He opened his mouth, but he didn't seem to have the power of speech.

My eyes darted to the barstool where I'd left Caitlin. The empty barstool now.

"Where's the girl?" I demanded. "Did they take her?"

"What girl?" Jerry grunted, wincing as he shifted.

I pulled my keys out of my pocket and fitted one into the handcuffs. All of ours were all keyed alike, so it only took a moment to free him. "The girl I left here, waiting until I came back. What did they look like? The guys who took her."

He rubbed his wrists. "Dunno. I didn't get a good look at them, but I figure it must've been at least two big guys to take both of us down. Maybe three. Armed, too. I walked in and saw Steve on the floor over there, handcuffed to the post, so I did what you just did and tried to free him. They hit me from behind and I woke up handcuffed to the other post and my pockets empty. No keys, no radio, no nothing." He nodded at Steve, who looked to be unconscious. "Wake him up. Maybe he knows."

I nodded. "I will. You start filling out an incident form before you forget anything important. I need details. All of them." Or I wouldn't be able to find who'd taken Caitlin. Shit, how'd they get in here?

I grabbed a bottle of water from the desk and poured it over Steve's face.

He woke, spluttering. "Where'she?" he slurred.

"Where's who?" I asked.

"Where's that girl?" His head jerked as he searched the room. "Knocked me out. I asked Jerry to help me get free and they got him again, then me. Must've been three big blokes, waiting to ambush me. I went down fighting, I swear, Miller."

For a bloke who'd gone down fighting, his face was remarkably unhurt. His knuckles, too, I noticed. No sign of damage except for a couple of tiny rips in the front of his shirt.

My bullshit meter overloaded. These guys were lying – one or both of them, I wasn't sure. Had someone paid them off to get to Caitlin?

"Did they say where they were taking the girl?" I asked slowly. "How long ago did they leave?"

Both hesitated for a moment too long before replying. While they argued over the correct answer, I ignored them and headed for the store room where we kept the spare equipment.

I caught a glimpse of movement out of the corner of my eye, but when I turned to face it, all I saw was our sole riot control shield. The clear plastic reflected the shelves when the light hit it just right and it took me a moment to realise what I was looking at. My breath whooshed out of me with relief and I reached up to the top shelf.

"Are you all right?" I asked as Caitlin took my hand, swinging her legs over the edge of the shelf. She nodded and waved me out of the way as she twisted to dangle from her hands before dropping to the floor. "What did the men look like? The ones who came in here?"

Her voice was barely louder than a whisper. "Security uniforms like yours. The first one tried to make me leave.

When he touched me, I took him out. The second came in as I was restraining the first. I had to knock him out, too, before I was sure whether he was a danger or not." She looked grave.

I had a crazy urge to burst out laughing. Caitlin had taken out my best security guards. Could tonight get any crazier?

"I'll protect you," I promised, curling an arm around her shoulders. To my surprise and relief, she leaned into my side, as if she welcomed the support.

Together, we returned to the office. "Steve, Jerry, this is…Alana." I hoped they didn't notice my hesitation as I stumbled over her name. "She's lucky she didn't end up trussed up like you, or worse."

Silence.

I peered at Jerry's report. "Biker helmets? So you didn't even see their faces?"

He shook his head.

"Should I search the security footage for them?"

"They took the tape?" he suggested, as if even he didn't believe his own cock-and-bull story.

I sighed. "Look, I can send you two to hospital to get checked out and we can file an incident report about what really happened, or I can ask a doctor to check you out here and we can pretend this was all a bad dream." There was no way in hell either of them would admit they were bested by a girl – let alone one as fragile-looking as Caitlin.

"Where'll you get a doctor this time of night?" Steve asked.

"Angel, would you be willing to help? Once we know they're okay to finish their shift, we can go."

Caitlin nodded and cautiously approached Steve. He flinched as she dropped to a crouch beside him, but he allowed her to examine him. Jerry didn't take his eyes off her all through his own examination until she returned to my side. I'd never seen these men scared before, but they were terrified of her. "I checked them earlier, while they were both stunned. They might have some residual muscle cramps from the taser, but those will subside in a day or so. They should be fine. If not, send them to me and I'll check them over again."

The taser? So that's how she'd knocked them out.

"That kid's a doctor?" Steve spluttered.

I inclined my head. "This is Dr Alana Miller. She's just taken a job at Fiona Stanley Hospital. She was waiting in here for me as it was supposed to be safer than outside. Given the helmeted, tape-stealing bikers, though, it's probably a good thing she hid in the store room and let you guys take the heat." I tried to grin, but it came out more like a grimace. "At least we're trained for it. We'll be headed off now. If there's any more signs of the mystery bikers, call me on my mobile, okay?"

Jerry nodded slowly as he buckled on his utility belt.

"Can you get these off me?" Steve grumbled, lifting his handcuffed wrists.

I left Steve and Jerry to it.

THIRTY NINE

I followed Caitlin's car back to her place, then walked her to the stairwell.

"Please, will you come up for a drink? Or two?" The quiet desperation in her tone tugged at my heart. I couldn't refuse her anything.

I agreed and followed her up.

"Just give me a moment to go tidy up. Help yourself to whatever you like while you're waiting." She waved vaguely at the kitchen as she headed to her bedroom.

When she returned, I was halfway through drinking my second glass of water.

"You don't want any alcohol?" she asked, still seeming more nervous than she should be.

I shrugged. "I figured I'd wait and see what you were having and water's not a bad thing to start with."

Slowly, she nodded as she opened the pantry and

stretched for something on the top shelf. I watched her for a few seconds before I gave in and offered, "Do you need help?"

She shook her head and edged a box off the shelf. When she set it on the bench, I couldn't hide my surprise. "After tonight, I think a stiff drink is in order. If I open it, will you share it with me?"

I eyed the bottle of Johnny Walker Blue Label she held out to me, the unbroken seal taunting me that I didn't deserve the expensive spirit it guarded. "Don't you have anything else? I mean, that stuff's supposed to be savoured. If all you want is to drown your sorrows and forget, you'd be better off with the Red Label."

Caitlin laughed. "That's what I usually have, a shot of that with a mixer when I get home. But tonight I just want to drink it straight, which calls for the good stuff. And I don't think even the whole bottle will make me forget, so it'd be pretty pointless to try." She reached into the cupboard and clunked two glasses to the counter. "So, will you join me in a drink?" A deft twist of her hand broke the seal and she poured a precise two fingers into one glass. The smell wafting up was potent, seductive.

I nodded and watched the amber liquid glug into my glass. The aroma stole into my nostrils and invaded my mind. I wondered if it could dissolve my brain – and whether I'd notice.

Caitlin's explosive coughing fit made me set the drink down again so I could stop her from choking, but she waved away my offers of assistance. "Shit, that's strong," she said hoarsely, squinting into her glass before taking another sip.

I gulped half of mine without tasting it, feeling it sear my throat on the way down. I held the second mouthful a little longer, rolling around until I tasted it, then let it burn my oesophagus, too. "It's like drinking petrol." My voice came out almost as hoarse as hers had.

She smiled and carried her glass over to the couch. When she slumped onto the seat, I realised just how exhausted she was. Cautiously, I sat on the opposite end, where I had a clear view of her face.

"You're taking this awfully well. Me being in Chaya and all, and me not saying anything."

I shrugged. "I didn't tell you I was a security guard, either, but that doesn't seem to worry you." After worrying about what she'd think of me, it was a relief. I hadn't even started thinking about the implications of her being a rock star. No, retired rock star – this was the last concert on her band's farewell tour.

Caitlin concentrated on sipping her drink for a moment before replying, "I already knew. Trevor makes me check all the security guards before a show, so I know who they are and if anyone's not there who should be. Also, if there's anyone I recognise who poses a greater risk than others. I told him I knew you, but that I wanted you on the security team. I was hoping to see you last night and I'd almost given up when you grabbed me tonight. All that instinct of wanting to fight back and escape, but I knew it was you who had me, so I didn't resist. Would you still have grabbed me if you knew I was carrying a taser?"

I swallowed more whisky. "Those things aren't legal in Australia, you know. If the police find out you have it…"

She laughed. "Oh, they're legal if you have a permit, and

I do. In all states and both territories, too. Right alongside my gun licences. It was one of the weird conditions of my witness protection – that I was supposed to carry a weapon. I always wondered if it was one of Mott's ploys to make sure I had a weapon on me when he sent someone to kill me. Dodgy bastard would've wanted me dead and suicide would've suited him nicely. I had a long talk with Trevor about it and he arranged for the taser permit. I think the argument was along the lines that, as a doctor, I didn't like the idea of shooting people to protect myself, as I'd be bound to provide medical assistance afterwards that would place me in even greater danger, but use of a non-lethal weapon with no long-term effects…"

"I can think of two men whose pride is going to be hurt for a long time, knowing you bested them with a taser." The minute the words were out of my mouth, I regretted them.

Tears flowed down her cheeks. "I'm so sorry, Nathan. I didn't mean for any of that to happen tonight. Those two men…shit, I'm sorry."

I desperately wanted to tell her that everything would be all right, but the words would be an empty promise I couldn't keep. "They're trained to be able to take down an attacker. If you managed to overcome them, they'll need more training. Simple as that. I don't think either of them wants to admit what happened tonight, so they won't spread stories. It could cost them their jobs. So it'll be a closely guarded secret that they'll do their best to forget. End of story."

She shook her head. "No. I'm not worried about that. It's that I attacked two men who weren't trying to hurt me – they were only doing their jobs. The guys from ASIO said

I'd be safe here. I'm beginning to think I'm paranoid, seeing threats everywhere when there aren't any. It wasn't this bad in Melbourne, but now I'm back here and with the mystery stalker and that house and even you – not that you're a bad thing, Nathan, just that I'm worried about you – I feel like I'm going crazy."

"You're not crazy." Perfectly true. "You are very protective of yourself and that's reasonable, given what you've been through." Mostly true. Most rape victims didn't have tasers. "If you say you have a stalker, then I believe you. It's not the first time government staff have lied to you about your safety." The last time I'd helped them, so I skipped to the next point quickly. "And what house? This one?"

She heaved a heartfelt sigh. "No, not this one. My grandfather's house. My cousin gave it to me as payment of a debt of honour or some crazy idea like that. At least, that's what he told my father. I don't even know what that means. Is it a good debt or a bad one? I mean, who gives someone a house? For all I know, the house could be wired to explode the minute someone sets foot inside. Why go to so much trouble? Surely an assassin would be cheaper and easier. But I can't sell it unless I know it's safe. I don't want someone else's death on my conscience – not even a ruthless real estate agent."

Something seemed fishy. A long-lost cousin offering an enormous inheritance was too good to be true. It sounded like a scam to me. "What does your security consultant say about it?"

Caitlin snorted. "Trevor? The minute I told him, he drove down there himself without telling me. It turns out the place gets cleaned weekly by a company in town. He chased up the cleaner and spoke to her. She believed it was a holiday house and she'd never met the owners. She was hired five years ago. About the time I moved to Melbourne." She blew out a breath. "Trevor told me to stay away from it. Just because the cleaner's never been blown up, doesn't mean I won't be. I've agreed to meet with my cousin to discuss it, but I need to see the house first before I agree to take it. There's something about it, lurking in the back of my mind. I know I'll stop worrying once I've seen it, but I'm scared of it, too. Scared of a house I never saw and probably never set foot in." Her eyes were on me now, looking deeper than I felt comfortable with.

I avoided her gaze and focussed on drinking my whisky.

"Will you come with me? Please?"

No. Fuck, no. I'd take a holiday in hell as the devil's personal whipping boy before I'd go within a hundred kilometres of a place that sounded like another nightmare we should both stay the hell away from. But for Caitlin, I'd do anything.

"Sure."

She threw herself at me, hugging me tightly. "Thank you. Thank you so much, Nathan. That'll be one less posse of demons to vanquish. I swear, I'll never ask anything of you ever again after this."

With her clinging to me, squirming in my lap, I wanted to ask her a few things. Things I shouldn't. Instead, I said, "Should we have another drink to celebrate? To crazy ideas and banishing demons?"

She laughed and agreed, so we poured a little more whisky into our glasses and toasted each other's health and the future.

Later that night, as I stretched out in bed, I reflected that if they existed, the devil and his demons would probably enjoy being beaten by someone as beautiful as Caitlin. I laughed quietly to myself and let the alcohol in my blood drag me under the surface of sleep.

FORTY

I woke up in the dark, hearing the sound of someone else's rapid breathing inside the room with me.

I sat up, looking for the source of it.

Caitlin. She lay on her side, facing away from me, silhouetted in the faint light coming from the window and the blind I hadn't closed properly. The curve of her shoulder, her arms bent and resting on the bed beside her. The smooth line down her side to the dip where her waist was, the swell of her hip, sloping down her leg to her foot. Smooth bare skin, not marred by any visible scar. I reached out to touch her, to find out if she was real, running my fingers lightly along her side as I pressed my lips to the back of her neck. Not wanting to wake her, I pulled my hand away as she moved.

"Nathan?" She sounded like she'd been crying. Her fingers touched my arm, then she turned and moved closer to me, her body pressed against mine. When she rested her head on my chest, her face was damp. She was crying.

"What's wrong?" I asked immediately, not daring to move in case she moved away.

"Nothing," she sniffled. "I just had a bad dream."

I grinned into the dark. "You know what you said last time I had a nightmare?"

"What?"

"That we needed to shape a new memory to replace the old one. If all my nightmares ended in phenomenal sex, they'd never frighten me again. Let me take your mind off it, angel."

I listened to her breathing, which wasn't slowing. Her voice was breathless as she said, "You mean it? You really mean it? You'd…make love to me?"

After a fashion. I wouldn't give her anything to complain about, that's for sure. "If you want me to, angel."

"Yes," she breathed. I heard the sound of satin sliding over skin before I felt it – her skin warm against mine, slippery with a thin sheen of sweat from the dream that had woken her. "Can you…can you turn the light on, though? I'm not good in the dark."

I reached over and clicked the switch. Now I could see her beautiful naked body – everything I wanted. I flicked my tongue over her nipple and felt it harden at the touch.

"More," she gasped, arching her back to offer me her breasts.

A gift I took willingly, sucking first one and then the other, before I slid my hand up her thigh.

"Oh yes," she breathed, parting her legs for me. She was slick with need, her core closing around my fingers as she moaned in pleasure and not pain. With Caitlin, I definitely knew the difference.

She rode my hand to her gasping peak and I kissed her mouth until her shuddering subsided.

"Better?" I asked, withdrawing my fingers.

"Fuck yes," she groaned, grabbing my hand. "Don't stop now. More to make me forget…forget everything. Everything…except you." The desire in her eyes was unmistakeable – I recognised it now.

Caitlin. Angel. Everything I'd ever wanted and more. My angel, whose body felt as heavenly as it looked. And I wanted her to feel it, too, deep inside. I wanted to make her forget everything that had ever happened to her before this moment so that she'd be mine.

I drove my fingers deep inside her, kissing her through every gasp until she climaxed, sobbing my name. I kissed my way down her neck and her breasts as she bucked beneath me, my fingers continuing their pleasurable onslaught. I slowed as my lips touched her belly, knowing she was close to her third. She came just as my tongue darted out to taste her essence. God, so sweet and I wanted more, so I didn't stop, tonguing that tiny bundle of nerve endings that made her fall apart all over again. And again. Until she shattered with a scream, sobbing my name and begging me to continue.

She might forget her own name, but she'd never forget mine. I plunged my fingers inside her, surging up the bed to kiss her with the taste of her still on my lips. She moaned at her next climax. I'd lost count of how many times she'd come and I didn't care.

"Have you had enough, angel?" I asked tenderly, kissing

her neck.

"No. I want more. More than your fingers and your tongue, Nathan. I want…" She cried out as my fingers caressed her insides again. She reached for me, running her hands across my chest as if she wanted to etch every muscle into her memory. "More. More!"

Blood rushed from her caressing fingers straight to my groin and I wanted to cheer. "Tell me what you'd like, angel, and I'll do it."

Her fingers tickled my belly, moving slowly down. "You could start with a kiss."

Mike's words.

Reality came crashing down, dousing my libido in freezing slush.

Not even her stroking hands could arouse me now, squeezing my flaccid length as if she could coax life back into it.

"You really don't want me." Her voice shook. "Oh God."

I wanted to tell her she was wrong, but she propelled herself out of bed and stumbled out of the room.

There. She finally knew my secret. I didn't deserve her. And she didn't deserve an impotent loser like me who could never satisfy her.

FORTY ONE

I'm ashamed to say I cried myself to sleep. What had I expected? Nathan had had years of being able to pull any girl he wanted. A damaged doctor who still had occasional nightmares from five years ago wasn't even a blip on his dating radar.

When the morning sun streamed in, reality dawned with it. Nathan had given me a precious gift last night, even if he hadn't given me all of himself. He was the only one who could play my body like that and I was profoundly grateful that he had. None of my dreams were nightmares after that. And he did want me – he'd said so and I'd seen it in his eyes. He wasn't the first man to suffer impotence as a result of psychological trauma. If I helped him with the trauma, maybe I'd be able to help him with other things, too. All in good time.

I bounced out of bed and into the shower, relishing the

hot water that was nothing compared to the caresses that felt burned into my body after last night. Trust selfless Nathan to use his extraordinary skills to make me feel this good without any thought of reward.

I needed to thank him.

I cautiously approached the guest room and knocked, but there was no answer. I pushed the door open slowly, glad that it was too new to creak, and stared at the made bed in an otherwise empty room. No Nathan.

Bathroom, maybe? I'd been too intent on my shower in the ensuite to notice if the other bathroom was occupied.

Nope.

I searched the house and even the parking lot downstairs before I knew for sure that Nathan had left and taken his car with him.

Did he think I was so shallow that I'd throw him out for not sleeping with me? He was my friend before he was anything else. Surely he knew me better than that.

Would he still come on holiday with me?

Doubt niggled, but he'd promised, and I knew Nathan kept his word. That much couldn't have changed in five years, even if everything else had. So sex with him was out. That was fine. I could live with that. I'd ignore my feelings and be what I needed to be – a friend who was helping him deal with the traumatic memories that plagued his dreams. And one who took him on holiday when he needed it.

I donned a dress and packed my things.

FORTY TWO

I knocked on the door a second time. His car was here, so I knew he was home. He might be asleep, though, given how little sleep either of us had gotten the night before, so I knocked harder in the hope that he'd hear me, wake up and come to answer the door. Just as long as it wasn't…

The door flew open and his angry little sister glared at me. "YOU! What are you doing here?"

I gave her my most professional smile, the one I gave difficult patients right before I decided only a rectal thermometer would suit my observations. "Good morning. I came to check on Nathan, to make sure he made it home okay last night."

Her lip curled in a sneer. "You're the slutty doctor who kidnapped him from hospital so you could suck his dick without losing your job? Figures. You're a selfish bitch, you know that? My brother is a sick man. You have no idea what he's been through. If you ever come back here again, I'll call the police and you can suck cock in a cell instead. I hope they charge you with kidnapping and send you to prison. The other prisoners will be queuing up to break a snotty bitch like you – I'm a lawyer and I've heard the stories. You'll be begging for mercy in a day and the hard cases in the women's prison don't know the meaning of the word."

I felt nauseated by her rant, but I swallowed my ire. Nathan's messed-up sister wasn't my problem. "Nathan's a grown man and perfectly capable of making his own decisions. Now I see why he was so eager to come home with me. *Fetch* him, please." I barely reached her shoulder, but I knew I was more than a match for her physically, though I hoped it wouldn't come to that.

Evidently she didn't share my sentiments as she braced herself in the doorway. "Go away. He's not home."

I blinked. "His car's here. So where is he, then?"

Her eyes darted around as she thought up a lie. "With his girlfriend. At the gym. At work. I don't fucking know. He's a grown man who does what he damn well pleases. And now he's already fucked you, he won't do it again, so just go away and don't waste my time. He doesn't want to see you."

I heard the sound of a door creaking, then the flow of liquid under pressure.

Nathan or her boyfriend. No, a shrew like this wouldn't have a boyfriend. "Sounds like he's here and he's awake, too. I suggest you ask him what he wants. If Nathan wants me to leave, he's more than capable of saying so." I winked. "I wasn't too hard on his tongue last night."

She reacted just as I expected. A shrieked stream of insults brought Nathan to the door, dressed quite demurely for him of a morning, with a pair of boxer shorts covering the essentials that he felt the need to draw attention to with a vigorous scratch.

"One of your ex-boyfriends, Chris? Or one of the girls who stole him from you?" he asked, peering over her shoulder.

I beamed and burst out laughing. "Not exactly."

"Angel," he breathed, disbelief written across his face. "You shouldn't be standing on the doorstep. Come in." He wrapped a hand around my upper arm and pulled me inside, shoving his irate sister out of his way. Behind me, he bumped the door shut. "What are you doing here so early? I didn't think you'd want to see me so soon after last night. I figured I'd call tomorrow or the next day to apologise. I meant to tell you, but I didn't know how…"

"I won't have that bitch in my house, Nathan!" Chris shrieked, pointing at me.

Nathan's arm curled around me. "Don't call her that. It's my house, too, and I've put up with enough of your douchebag boyfriends. More tattoos than brain cells and worse at keeping their dicks in their pants than I am, and that's saying something."

I smothered a laugh. The mental image of Chris's dissatisfied biker boyfriends was just too funny. Little Miss Bitchy Lawyer buckled down in the bedroom for bikers…or maybe she didn't, and that was the problem. I bet they didn't like her sharp tongue, either. Oh God, I couldn't hold in my laughter for much longer. Even the thought of this proud harpy on her knees for some bloke in sweaty leather pants...

"I'm going out," Chris announced. "She better not be here when I get back." She grabbed her bag, flounced out and slammed the door behind her.

Nathan led me to the couch. "I'm really sorry. I've never seen her like this. I mean, she screams at me occasionally but never at someone she doesn't know. I'll talk to her when she cools down and get her to apologise."

Now the girl was gone, I summoned a real smile. "How about we leave her to cool down for a bit longer? I'm heading down to Busselton today. Are you still coming with me?" I met his surprised eyes. "I really want you to come."

He flushed as if he'd caught my double meaning. His unfortunate problem last night was too fresh in both of our minds for him not to. "Are you sure? I might not be the most cheerful holiday companion. I'd only drag you down."

"I haven't been on a holiday in ages, Nathan, and you need a break as much as I do. You said you'd come and I've really been looking forward to spending the time with you." I glanced at the front door. "Without anyone else interfering."

"I still want to, but Chris will hit the roof when I tell her. It'd probably be best if you're not here for that."

I laughed softly. "I think it'd be best if you're not here for that either. Pack your things and leave her a note. She's your little sister, not your keeper, and she doesn't own you. My bags are in the boot of the car. As soon as you throw your stuff in, we can go." I gazed into his eyes as I saw the glimmering of his acquiescence. "I promise I'll take care of you."

He grinned. "Angel, if I'm coming with you, it'll be me

taking care of you, not the other way 'round." The look in his eyes mystified me for a moment, until I identified it as gratitude.

"Then get some clothes on so we can go. Check-in's at two, so we have three hours to get there. I want to watch the sunset from the end of the jetty with you."

Half an hour later, he locked the front door and stared wistfully at my car. "Can I drive?"

FORTY THREE

Gravel grated under the tyres, startling me from sleep. I peeled my tongue from the roof of my mouth as I twisted my neck to ease the kinks out of it. How long had I slept?

Nathan's hand touched my shoulder. "Angel? We're here. This is the guesthouse."

I pried my eyes open and was surprised to find that he was telling the truth. Nathan wouldn't have kidnapped me again, I scolded myself. He's a good man and one of the few I trust. I was safer with him than with anyone else I knew. I just needed to get used to trusting someone again.

His eyes told me he knew about my doubts, though not the reassurances I banished them with.

I leaned over and kissed his cheek, but he pulled away before I could take it any further. Annoyed but understanding, I also got out of the car and stretched my legs.

"I haven't been here since I was a kid," Nathan said, peering through the front door. "Chris was only a baby and Alanna and I shared a room, so we must've been about five or six. Dad took us fishing off the jetty, we went down the beach for a swim every day. Mum said this is where her parents came on their honeymoon. And it's still a guesthouse, more than fifty years later."

"Actually, the buildings were brought from the old RAAF World War II airbase over near Bunnings. Three buildings and you can still see where the joins are, too," a new voice said as the door swung open. The blonde woman grinned. "Beth. My husband and I run the place now." She stuck her hand out and looked expectant.

Nathan saved me by shaking her hand. "Nathan and Alana Miller. We had…two rooms booked? Next to each other, please."

Beth looked from him to me. "Are you expecting anyone else?"

Shit, I'd never thought that now we had the same last name, but didn't look alike, people would assume we were married. "No," I answered.

She waited as if she expected me to say more, then hitched her smile back up. "Well, I've given you three and four. They're not quite next to each other, as the linen room's between them, but they're across the hall from each other at the end." She led us inside, pointing as she went. "That's the TV room. Through those double doors to the guest dining room, where your breakfast will be served. There's a fridge and microwave in there for you to use, and tea and coffee all day. Games room and reading nook's through there. Outside is that way, to the back deck and the spa. And these are your rooms." Behind her, the passage ended in an alcove lined with linen-filled shelves. Her spread arms indicated the numbered doors on either side of her.

I peeked into one at the same time as Nathan. He wheeled my little suitcase inside. "You take this one. I'll have the other one." I nodded.

"Breakfast menus are on your dresser. Leave them in the kitchen tonight and I'll have everything prepared for you tomorrow. If you need anything, just let me know," Beth finished with a final smile before she left.

I unpacked quickly, kicking my suitcase under the sofa so it wouldn't be in the way, before heading across the hall to see Nathan's room. His was much smaller than mine, with just a bed and no sofa. I hadn't known we'd get such disparate rooms – I thought they were both the same. I opened my mouth to apologise and offer him the better accommodation.

"You're funding this trip, so you get a better room. Closer to the car, too, if for any reason we need to leave in a hurry."

I stared at him in alarm.

"Your stalker, remember? If he tracks us here, I want you to go out the window and drive off. Don't wait for me."

Slowly, I nodded. "Trevor would say that, too." I wet my lips. "He'd also lock my door when I retire for the night, so he'd be the only one with a key. I want you to do the same." Suddenly, the thought of a stalker here even on our holiday made the whole thing seem like a terrible idea. Would this never be over?

Nathan's arms slid around me, pulling me against him. Warm, firm and safe. "No one followed us, angel. Believe me, I half expected someone to, but not a single car from Perth was with us when we turned off the highway for Busselton. I'm just protecting you, like I said I would."

Yes. And I couldn't ask for a better protector than the man who saved my life. My hero.

FORTY FOUR

A gentle knock sounded on my open door. I looked up to meet Caitlin's smile. "Want to go for a walk along the jetty to see the sunset? Apparently, there's an underwater viewing deck at the end and everything."

It was hard to resist her enthusiasm. "Sure. I probably need to stretch my legs after that long drive, anyway. Even if your car is so much nicer to drive than mine. I'll warn you, it's a long walk, though – the jetty's almost two kilometres long and the observatory's at the deep end."

Her smile only brightened. "After walking the wards all day and night at work, it sounds like a lovely stroll. C'mon, let's go be tourists."

I shoved my feet into my sneakers and followed her out. "Do you want to drive or should I?" I asked, raising the remote to deactivate the central locking.

"You can drive if you want, but I'm walking," she

replied, heading toward the sound of breaking waves. I couldn't see the beach, but there was no mistaking it. I hurried to catch up.

Caitlin reached for my hand and I clasped her cold fingers in mine. I couldn't take my eyes off her and I know she noticed, but she didn't seem to mind.

Whatever we had was weird, I decided. We'd been through hell together, she'd saved my life and I'd done the same for her, even if I'd been the one who put her in danger in the first place. Yet I'd never taken her on a date. No movie, no dinner…well, there was that disastrous drink in a nightclub that I'd prefer to forget, but that didn't count. My love for her was forged in blood and pain, and it would be a part of me for as long as I lived. But I'd hurt her too much for her ever to see me in the same way as I saw her. Maybe when her security guy retired, she'd let me take his place. Then at least I could protect her and keep her safe. Shit, I'd probably need a lot more training before she'd agree to that. After all, she could afford her own bodyguard. Why would she settle for me when she could have the best money could buy?

Caitlin pressed against my side, pulling my arm around her to hold her against me. "The ocean breeze in winter…I should have brought a coat."

Automatically, I opened my jacket to share its warmth with her. With her nestled against my shirt, hope flowered in my heart. Of course I'd protect her. Keep her warm. Whatever she needed me to do. I'd give my life for her, now, because I knew she'd be all right without me. But that didn't mean I couldn't enjoy her closeness while it lasted.

Cloudy skies turned the water grey, capped with white as

the wind churned up waves that washed over the short jetty beside the much longer one. It wasn't the welcoming water I remembered from my childhood, but this bleakness suited the stark reality of adulthood. Life was no longer a stream of sunshine and sandcastles, shared with a sister I'd never see again.

Caitlin tugged on my arm. "Let's get tickets to the observatory before the ticket office closes." She pulled me inside the shop that housed the ticket office, a strange selection of maritime-themed knickknacks and a small museum with the history of the jetty.

The black and white photos of sailing ships and steamships caught my attention, alongside some large, colour pictures of broken-off pylons where chunks of the jetty were missing. The forlorn pylons tugged at my memory – I was certain I'd seen them. A placard beside them described how a cyclone had destroyed the jetty in the seventies, years before I was born. How could I remember it, then?

"Look at this!' Caitlin exclaimed, holding up a statue of a buxom mermaid whose breasts were barely restrained by two tiny, strung-together seashells. "I don't know why anyone would wear such an uncomfortable bra. If mermaids exist, I hope someone's told them about women's liberation." She set the figurine carefully back on the shelf.

"Good thing they're just mythical," I replied. There was something in the statue's expression that looked like proud disdain. I wouldn't want to tell her she couldn't wear whatever mermaid fashion she wanted.

"Can we get two tickets for the observatory, please?" I heard Caitlin ask and realised she was speaking to the women behind the shop counter.

Both exchanged glances and shook their heads. "It's closed for today. Visibility isn't all that good with the waves stirring everything up at the moment, anyway." The older woman pointed at the screen on the wall, which showed a murky green picture. The shadow of something tall and straight seemed to move in and out of focus. "See? You can barely see the pylon. Come back tomorrow or on the weekend, when the weather's meant to be better. Or summer, when visibility's the best."

"But the sunset looks pretty from the end of the jetty, if you're up for a walk," the younger one added. "Romantic and all." She eyed me with a certain degree of calculation.

I knew that look. Years ago, I'd have winked and grinned, but now I turned my gaze to Caitlin. "Do you still want to walk along the jetty?"

Caitlin beamed. "Of course. We've come this far. It'd be a shame not to enjoy the view and a leisurely stroll."

FORTY FIVE

Caitlin took my arm and we set off through the gate. Our footsteps thumped dully on the concrete, jarring with the hollow-sounding timber boards in my memories.

"This isn't how I remember the jetty," I blurted out. "It was wood – I remember, all timber, and old timber, too. Grey from age, not because of concrete." I tapped the railway track with my shoe. "And it was narrower, too. There wasn't space to walk beside the tracks. And there weren't handrails on both sides, either. I remember walking on the edge of the boards, having to put one foot in front of the other like I was on a balancing beam, until Alanna shouted at me and Dad made me get away from the edge. She walked right in the middle of the tracks – she was afraid of falling in." I laughed softly. "She wasn't as tough back then."

How tough had she really been, though? If Caitlin had

survived her kidnapping, and Alanna hadn't? With Caitlin so delicate, Alanna should've had more of a chance against them. But somehow she gave up and left me to deal with the consequences. Identifying her dead body. Coping with her loss. Seeking vengeance for her murder. And having to watch as they took Caitlin…

I stumbled over a dead fish, which demonstrated that it wasn't quite dead yet as it ballooned into an angry, fishy ball. I kicked it, launching the blowfish back into the water.

"Dad took us fishing off this jetty. Just Alanna and I – we left Mum and Chris at home. I had to bait up her hooks with the squishy little prawns because she wouldn't touch them. They were too yucky, she said. We just had those little handlines – you know, round, plastic rings with line wrapped around them, and a hook and sinker on the end. Dad had a rod and reel, but he was so busy helping us pull our fish off the hooks and baiting them up again that he didn't get to use it much. I think I caught forty blowies that day – they just kept biting. I didn't understand why Dad wouldn't put them in the bucket, though. Instead, he just unhooked them and let them flap around, blowing themselves up on the jetty until I kicked them off the edge." I peered over the side, but I couldn't see the one I'd thrown back. Maybe it'd swum away to enjoy its good fortune.

Caitlin glanced at me and smiled, but didn't say anything.

A seagull landed on the railing, screeching its displeasure at whatever had pissed it off.

"Alanna eventually gave up on catching fish and just sat next to me, watching my line. That's when Dad decided to give his rod a go. He baited it up, threw it over his shoulder and I heard the line whizz out over the water. I looked just in time to see the seagull diving for something, then fly up again, flapping frantically. Dad started reeling in his line right away, but I didn't understand why until the seagull started flying toward us, even though it looked like it was trying to fly away. The stupid bird had gone for the bait and taken the hook as well. Dad tried to reel that seagull in so he could try and free it, but the closer he got, the more the bird flapped until it was almost at the end of the rod, it was so close. Dad dropped the rod on the jetty and tried to grab the seagull to cut it free. The bloody bird went berserk. It flew up, hook, rod, and all, and then splashed down again because the rod was too heavy for it to carry. It splashed around on the surface for a bit before it took flight — without the line or the rod, which sank under the jetty. Dad started shouting and swearing at the stupid bird, Alanna giggled and then I caught another fish. Dad packed everything up, but he had to wait until I'd managed to reel up my fish. He yanked it off the line and threw it at the seagull, but the bird flew away and the fish landed in the water instead." I smiled at the memory. "When we got home, Mum went nuts. We'd been sitting on the rusty old tracks, dangling our legs off the edge of the jetty, and our pants were covered in rust stains. Alanna was horrified that she'd been walking around with a brown bum. She burst into tears and Mum blamed Dad for the whole mess, but it was my idea to sit on the train tracks."

I kicked at the tracks beneath my feet now, which weren't rusty at all. "This jetty isn't the same. It's like even my memories are gone. Stolen, somehow, like Alanna was. I remember her as really tough when we were in high school and uni, but I guess she wasn't, not really. The way she shrieked and danced around in fright when she caught her first fish and it moved..."

Not tough enough to survive. What I'd give for her advice now on what to do about Caitlin. I mean, here we were together at the end of the jetty, with no one else around and the sun setting over the ocean. I knew this sort of romantic shit worked. Any other girl five years ago and I'd have grabbed her and kissed her until she was helpless to resist me. With Caitlin, I couldn't. She needed to resist me, just like I had to resist giving in to my feelings about her. But I wanted...

Caitlin's eyes met mine, filled with sympathy and pain. I wanted to kiss it all away and turn her sadness to joy in my arms. Mine. No one else's. But I couldn't. I wasn't good enough for her.

As if to taunt me, she pressed closer. "It's even colder in the breeze out here," she said softly.

Every bit of my being wanted to wrap myself around her and never let her feel the cold again, but I forced myself to pull away. Shit, it felt like I was tearing myself in two.

I shrugged out of my jacket and draped it around her shoulders. "Take it. You need it more than I do."

A tear sparkled on her cheek, tinted with gold in the sunset, but she wiped it away. "We should head back and get dinner. The ladies at the ticket office mentioned a fish and chip shop in town – Cod Rocks, they said it was called. They have fresh Spanish mackerel and whiting. We could bring it back to the beach to watch the stars come out." She ducked her head to slip her arms into the sleeves of my jacket before she zipped it up. Her arms folded across her chest, shutting me out of her warmth and her heart.

Trust me to mess things up for her. At least I was good at something.

"Sure. Whatever you want," I replied dully. Shivering in the cold, I led the way back down the jetty to the shore. Wishing the stiff breeze could ice over my heart.

FORTY SIX

The sound of screaming jolted me awake. I was out of bed and charging across the hall before my brain had caught up with my body, but the thought of Caitlin in danger only quickened my stride. Of course I recognised her scream. It had haunted me for five years.

I tried her door, but it was locked. Shoving my shoulder against it, I cursed the sturdiness of wartime building materials, then remembered I was the one who'd locked it, at her request. Ignoring the sleepy onlookers who'd emerged from their rooms to find out what was going on, I snatched up the key from my dresser and frantically tried to fit it into the lock. My fingers were slippery with sweat as the screaming continued. Oh God, I couldn't lose her now. Not now…

I wrenched the door open and strode into the room. A quick scan told me the windows were closed and Caitlin appeared to be alone — but she gasped for breath and let out another agonised scream.

Nightmare. I dropped to my knees and reached for her, trying desperately not to listen to what she was screaming. If I let the words in, I'd be a gibbering mess on the floor and I couldn't help her. Besides, when she woke up, she'd tase me anyway. I just had to rouse her…

Swallowing, I pulled her into my arms, tightening my hold as she struggled. One flailing fist struck me hard enough to summon stars, but I didn't let go. Her body might have recovered, but her mind was locked in a nightmare that I needed to free her from. Caitlin didn't deserve a messed-up head like mine. I heard my own voice murmur the same soothing litany that I'd said so many times in the past. Who I was, that I was here and that everything would be all right. This time it was true.

A throat cleared behind me. "Mate, I think you should step away from the girl." Beth's husband, who'd helped us with the pool table last night, stood in the doorway. His expression was grim.

"Not until she's —" I glanced at Caitlin. Panicked, wide-awake eyes stared back, "— awake." I eased her onto the pillow and rose.

"Probably best if you go back to your own room now," the man continued. Behind him stood a bathrobed Beth and a small crowd of pyjama-clad, whispering onlookers.

I wanted to shout at the lot of them. People judging what they didn't understand. Yes, I locked her in her room because she asked me to. Yes, I grabbed her while she was asleep and screaming at me to let her go. Yes, she's been horribly abused and it was my fault, because I was there and did nothing to stop them. Yes, I'm a lower form of life than pond scum. And yes, I'm allowed to live – outside of prison, no less – because she saved my life and spoke in my defence. Though I didn't deserve it. Instead, I shoved through them to my room and the faint hope of sleep. A forlorn hope, but one I clung to.

"Are you all right? Do you want me to call the police?" I heard the man say.

Yes and no. I already knew her answers, so I didn't stay to hear them.

"Get out of my way. Don't touch me!" Caitlin's sharp tone cut through the low hum of strangers' voices. "Nathan. Nathan, please don't go."

I turned.

She stood in the doorway, wearing a soft cotton nightdress that proclaimed to the world that she was no angel, playing with one of the thin straps as her eyes pleaded with me. "Nathan, I want you to stay with me." She hugged herself, the way she used to when she was close to tears. If it wasn't dark, I knew I'd see the familiar shimmer.

I couldn't refuse and she knew it. As soon as I was close enough, she grabbed my hand and yanked me into her room, but someone's foot stopped her from closing the door behind her.

"I don't think that's a good idea. Let me call the police," the same man said.

"I'll be fine," Caitlin replied. Her clipped tone implied that no one else would be if they didn't follow her orders. "If you need to call the police, or an ambulance after I'm done with him, I'll let you know."

An ambulance? Was she going to shoot me instead of

using a taser?

I waited for her to close the door before I said, "If you're going to shoot me, better take me out into the bush where there won't be any witnesses. Burial's easier, too. Plenty of caves and sinkholes south of here."

Her eyes bored into mine. "And you said you weren't suicidal."

I shrugged. "I'm not. But if you want to kill me, I won't fight you, that's all. And I wouldn't want you to get into trouble for what I see as justice. If you feel I need to die for what I've done, then I agree with you."

Caitlin shook her head irritably. "Nathan…I didn't ask you to stay so I could shoot you, okay? I wanted to thank you. Thank you for waking me up from that…that…and for being there to reassure me. It's been a long time since anyone…and I'm grateful not to have to deal with it alone."

"Do you have nightmares often?" I asked, unable to stop myself. It was none of my business. None of my damn business and she'd tell me so, right before she kicked me out into the condemning crowd outside…

"No. Honestly, I don't. Maybe once a week or a fortnight. It's just the memories and the stress and being in a new place and…well, I can't help but remember things around you." Her rueful look turned to panic as she tightened her grip on my hand. "It's not your fault! It's not, I swear. Being in Perth stirs up the memories, too. Please…please can you stay?"

She already knew my answer, but she'd asked anyway. "You know I can't sleep with you." Even now, I couldn't call my curse by its name. Impotence…hissing in my head like a snake. A limp snake.

"I know, but…if I have any more dreams, you're the only person I trust to wake me. If anyone else touches me, I'll…unless it's you. You're the only one who can touch me without making me want to run, screaming, in the opposite direction." Her watery smile didn't reach her frightened eyes. I knew what it was to be terrified of your own dreams.

I nodded once. "I'll get a blanket and a pillow and I'll sleep on your couch. If you have any more bad dreams, I'll be here."

"Thank you." This time, her smile was heartfelt.

Ten minutes later, I stretched out on the sofa, my eyes fixed on her as I swore to guard her until morning. I'd even save her from her dreams if she needed it. There was nothing I wouldn't do for her. I only wished I could do more.

FORTY SEVEN

Sunlight and sweet singing...I knew it couldn't be heaven because I didn't belong there, but for a moment I wondered if someone had made a mistake. A hissing sound I hadn't noticed ceased and so did the singing. I opened my eyes to Caitlin exiting the bathroom, a towel tucked tantalisingly around her breasts. Shit, my head wasn't the only part of my anatomy waking up. Of all the times for my dick to decide to check in...

The towel came off and I bit down on my tongue to stop myself from moaning. I swallowed, trying to ignore the salty tang of blood. "I should go."

Caitlin's gentle laughter was music to my ears. "I don't mind. You've seen it all before, Nathan." She slipped on some lacy little knickers.

My dick shot up in salute. Fuck. Think of something, anything, to settle down. Caitlin screaming and squirming in my arms last night. Nope, that didn't work.

I glanced again, just in time to see her turn as she fastened a matching lacy bra. Sweet handfuls of heaven. God, I wanted to slip my hands inside the cups and scoop her out like...

Cold shower. I needed a cold shower.

I scrambled off the sofa, bundling the blanket in front of me to hide what she did to me. No way in hell would she let me near her if she knew how much I wanted to help her out of that underwear and take her on the bed. I mumbled something about a shower and fled.

Fifteen minutes later, still shivering from my wintry shower, I stumbled on half-numb feet to the dining room. Avoiding the coffee with a glass of orange juice, I set my breakfast beside Caitlin and slid into the chair next to her.

She swallowed a mouthful of croissant. "Good morning."

I mumbled a response through my toast – even after five years, I couldn't stomach breakfast cereal and it looked like she couldn't, either – and watched as she popped a strawberry into her mouth.

"Oh, you're up." Beth seemed stunned to see me, but she managed a smile all the same. "Are you ready for your cooked breakfast now? The one you ordered yesterday?"

I nodded, not remembering what I'd ordered yesterday. Pancakes or eggs or a whole buffet – I had no idea.

Caitlin parted her lips to permit another strawberry inside.

Dead bodies, morgues, hospital theatres with lots of blood, tears, the nauseating smell of disinfectant...anything I could dredge up from my brain to stop myself from walking around with a hard-on all day. Shit, what was wrong with me this morning?

Breakfast arrived, in the form of a huge plate of steaming…well, everything, really. I wasn't sure I could eat it all. I stuck half the grilled tomato in my mouth and bit down. Cooked to perfection.

"So what were you planning to do today?" Beth asked cheerfully.

I struggled to chew and swallow so I could answer.

Caitlin beat me to it. "Nathan and I were discussing the caves down south last night. I was hoping we might get to explore one today. I heard there were some unusual fossils from animals that fell down sinkholes and died in the caves, their bodies perfectly preserved. Is it true there was a thylacine – one of those Tasmanian tiger things? I thought they only lived in Tasmania."

I choked. The caves. Sure we'd talked about them – as a place to dump my dead body. My libido withered and perished.

Beth and Caitlin were both looking at me. "Lake Cave, Nathan? Or would you prefer Jewel or Mammoth?"

I coughed and managed to say, "Sure. Whatever you want." I shovelled a crispy piece of bacon in my mouth, relishing the taste. If I was going to die today, at least I'd get to enjoy my last meal. And death would be delivered by the hands of a beautiful woman I'd do anything for. Death row inmates never had it this good.

FORTY EIGHT

A gust of wind slammed the ticket office door, echoing like a gunshot. Nathan, who'd been crossing the deck to the start of the stairs, dropped to a crouch, covering his head in panic. I wasn't sure what had gotten into him this morning – he seemed frightened of his own shadow. Was it because of my nightmare last night or something else entirely? He'd barely said a word to me in the car on the way down to Lake Cave.

"Well, he looks like he's one wrong word away from suicide. I haven't seen a case of PTSD that bad since the Fourth of July in the US. Where do you bet he was stationed, Afghanistan or Iraq?"

I stopped mid-stride and stared at the man who'd spoken. What the hell did he know about it? I gritted my teeth as I replied, "There are worse things than war that can do that to a man."

He grinned as if my cold gaze had no power over him. His eyes seemed unnaturally dark. "So you're his friend – girlfriend, maybe? Get out while you can. You don't want to be the one to find him when he offs himself. No one needs to…"

Suicidal. I knew it, this prick knew it, but Nathan wouldn't admit it. I'd give anything to be able to help him, if only he'd let me in and tell me what he was thinking.

"My love, are you scaring people? Maybe we should have spent the day at home," a gentle voice said. The woman who owned it kissed the man's lips and smiled.

"Hey, if you want to chain me to the bed, you know I'm up for that, Mel. Like I said…" His dark eyes bored into mine and I found I couldn't breathe. They weren't just dark – they were like black holes, sucking at my soul. The man was evil. Ultimate evil and…

"Don't let him scare you, honey. He sees the worst in any situation. He's been through hell for longer than anyone should. Bringing him back is a challenge, but he's worth saving. I'm sure you understand. Sometimes they're strong for too long that they forget how to ask for help from those they love and that's when a kickass heroine has to save the day. But not in a single blaze of glory. With patience and persistence and maybe even love." She cleared her throat. I realised her hand gripped my wrist while my fingers were firmly wrapped around the hilt of my hidden knife. I looked from her hand to her friend. His eyes didn't seem so dark any more – in fact, they were the same light grey as the woman's. And he looked worried – concerned for the woman. Shit, he looked at her the way Nathan stared at me.

My mouth opened, but no sound came out. How had

she touched me without me noticing? And was she talking about Nathan as if she knew him or her demon-beset friend?

"Angel, are you okay?" Nathan rose from his crouch and continued walking toward me, quickening his pace.

The strange woman removed her hand and it felt like she withdrew comfort with it. "I think you know exactly what I mean, for you have your own hero to save. Good luck." She bobbed her head and took the questionably evil man's arm. "All souls deserve a chance at redemption, don't they, my love?"

Her companion nodded, keeping his eyes firmly on the decking as they walked away.

"Honestly, Luce, I'm beginning to think chaining you to the bed wasn't such a bad idea after all." Her soft footsteps carried her down the stairs to the level below us.

"Of course it's not a bad idea. I suggested it. But it only works if you're there with me…" the man replied, his voice fading as they descended.

I forced myself to place my hands by my sides. I wanted to shake the strange woman's words out of my head, but they rang too true for that. From the worried look in Nathan's eyes to the way he broke into a trot when he thought I was in danger…I'd known it all along. After all these years, he still carried a torch for me that he was terrified to light.

"Is everything all right? I saw you reach for…for your knife and I thought you needed help. Did you know them? Did those people hurt you – now or before? Were they…" His eyes widened in what I recognised as fright. Nathan couldn't hack being my bodyguard any more, no matter how much he wanted to protect me. Last night's nightmare had traumatised him more than it had me. Like the strange woman had said, it was the heroine's turn to kick arse. And the first one that needed a kick was mine. Enough stalling. I needed to see the house Mohsen wanted to give me so I'd stop worrying. Once I was no longer having nightmares about nothing, then I'd kick Nathan's supposedly sacred arse.

I took his arm, trying to share some of the calm the woman had infused in me. "I'm fine. I was just talking to that couple and I..." I trailed off as the names they'd used sank in. "I just had a really crazy thought. Do you think when God gets bored, he or she chains the devil up and tries to brainwash him into being a decent citizen?"

Nathan stared at me. "I don't know. I'd have thought they played chess or arm wrestled or something like that, with souls or the world at stake. I don't think chains and bondage would be...would be..." He doubled over, breathing hard.

"Nathan. Nathan. Oh shit, I shouldn't have...Let's just go home. Stuff the caves – it was a bad idea and I'm scared of the dark, anyway. Give me the keys. I'll drive." I fished the keys out of his pocket. "Let's get you home."

FORTY NINE

Maybe halfway back to Busselton, just after Yallingup, the car started making a strange sound. I strained my ears, trying to work out what it was.

Nathan drowned it out as he turned the music up.

"Stop it! Turn that down. I'm trying to work out what that noise was," I scolded, clicking the stereo off.

Nathan cleared his throat uncomfortably. "Um, it was me. My stomach's growling because I'm starving. Any chance we can stop for lunch?"

I reached into the glove compartment and pulled out the map from the tourist office. Beth had given it to me at breakfast, marking the caves and some chocolate places she recommended we visit. "Pick a winery along the way and we'll pull in there for lunch. Lots of them have restaurants."

"I don't drink wine," Nathan said, shuddering. "I could go a cold beer, though."

An arrowed sign ahead pointed the way to a brewery on the left. "Beer it is, then." I indicated and turned off Caves Road.

The side street meandered through paddocks until it ended in a gravel car park outside a pretty ordinary-looking building with a tin roof. Between the pool table on the veranda and tables and chairs scattered around the grass and inside the place, it looked like it served something to make people want to stay. Not that there were many around – after two on a weekday was too late for lunch...for everyone except Nathan, apparently.

We ordered our food and drank some oddly named beers while we waited for lunch to be prepared. I wasn't sure what Nathan's murky brew was called, nor what was in it, but I'd capitulated and ordered a beer that claimed to have been made with strawberries. After one mouthful, I figured it was true – but beer and strawberries were a strange mix. I took another sip, trying to decide if I liked it or I hated it.

A sharp crack made Nathan shoot to his feet, scanning the room for the source of the shot.

I twisted in my seat and realised the strange round table I'd dismissed earlier was a peculiar pool table – the report I'd heard came from a bloke's smooth break of the balls.

Nathan's swearing drew my eyes back to him. He'd managed to knock his beer over and even his frantic efforts to clean the beer splashes off his shirt didn't hide how badly his hands were shaking. Nathan sure was a nervous wreck today. Had he spotted some risk to our safety that he hadn't told me about? Or were his demons catching up with him, overwhelming him so that he needed help he was too proud to ask for, and the sudden sound had just brought his shattered nerves to breaking point?

Recalling the strange woman's words, I summoned a smile and said, "Would you like to play a game of pool after he's done? I want a rematch after last night. I don't think I've ever played so badly in my life."

Nathan seemed to relax a bit as he agreed, then headed up to the counter to order a replacement beer. His hands shook less as he ate his nachos – thankfully, as the abundant fresh salsa would've gone everywhere otherwise.

I let him break when it was our turn on the pool table, knowing he'd do a better job of it than I could. He winced at the sound though he tried to hide it. I said nothing, just moving forward to take my shot. If anything, I played worse than I had last night – Nathan was going to win for sure.

After he'd sunk about half his balls and I'd managed to sink exactly one – and one of his, at that – I summoned the courage to mention the house.

"Do you mind if we take a detour on the way back to the guesthouse?" I asked casually, lining up my next shot.

"What? Where?" He stiffened as if I'd shoved my cue up his bum.

My shot went wide again. I sighed and straightened. "The house my cousin wants me to inherit. It's on the way back and I think worrying about it is one of the reasons I'm having nightmares again. The sooner I see it, the sooner I can decide what to do with it." And the sooner I could take Nathan on a proper holiday with the proceeds. It'd been a mistake to take him somewhere so close to Perth, where he jumped at his own shadow. A deserted tropical island, maybe, where no one knew us and they only had one flight in a day, or, better yet, once a week.

Nathan relaxed again. "Oh. Sure. Whatever you want." In three shots, he sank his two remaining balls and the black. "Do you want me to beat you a third time at the guesthouse tonight, or would you like another attempt on this table first?" He carefully chalked his cue before returning it to the wall rack.

I set mine in place beside it. "You're not going to beat me. Violence isn't your style, Nathan. But I'll lose my next game at the guesthouse, I think. Time to go see that house while we still have a bit of daylight left."

FIFTY

I gave in to curiosity and asked, "So, where is this house?"

"Osprey Bay."

I spluttered. "You can't be serious. That's where Alanna's body was dumped. Where you…where I…that's the beach where you…" Did she know how few houses there were in Osprey Bay? Hers could be right next door to where she'd been held captive. Hell, Alanna could have been murdered on her back lawn. And while she'd been locked in that underground dungeon, I'd lived in a house there for weeks, agonising over a decision that should have been crystal clear.

"I know. But I've inherited this property there and I need to see it to decide whether to sell it or keep it. The real estate agent said it's both a goldmine and heaven on Earth, which doesn't help me decide anything except not to trust the real estate agent." She managed a weak grin.

I hesitated. "I'll come to the house, but I'm not setting foot on that beach again. I'll have nightmares just thinking about it. I don't even need to see it."

Caitlin's fingers crept over mine, clinging tightly. "Nathan, I need to go there at some point. I need to see where I almost died. Where you almost died. You don't have to come with me, but I need to stand there. It's part of letting go."

Fuck. The only thing worse than me going there was her alone there without me. "No. I won't let you go there by yourself."

Her eyes blazed. "Nathan, you try and stop me and I will fucking tase you and leave you where you fall. You don't control me. You could never control me and if you think I'll let you get away with being an overprotective asshole –"

"I've changed my mind. I'll go with you. Call me whatever names you want. I'll go crazy with worry if you go without me. I'm terrified of seeing that bloody beach, but what frightens me more is you there alone. The last time I left you there alone, I had to kill someone and I don't know what he did to you while I wasn't there."

She grinned fiercely. "So you're coming? Don't worry, I'll hold your hand, Nathan. Anyone else comes after me and they won't survive to regret it. I've had enough of living in fear."

My head told me to be terrified. Caitlin had killed and she'd do it again if she had to. I didn't doubt that for a minute. And if she wanted to shoot me on the beach where I'd failed her, so be it. I'd open my arms and welcome justice at her hands.

What scared me is how much it turned me on, because I

wanted her. Bad. Shit, how fucked up did that make me?

I stayed silent as we headed north and then west on Osprey Bay Road. I didn't say a word as we passed the resort, though I knew there were only a handful of houses between the resort and the national park. And one of them was the one where…

"There. Number one hundred," she said in satisfaction. The black, bulbous driveway marker taunted me as we pulled up beside it. Sure enough, it bore the number I'd never noticed before. Caitlin leaned out the window. "That looks like one of those old World War II sea mines that sank ships. I didn't think we had any of those here. Must have washed up here, carried on the current. I hope it's not still armed." She accelerated slightly along the rutted driveway as I fought down my panic.

So much for not going anywhere near places that scared me.

"What? What is it?" Caitlin asked, staring at me.

I had to swallow three times before I could get the words out. "Angel, this is their house. The house your kidnappers lived in. And that –" I pointed a shaking finger at a track leading from the house into the national park "– THAT is the way to the bunker where they almost killed you. I think your so-called cousin is a lying sack of shit who's trying to kill you and we should get the hell out of here."

"You could be right," Caitlin said grimly, unbuckling her seatbelt. "But no one knows we're here, so no one's expecting us. This could be our only chance to see this place without a welcoming party." She opened her door and stood on the gravel drive. "C'mon, Nathan, let's lay some ghosts to rest."

"And if any of them aren't ghosts yet?" I couldn't help asking.

My avenging angel grinned as she pulled a bulky, metal torch and her taser from the boot of the car. "Demons, you mean? Then we can fucking tag team them. I want my life back."

My mouth went dry. Shit, how could I back down when she had so much courage? I looked like a coward compared to her if I didn't do this. And I'd never forgive myself if anything else happened to her. She could shoot me later – but not before I'd protected her one last time. I took a deep, shaky breath, praying my voice wouldn't squeak with the terror coursing through my veins. "Then let's check out the bunker first before it's completely dark outside."

FIFTY ONE

"So this is where I was held." Caitlin's voice was flat as her torch swept across the floor. She didn't mention the dark stains that still streaked the concrete.

"Yes," I replied hoarsely, clearing my throat. I glanced at the door, lying in a nest of crime scene tape. Dust had covered my boot marks, so you could barely see where I'd kicked it off the hinges the last time I'd been here. "I'm so sorry. If it wasn't for my parents, if they hadn't taken Alanna…"

"She died here, didn't she?" Caitlin asked sharply.

"I don't know where she died," I whispered. "The police said she'd already been dead for a few hours when she was dumped on the beach. They never found where she'd been killed."

"The bloodstains here aren't mine. I was near the door when the bitch cut me – tied up too tightly to move this far.

They killed her here. She must've bled out before they dumped her body on the beach so it'd be found. Here, no one would have found her." Caitlin's voice sounded so clinical, it was scary.

My feet moved on autopilot, carrying me to her side. I needed to see her gory find for myself. I stumbled over the rubble littered across the floor, almost falling. I managed to right myself before I face-planted, but the torch flew out of my hands and smashed against the brick wall. The light died, leaving only the little key-ring torch in Caitlin's hand.

She held out her other hand to me, keeping her torch beam steady on the dark streaks on the floor. My fingers clasped hers for strength as I looked down at my sister's last, live resting place. A glint caught my eye and I dropped to my knees, scrabbling in the dust. Half hidden beneath a broken brick was a twisted scrap of silver. I blew the dust off it and held it up to Caitlin's torch.

The tiny, red crystal in Alanna's crushed signet ring winked at me like the eye of some sort of demon.

"Oh God." I barely managed to get the words out. My fingers formed a fist around the precious piece of silver, as if by holding it tightly I could hold back the tears threatening to spill from my eyes. I didn't want Caitlin to see me cry.

I rushed across the room, stubbing my toes on bricks, but I didn't stop. Taking the rough steps two at a time, I burst into the bush at the surface, breathing hard. The sun had well and truly set and clouds hid the moon – I couldn't even see the stars. I could see the shadowy bulk of the house and that's what I staggered towards, even as tears blurred my vision and tree roots tried to trip me.

I blundered through a prickly bush and plunged on, but the ground vanished beneath my feet and I fell. I heard the crack before I felt it – after that, all I could hear was my own agonised voice, swearing loud enough to wake the dead.

FIFTY TWO

My vision was hazy, so it took me a minute to realise that Caitlin was close enough for her torch beam to illuminate me. I was sprawled across some rusted, corrugated iron in the bottom of a circular pit. My right leg had snapped over the edge of the brick surround – it looked like I had an extra knee between the first and my ankle. Fuck, it hurt.

"Nathan. Nathan!" Caitlin shouted. She stood on the lip of the hole, staring at me. I wondered how long she'd been calling me.

"I can't get up," I told her. "It's broken." I waved limply at my double-jointed leg. A dark stain started seeping through my jeans, much like the bloodstains in the bunker. The torchlight stole the colour and turned my blood to black.

"It's all right, Nathan. I'm going to help you," she said calmly, placing the torch carefully on top of the bricks. She sat on the edge, lowering herself to the ground beside me. Waist deep in the pit, she edged around the rusted iron to reach me.

"Don't," I groaned as her light touch sent pain shooting up my leg.

"We have to get you to hospital. I should splint this, though, before we can move you," her soothing voice continued as if I hadn't said a word.

I fumbled in my pocket for my phone. My hands were shaking so badly I almost dropped it. "Here. Call for help. You can't lift me out by yourself. Don't…please don't leave me here."

She took the phone from my fingers and dialled 000. I heard her coolly request an ambulance, then state the address and say she'd wait for them by the house to guide the paramedics to where I'd fallen into a disused water tank. She ended the call and handed the phone back to me.

Her lips touched my forehead. "I'm going back up to the house for the first aid kit in the car, and to see if I can find something to use for a splint."

"No…Caitlin, PLEASE. Don't leave me here alone in the dark," I begged. Like I did to her, alone in the bunker in the dark as they hurt her. God, talk about ironic. I deserved to be left here to die. She wouldn't even need to shoot me.

"I'll be right back, Nathan. You hold that phone, in case they call for directions." She hoisted herself easily onto the lip of the bricks, her boots level with my face for a moment before they swung up and out of sight.

"Please!" I called after her, but I'm not sure if she heard. The crunch of her footsteps faded into the dark as my phone's backlit screen went black. She deserved her revenge, leaving me to rot in this hidden hole. Fuck, if she wanted me dead, she should stab me like she did Simon, or shoot me the way she slaughtered Laura. Fuck suicide. Fuck justice. I wasn't going to curl up and die in the dark. If she could climb out of this hole, so could I.

I stretched my arms up, hooking my fingers around the bricks so I could haul myself upright onto my good leg. I paused to swear as the pain almost made me pass out. This hurt worse than being shot, and watching my foot dangle limply was making me queasy.

I swung around, grunting as my bad leg gave another twinge. I wrapped my hands around the trunk of that shrub that dropped me into this mess and heaved until my hips rested on the top layer of bricks. Panting, I paused for a moment before I used all my strength to pull again. Stretched out on the sand, I could hear my breath whistling as I inhaled. If I had to crawl the whole way, I had to get to the house. Or, failing that, the driveway up to the road. That's where there'd be an ambulance and help.

I dug my fingers into the pale sand, dragging my body behind me. I let out a steady stream of swearing so that anyone nearby would hear me and, hopefully, help me. My vision blurred, but I could see the dark house and that's where I was headed.

A bolt of agony lanced through my leg and I yelped, barely recognising the voice as my own. I looked back, holding my phone out to light up the problem. My dangling foot was caught on a tree root. Shuffling back through the sand, it took me a few panicked minutes to free myself before I could start moving forward again.

It felt like I'd been crawling forever. Fuck, maybe I

would be crawling forever – for the rest of it I had left, anyway.

Caitlin wasn't coming back. She'd left me to the fate I deserved. How many times had I headed through the dark to the bunker and not stumbled into the treacherous pit? She didn't need me any more and karma had come back to bite my arse, big time. She'd just been biding her time as I got complacent.

I paused to rest, gasping for breath. My vision was starting to dim. I couldn't see the house.

The last thing I saw before everything faded to black was an exquisitely small boot. It had to be a hallucination, because there wasn't enough light to see Caitlin's boot in anything but my imagination.

FIFTY THREE

"He's awake. Someone go get Dr Miller."

I blinked and the light blinded me. I had a hangover from hell and I couldn't even remember what I'd drunk. And why did my leg hurt so much?

Oh shit – whatever I'd drunk wasn't going to stay drunk. A vomit bag appeared in front of my face and I heaved, coughed and spluttered until all I brought up was bile. Maybe I hadn't had that much to drink after all. Or maybe they'd pumped my stomach while I was unconscious and this was just…

"Morphine withdrawal really sucks, but you got the good stuff, what with your broken leg and all." This time, I recognised that the voice had an owner – a grinning one, even though the orderly was holding a bag of vomit in one hand. "I'll just get rid of this and I'll be right back with something to wash the taste out of your mouth. You've just missed the lunch trolley, but I think the ladies will make an exception." He darted out of the room, his tied-back dreadlocks swaying like tentacles behind him.

I surveyed the room and found nothing more interesting than my own body, with my leg immobilised in a cast most of the way up my thigh. My memories returned with a kick in the teeth as soon as I saw that. I'd broken it, running from the bunker into some rust-lined death pit, and then hauled myself out when Caitlin left me to die. So much for suicidal – when it came down to it, I did want to live after all. I bet she'd laugh if she knew.

Orderly Dreads Dude returned with a full meal tray, but even the smell made me nauseous again. I grabbed the glass of water and pushed the rest of it away. After I'd gulped down the liquid, I tried to find the right words. "Has Caitlin come to visit me?"

His confusion sent my heart plummeting before he'd even opened his mouth. "Nope, no Caitlins. Just the doctor. You got a guardian angel worth its weight in gold when you scored a doctor that hot. She makes me want to meet a shark surfing one morning just so I can end up in her tender hands."

A giggle stopped him dead. "Josh, if a shark bites your backside when you're surfing, you know one of the qualified doctors here will be stitching you up, not me. I'm only here until Nathan's discharged."

Josh flushed and mumbled something as he left.

"Angel," I breathed. "He told me you hadn't come to visit. Just some –"

"Hot doctor?" she asked, raising her eyebrows. "Dr Alana Angel Miller, thank you very much. I earned it."

Now it was my turn to blush. "I didn't mean it like that. I forgot that you're all qualified and stuff now. Sometimes it feels like five years haven't passed and we're the same as we were then, only you're better. And me, I'm..." Worse, I wanted to say, but I didn't dare. She didn't deserve the excuse for a man that I'd become. She should have run and left me to die.

"I'll help you get better, too," she said, lowering herself into the plastic visitor chair like it was a throne. "Locking up the past and not telling anyone about it is eating you up inside. I can see it. You should talk to me, Nathan. Tell me about your nightmares and your memories and let me help you banish them like you did for me."

I pressed my lips together and shook my head.

"Your sister will have you committed. She's got Dr Hogan and a lot of medical reports on her side."

I laughed. "Even if she does, I'll be out in a week. I'm not hallucinating. I'm not a danger to anyone but myself and I know all the right answers to the depression tests to make me sound sane. If I tell you what I did, will you kill me like we did the others? I'm no less guilty than any of them. Will you forgive me and give me the mercy of a clean end?"

Her expression was unreadable. "I forgave you years ago. I told you that before I left for Melbourne. But it wasn't enough for you to leave your job and come with me. I could have helped you then, but you wanted to go save the world, one terrorist at a time, and mess your mind up worse."

I laughed so hard I nearly choked. "What job? I lost my job before you left. I was an unemployed bum with no degree and no references. The dole office got me trained as a security guard, because that's what they figured I was good at, and I've been working as one ever since. The compensation money I got paid – the ex gratia thing? It was barely enough to cover the cost of a car to replace mine. Not even a new car – just a second-hand one, something cheap. You're right. I am worse. I didn't deserve you then and I sure as hell don't deserve you now. You should've left me in the bush to die. That's what I deserve."

"Damn it, Nathan!" Her fist slammed into the bed, jarring my leg and sending pain shooting through it. I let out an agonised whimper before I bit my tongue, knowing I deserved the pain. "Shit, I'm sorry. You saved my life and nursed me back to health with a single-mindedness that even I can't summon for my patients. You know that all I had in my head was vengeance, the whole time I was in hospital and when I was supposed to be recovering? I would have happily died to know I was taking out the last of those bastards with me. And they are gone. All of them. I saw the bodies and so did you. You've made amends for whatever you did. You never hurt me, but you went without sleep, without your family, without your own damn sanity to put me back together again and show me that life was worth living. If you'd personally murdered my whole family and then tried to kill me, you'd have made amends a dozen times over for…oh God. I'm sorry."

Caitlin flung her arms around me and I buried my face in her shoulder to hide the tears. Tears of self-pity that I was at least twenty-five years too old for. But they just wouldn't stop. If nothing else could put her off, maybe this disgusting display would do it.

"I love you, Nathan. Talk to me and let me help you," she whispered. "I won't give up on you. I swear I won't. I owe you my life."

I forced myself to pull away from her, wiping my nose on my sleeve. "You wouldn't say that if you knew what I'd done."

She folded her arms. "Try me."

I stared into her eyes. Those perfect, dark pools that drew me in from the first moment I saw her. I hung my head. "I can't."

She smiled and kissed my cheek. "Then I guess you'll just have to put up with me until you can. And you might be surprised about afterwards."

It was on the tip of my tongue to talk about restraining orders, but we both knew I wouldn't. Even if it tortured me to see her, I'd cherish every moment until she left me again.

"Oh, I almost forgot." She clasped her hands together, then slowly drew them apart and held something out. "This is yours. I found it in the dirt you'd dragged yourself through. It must've fallen out of your pocket. I hope you don't mind – I've been wearing it so I could give it back to you the moment you woke up."

Alanna's signet ring glittered on her palm. Scratched and warped, yet unmistakably hers. Caitlin had cleaned it and tried to twist it back into shape, but the damage was still there. I took it with shaking hands and attempted to slip it onto my smallest finger.

Even Caitlin laughed when it sat like a little crown on my fingertip, too small to even make it over my fingernail.

I swallowed. "You keep it. Then if anything happens to me, at least I'll know that someone still cherishes her memory, even if you never knew her."

"Nathan…"

"Please." My voice died.

She nodded and slipped it back onto her finger, the one where she'd one day place an engagement ring. Or a wedding ring. Her fingers were so tiny compared to Alanna's.

For a moment, staring at my ring on her hand, I dared to hope. Her hand was warm in mine as I brought it to my lips.

"I'll take care of it until you're ready for me to return it," she promised.

My heart plummeted again. Nothing lasted forever and it was only a matter of time before she left me again for good.

FIFTY FOUR

When we pulled up in front of my place, my heart sank. The last place I wanted to be was the house I shared with Chris. Grimly, I hauled myself out of the car and struggled with my crutches.

"What is it? Do you want me to grab some more of your pain meds?" Caitlin asked, looking worried.

I shook my head. "No, I'm good. I'm just thinking about how much I wish I was going back to your place instead of staying here with my sister. She'll flip when she finds out I've managed to break my leg."

Caitlin seemed unusually nervous – I wasn't sure I'd ever seen her wring her hands before. "I'm sorry. But there's no way you could make it up six flights of stairs to my place. And if we did manage to get you up, I don't know how we'd get you down again…"

I grinned. I had a few ideas. And having her to myself in

her house, alone, certainly featured in them. The pain pills must've been making me loopy – I was having sexy thoughts and they were definitely having an effect. Oh, hello… I figured I should probably get inside before Caitlin realised I'd hoisted a flagpole ready to communicate my surrender to her. Oh God, and I needed to take a piss. Three hours of driving after being on an IV drip for days were a bad combination.

With Caitlin's help holding the door, I lurched into the house and the blessed bathroom. I took my time, seeing as I wasn't looking forward to getting back out there. Even washing my hands was a challenge when my crutches slipped to the floor and I didn't know how to pick them up again. How had Caitlin managed when she couldn't walk?

She was amazing, I decided. A walking miracle. Fuck, dropped it again. Just a couple more inches and I'd be able to reach it…

I managed to get my crutches under me again and opened the bathroom door. The sound of shouting grew in volume as I laboured to get me and my crutches through the doorway and out into the hall.

"Leave him alone!" Chris demanded. "You have no idea what he's been through. First our sister, then you. When you dumped him last time, it broke him. The only pieces I'll be picking up this time are the bits of your broken body if you hurt him again. Fuck off and leave us alone!"

"Do you know how to break a man?" Caitlin didn't wait for her to reply. "First, you take away the one person he loves most and slaughter them in the most brutal way possible. And you make sure he knows about it. Then, you tell him you know who did it and tantalise him with the whiff of revenge. But you don't give it to him. Instead, you show him the girl of his dreams and tell him that he has to hurt her, just like his loved one was. And if he doesn't, they'll kill her and torture someone else he loves instead. And this time, they'll make him watch." She paused and I struggled to stay silent. "And after he's done everything they asked – or refused and tried to save everyone's lives – they don't kill him. They throw him to the police as the culprit for both crimes, until the grief overwhelms him and he takes his own life, because he can't live with what he's done. What THEY forced him to do." There was the sound of a zip being forced down and fabric sliding over skin. "These scars are the price your brother and I paid to save your life. They carved your fucking name into my flesh as a threat to him. So don't you DARE tell me I don't know what he's been through. I had to look into his eyes every day as he shared my pain and there are no drugs to numb the agony he went through."

Chris's voice wavered as if she was about to cry, the tears only held back by a thin dam of anger. "You think you're the one he loves most?"

Yes, damn it, she is the one I love most. And I can never tell her because I don't deserve her.

"No," Caitlin said quietly. "The girl he loved most was Alanna. I'm the girl of his dreams. Dreams that turn into nightmares, every night."

"No," she countered. "He dreams of her. Not you."

"That's what he tells his doctor and you. Lies to keep you from the painful truth. Your brother was abducted, just like Alanna and I were, but he was forced to hurt me instead of being tortured. And it broke him. All that time he helped me heal and he was hurting just as much. I owe him the same and you won't stop me from taking him anywhere he wishes to go. To hell with you and your sheltered illusions. You can't help your brother. I can and I'll do it, too." A pause. "You know what? I don't have to listen to your shit. It's a wonder Nathan does. Tell him I'll come over tomorrow afternoon to check on him."

I reached the lounge room just in time to see the front screen door swing shut behind Caitlin. I made it to the steps to the front door, but crutches and stairs were a nightmare I couldn't negotiate yet, so I rounded on Chris instead.

My sister's mouth was wide open as she stared at me, taking in my crutches and walking cast before her face turned red with anger and she turned to yell at Caitlin's departing back. "Don't you dare! By tomorrow afternoon, he'll have taken out a restraining order against you!"

I laughed as Caitlin raised one arm and gave Chris the one-fingered salute.

"I'll do it," Chris said through gritted teeth. "She did that to you, didn't she? I'll drive you to the police station so they can see. She's not coming in here again."

I cleared my throat. "Actually, I managed to fall into a hole and break my leg all by myself. She called an ambulance and stayed with me until the hospital released me."

Chris snorted. "I bet she set you up, just so she could get you back into bed and nurse you back to health between her thighs. That girl's full of shit."

"She's not," I said softly, my voice so carefully controlled that every word was clear. "She and I did go through hell to save your life. And she's forgiven me for my part in it because she knows why. And you know what? I'm not sure I'll ever forgive myself for it because I'm not sure her sacrifice was worth it. Maybe I should've let them take you instead. And if you go to a police station and accuse her of a crime, you'll have the police and ASIO doing everything in their power to shut you up, because of what that girl's witnessed. You're not a lawyer yet, Chris, and trying to take on federal security legislation you don't understand is just fucking stupid."

Her eyes filled with tears, but her face was still screwed up in anger. "I'm just trying to take care of you like Alanna would."

I shook my head. "You're not Alanna or our parents and you never will be. She never tried to control my life because she knew she couldn't. Stay out of my life, Chris, and the only thing I ever want to hear you say to or about Caitlin is how sorry you are for what you've said to her. Or I'll tell Mum and Dad about your string of biker boyfriends and we'll see how you like someone telling you how to live your life."

I hobbled away, leaving her to her disturbing thoughts. For a moment, I was relieved that Chris knew and I didn't have to be the one to tell her. Relief died in the realisation that she also knew I was responsible for everything Caitlin had been through. Ah, fuck it. Maybe it'd make her decide I wasn't worth saving and she'd finally leave me alone.

FIFTY FIVE

What do you do when meeting a man who employed thuggish bodyguards and gifted you with the house where you were held captive and almost killed? He might have been family, but that didn't mean I had to trust him.

I didn't know him. Didn't know whether he'd want to kill me, kidnap me or kiss me. Didn't even know what he looked like. And I didn't have Nathan here to hold my hand if I felt frightened. Or kill for me if things went wrong.

And I didn't want him here, I told myself. I didn't want him mixed up in my family's mess. He'd been messed up by them enough already. If Mohsen wanted to kill me, Nathan wouldn't be able to stop him, anyway.

But he'd been the landlord of a known terrorist. Surely that meant he was under surveillance. I brightened a little at the thought. ASIO might not have been much use protecting me before, but they were better than nothing.

Maybe they'd improved over the last five years, especially as Mott, Nathan's dodgy old boss, didn't work there any more.

The big question was whether to arrive early, so I could choose a table and scope him out the moment he came in, before he saw me, or to arrive late, so I could see if he'd brought his bodyguards or an anti-terrorist tail that I could wave down for help if things turned bad?

Force of habit won: I entered the café fifteen minutes early and chose a corner table. I was armed with both a knife and a taser, plus I had some pepper spray in my bag. I prayed I wouldn't have to use any of them. I glanced around the café, hoping I'd recognise an ASIO agent if I saw them. I tried not to laugh when I caught Navid's nod and wave. The man had aged, growing grey hair he hadn't had five years ago, but he also looked like the intervening time had hardened him. If he was here, it was no coincidence. When Mohsen arrived, I wouldn't be alone at all.

So much for not knowing him. A short, athletic man with dark hair entered and I knew immediately he was Mohsen. The expensive suit and shoes only confirmed it. He peered around, as if the bright afternoon sun had blinded him to the dim interior of the café, and I waved to get his attention. His smile of recognition seemed professional and practiced – this man was dangerous.

I clenched my fists. So what if he was dangerous? So was I.

He held up a finger and mouthed, "One moment," as he paused at the counter to order before crossing the floor to my table. "You have not ordered anything, Kiana. May I buy you coffee?" At my hesitation, he added, "If you are worried about accepting a drink from a stranger, consider it a tiny advance on your inheritance."

Grudgingly, I asked for a cappuccino and one of the strawberry tarts I'd seen as I walked in. He returned to the counter, paid and made his way back to the table. As he removed his jacket, draped it over the back of his chair and enthroned himself, his eyes seemed to be drinking me in. There was no lust in his gaze – just satisfaction, I thought. If he were the villain in a movie, he'd give a pretty impressive monologue, my mind added and I had to swallow my burst of laughter.

"I would like to hug you, but I don't think you would feel comfortable with that yet, so I would like to shake your hand instead. I am Mohsen Rezaei, a cousin of your mother's." I took the proffered hand and accepted the light pressure of his fingers as I shook them. "I am so sorry for her loss, Kiana."

I pulled my hand back. "You know my name isn't Kiana."

He nodded. "Yes, but it is the name she gave you and you did not tell me what else I should call you instead."

I reflected for a moment before replying, "I think Kiana's as good as anything, don't you? You don't know anything about me, or you'd never have sent me to that house. Do you know what happened there?" Despite my resolve to stay calm, I could already feel my temper rising. I forced myself to focus on my breathing, keeping it slow and steady.

His smile lifted his lips but didn't reach his eyes. "I know more than you might guess and I'm sure you have questions, but I will ask you to keep those until I have said what I must. I would like to talk about –"

"I'm not interested in what you want," I interrupted. "You may come from a country where men are considered second only to God and women are worthless, but you're in Australia now, mate, and you sent me to a house where someone tried to kill me. I want answers or you don't deserve my time. I don't care how much money you're offering. If you're not answering my questions, you don't get another minute of my time." I rose.

"You are certainly Fatima's daughter, with a fire I know she'd be proud of." He pulled out his wallet and ripped something out. "I would like to talk about my sister. This is my sister." He slapped a photograph on the table.

I squinted at it, then grabbed it and held it up so I could see it better. The picture showed a young man and two conservatively dressed women, all with the same dark hair, seated on a sofa. The man was Mohsen. The girl who looked like me held a blanket-wrapped bundle that might have been a baby. Her smile matched the man's as they beamed at the camera. Mum. The other woman's glower made me want to take a step back because I knew it well. Instead, I sank into my seat.

"My sister's name was Lilupar, but when she moved to Australia with her second husband Michael Page, she changed it to Laura Page. She died five years ago, from a combination of poison, asphyxiation and a gunshot to the head."

I met his eyes. "She was alive when I shot her. And it was toilet cleaner."

"Then I owe you a debt," he responded, "but first I think I need to tell you about what happened before my sister died, so you understand."

Under the table, I slipped my hand into my bag to arm my taser. Let the monologuing commence. When he tried to kill me, I'd be ready for him.

FIFTY SIX

"My sister was an angry, unruly child, but she was my father's favourite. He never believed a word of what my brothers and I told him of her behaviour. No toy, pet or servant was safe around her – but he said his sweet waterlily, for that is what Lilupar means, would never harm anything. I knew better.

"When war broke out and Fatima's family fled, of course my father offered to let her stay in our house in Riyadh. I was delighted to see her again, for she was my favourite cousin. Like me, Fatima wanted to see the world. The furthest she'd ever travelled from home was Egypt to see the pyramids and the other ruins there, but she wanted so much more. She was thrilled for me that I'd be studying in France and she made me promise to visit her in Australia. She'd fallen in love with an Englishman and she and her daughters were going to live with her husband in Australia.

She could talk of nothing else, she was so happy. And even when she went into labour with you, she was excited. In pain and still smiling." Mohsen shook his head.

I thought about asking what my mother had to do with his sister, but I pressed my lips together and stayed silent.

"And one day she came to me with a smile that seemed less than happy, saying she was worried about my sister. Her room was next to Lilu's and she'd heard sounds like the girl was in pain, so she'd gone in to investigate and found Lilu with one of the servants. A naked man. Knowing the dishonour Lilu could bring on herself and her family, Fatima had come to me so that I could tell my father.

"I did, but it was hard. He didn't believe me at first, but I managed to persuade him that even if Lilu didn't mean to do it, she was in danger of seducing our staff, and she needed a husband. I truly thought it would help.

"I left for Paris, and Fatima made you wave your little hand at me, insisting that she would see me in Australia before the year was out. I never saw her alive again.

"Her funeral was strained. Your father's grief is still fresh after twenty years, so I didn't want to burden him, but the atmosphere was angry. And my father's house was worse. Her father accused mine of treachery in allowing Fatima to be murdered beneath his roof while my father insisted she'd killed herself. I knew Fatima better than anyone and she would never have killed herself. She had too much to live for. So I swore vengeance on her murderer, because she deserved to see justice. And so did you, her orphaned daughter."

I blinked, delighted by the distraction offered by a waitress with my coffee and what looked like enough food for a small army. "What is that?"

Mohsen waved at the tiered plates a waitress hoisted onto the table. "High tea. It's an English custom, I'm told. Isn't this what you normally have at this time of the afternoon?"

I burst out laughing. "No. Maybe the Queen of England does and maybe people did a hundred years ago, but I've never eaten something called high tea in my life."

"Then it's a first for both of us, cousin." His practiced smile returned as we both listened to the waitress' explanation of how to eat a high tea.

I sipped my coffee as he took a tart and placed the whole thing in his mouth. I watched as he struggled to chew the thick, crusty pastry before I asked, "So, who killed her? I'm pretty sure it wasn't me."

He almost choked on his tart, trying to swallow it whole so he could answer, but he resigned himself to chewing it while keeping his annoyed gaze on me. Evidently he could have spun his rambling tale all afternoon.

I selected a quiche and nibbled at it, careful not to make his mistake.

"Lilu did it, I'm certain of it. She said she found Fatima with a knife through her chest, but my sister always liked playing with knives." Mohsen took a large mouthful of tea, seemingly oblivious to the heat. "But at the time I was too shocked at Fatima's death to realise it. My sister was soon married to the poor man my father had selected for her and I returned to university. As you probably already know, Fatima's father took responsibility for you and her two younger sisters probably spoiled you as much as he did. I don't know. I kept to my studies until I graduated and returned home. My father needed a trusted executive to look after his business interests and I was only too happy to help.

"Our businesses prospered under my care for some time until my sister's husband died very suddenly. Suicide, I was told. My father's health suffered and I found myself doing both his job and mine. Lilu moved back into our house and my father teetered between anger and despair. He didn't let her leave the house for her entire mourning period, when he announced he'd found a new husband for her. She screeched that she wouldn't have him and she'd kill him too, and it occurred to me that perhaps the man had pre-empted her attack by ending his own life. Then I started wondering about other supposed suicides…"

I nodded impatiently, waiting for him to get to the point. My coffee was almost gone.

"My father shipped her off with her new husband to Australia and I forgot about her. His health continued to suffer and my duties only increased. When he died, seven years ago now, I discovered that there were several, substantial drains on our profits and I sought to weed these out. One was a sequence of regular transfers to a mysterious foreign account that I had no knowledge of, while others turned out to be political causes he'd supported. Some might call the groups terrorists, perhaps. Bad for business, was all I knew, as there was a pair of investment advisers who were trumpeting this message at every forum they could find. Australians, too, which I wondered about. I stopped all of the payments to accounts I didn't recognise and waited to see the result.

"The first contact was a screeching phone call from Lilu

– she wanted to know why her allowance had been cut off. The foreign account was hers. My father had been paying her an allowance for living in Australia, so far from her family. That's why she'd consented to the marriage. He'd bribed her and sent her out of the country where no one knew she'd murdered her husband or her cousin. I told her that there had been a reduction in profits due to bad investments my father had made into terrorist groups, which I'd realised thanks to the Australian couple, so she would have to find her own source of income. Perhaps even find a job.

"She threatened to come home, but I said I'd tell the police here about the people she'd killed. So she swore she'd sort it out herself." He poured another cup of tea from his little pot. "It wasn't until several months later, when Australian security agents started to make enquiries about my business, that I realised Lilu had actually done something. Killed a girl, I understood, and tried to kill another – you. I recognised you immediately – you do look like Fatima. This news was quickly followed by the report of my sister's death and that of her husband. I tracked down the reports to one security agent, who she'd corrupted. If he provided me with information and maintained his position in the security agency, I'd continue to support him financially as long as he ensured my family's name wasn't dishonoured. My sister was crazy and she'd done terrible things, but the Australian justice system couldn't do anything to her after her death. I insisted he give me all the details he had on your whereabouts, so that I could find you, but no one else could." His stare was almost imperious, as if he was daring me to complain.

"You stole records about my name and address changes, all about me being placed in witness protection, but you didn't make a move all this time? Why now?"

My question seemed to surprise him. "The agent was about to lose his job and he faced an inquiry, when he might reveal everything. I arranged his suicide and he told me about my sister's death, attempting to get me to go after you out of vengeance."

My mouth went dry. "And you have. Here we are. Will I get to finish my strawberry tart before you decide you want to end this?" I stabbed my fork into a syrupy strawberry and lifted it to my lips.

He stared at me. "I don't understand. He told me you'd killed my sister – quite inventively, too. A fitting, painful end for the woman who murdered your mother and tried to do the same to you. You are Kiana – a true force of nature, as your mother named you. I'm in your debt because you did what I swore I'd do." He wiped his lips with a napkin. "I offer you her house, her dowry, and anything else you want of me. I will pay for personal bodyguards for you for the rest of your life if you wish. Or I will set you up in a palace of your own at home if you don't want to live in this country any longer." For the first time, this polished man seemed uncertain. And sincere.

I swallowed. "I don't want or need any of those things. I'll accept the house here, but only because of what happened there. I think I need to visit the place again, maybe more than once, before I can properly come to terms with what your sister – my cousin! – did to me there. The rest…Mohsen, I just want to live a normal life, like any other Australian. No servants, no bodyguards, no dowry or allowances…I don't need it. I'm a doctor – my income is enough and I'll never lack for a job. I want the security of knowing that no one will come seeking retribution. Not from me, and not from the Australian couple's family. I want the Millers left alone – all of the ones who are left."

He grinned fiercely. "I will make sure it is known. Neither your family or the other one is to be touched or they will answer to me."

For a moment, I shivered. Laura had been crazy, but this man was chillingly sane. And when he said that, I could imagine a world of pain for anyone who disobeyed his orders. But he was my cousin, and he owed me. I matched his grin. "You do that. And when I die of old age, I'll consider your debt paid."

His smile turned indulgent. "You speak confidently, yet you're defenceless. I have two bodyguards waiting outside and at my signal –"

I pressed my taser to his groin under the table. "They can come and collect your stunned body while I leave unharmed. Your sister taught me never to be defenceless and I carry the knife she tried to kill me with as a reminder. I am my mother's daughter, but I'm related to you, too."

His wide eyes weren't smiling any more. "Kiana…"

I pulled the taser away. "Yes. I have many names, but you can call me that. Thank you for what you've told me, for everything you've done and for your actions in the future, too. It's good to have family who will look out for you. If you're ever in Perth again, we could have high tea." I picked up my strawberry tart and walked out of the café, happily headed for the train station and home. Hoping I wouldn't crumple into a little relieved puddle on the train carpet when it finally hit me that Laura's brother wasn't going to kill me – and he'd kill anyone who tried to. And Nathan…both he and his family were safe.

FIFTY SEVEN

I trudged up the steps to my apartment, feeling more exhausted with every flight of stairs. Politics and difficult negotiations and risking my life…who knew they'd be so tiring? Good thing I didn't hanker to the next female James Bond.

As I reached the top level, I stopped in horror. While I'd been in the café with Mohsen, someone had left a corpse on my doorstep. The timing was too good for it to be a coincidence. If this was a message from my cousin that he wouldn't pay his imaginary debt to me, then I was going to…

"Angel? Oh, thank God, you're home," the corpse mumbled, rolling over to reveal Nathan's bleary-eyed face.

My heart started beating again. "Nathan? What are you doing, sleeping on my doormat? I gave you keys weeks ago, when you were staying here. And you…shit, you climbed six flights of stairs with your cast? You shouldn't do that!" I dropped to my knees to help him up, my knees almost buckling under his weight as I struggled to unlock the door. Somehow, we managed to get him inside and onto my couch, before I put my bag away.

"Where were you?" he asked.

"You remember how my mother's cousin wanted to meet with me about the transfer of the house? That was today," I admitted, not willing to look at him.

He lurched to his feet. "You still went? Alone? You could've been killed!"

I smiled weakly. "Yeah, I could've. I didn't know that he was Laura's brother. Turns out he knew she was crazy, but his father sent her here so she wouldn't kill anyone back home. He was grateful that I'd solved his dilemma over what to do with her, actually. Even offered me money. For a minute there, I seriously thought about a career as an assassin."

Nathan's eyes widened. "Angel, I know you're good, but please...I'd never sleep again if I knew you were out killing people every night, and that one night you might not come back..."

"Come back? You mean you want to stay with me again? Is that why you climbed all those stairs against your doctor's orders? I thought we agreed that you'd be better off at your place with no steps."

He stared at his feet. "Yeah, but bumping up and down six flights of stairs on my bum is better than spending another day in that house with Chris. She carps at me constantly over everything I do. I can't believe I considered hurting you to save her. It's like my punishment for saving her life is to want to kill her myself for the rest of my life."

I folded my arms. "So you're saying that I should take you in to save the life of a girl who called me all sorts of uncomplimentary names, tried to keep us apart by lying to me and generally tries to make your life hell?" I owed her nothing. Less than nothing, seeing as I'd already given far too much for Nathan's bitch of a sister.

Nathan's eyes were hard when they met mine. "No. I'm asking you to take me in so I don't commit murder and go to prison for it. I'll pay rent and I know how to vacuum and clean the toilet."

I didn't want to know what that meant, but it'd be a relief to have someone else home. Not so lonely any more. "All right, you can stay," I relented. "But keep my vacuum cleaner out of the toilet. Toilet brush only."

FIFTY EIGHT

"So what do you plan to do next?" Caitlin picked delicately at her chicken salad, managing to skewer a piece of lettuce perfectly before transferring it to her mouth without a drop of dressing landing outside her lips.

I shrugged. "First, I'm going to rest and let this broken leg heal. As soon as I'm out of the cast, I'll be back at work, breaking up drunken brawls and chasing away graffiti artists in between events." I considered the event line-up for the next few weeks. "Hey, I think this'll get me out of the Wiggles concerts this year. It's worth breaking my leg just for that. I can't stand all those crazy parents." I took a huge bite of my burger, showering crumbs everywhere. Shit, Caitlin must've thought I was some sort of barbarian. I tried to gather up some of the mess and put it back on my plate.

She swallowed a morsel of chicken and sipped her drink. "There's more to life than working security at events. Look,

I'm sure it's paid the bills, but you were only a year off finishing a degree in medicine. You could still go back to university, finish the course and be working in a hospital the following year. Wouldn't Alanna have wanted you to finish your degree and do more than work security all your life?"

Yes. God, how did I tell her that without revealing that some of my nightmares were back at uni in the necropsy labs? The last day I saw Alanna, too?

"I tried going back. I enrolled and went to class and everything was fine until we had a lab and I couldn't..." I choked up and couldn't continue. Instead, I bit into my burger.

"Cadavers? After having to identify Alanna in the morgue, that must have been really hard for you."

I nodded, chewing slowly in the hope that she'd change the subject before I could swallow.

"It's been five — no, almost six years, though. Do you think if you went back now, you might be able to..." She trailed off as she saw how adamantly I shook my head.

Not a hope in hell. If anything, it'd be worse now.

Caitlin nodded as if she understood, intent on fishing the last few pieces of chicken from her bowl. "You know, there are other courses you could do instead. Ones that don't involve cadaver dissection, but that'll give you credit for what you've already done. Nursing. Biology. Biomedical science. Psychology. Even physiotherapy."

"What?" I couldn't seem to close my mouth. A different course? Why hadn't I thought of that?

"Physiotherapy. It's the reason I recovered as fast as I did five years ago. Working with an experienced physio and religiously doing the exercises she gave me. They deal with injuries, but also pregnancy related stuff. If you ran one of the physio sessions on core fitness, you'd have every nubile woman in the class lusting after you. The male physios get way more interest than the female instructors. A bit sexist, but when you see some of those guys in their gym gear..."

My mind was too busy exploding with the possibilities of what I could study next for me to even summon up some jealousy at the thought of Caitlin checking out the men she worked with. Shit, if I could transfer courses, the man she checked out might be me...

"I'll look into it first thing tomorrow," I swore.

She managed a smile. "You don't have to if you don't want to, Nathan. It was just a suggestion. I mean, a job's a job. If you're happy doing security, it's none of my business. I just thought..."

I grabbed her and kissed her. She was too stunned to resist and by the time she'd recovered, I'd already let go. I laughed freely for the first time in what felt like years. "You're an angel. You really are an angel, you know that? I only thought of medicine...that if I couldn't be a doctor, then there was no point in going back. Chalk it up to four wasted years. But if I can use that...and finish a degree...get a job as a graduate...shit, angel, I'll owe you my first paycheck. Dinner in the most expensive restaurant in the city. You'll have to tell me which one that is, though, because I can't afford it on a security guard's salary."

Caitlin covered her cheeks, as if she was trying to hide her blush. I wished I'd kissed her with more passion. She deserved it. "My laptop's in the spare room, the one I'm using as a study. You can use it while I'm at work tomorrow if you like."

I shrugged. "I brought my one, but I had to leave it in the car with all my stuff. Hauling my own arse up here was hard enough. I'm not sure I'd have managed it with a bag."

"So you're up here without even a toothbrush? I might be able to carry your bags up, but I'd prefer to wait until morning when I can ask someone to help me." Caitlin looked torn. "The stalker will be down there. I didn't see him at all down south, but last night I saw someone lurking in the car park as I headed up the stairs. I don't know if my cousin's called him off or if he works for someone else entirely."

Shit, the stalker. I'd forgotten about him. I'd meant to accost him and make him tell me why he was following Caitlin around, before making sure he left her alone. With my broken leg, I'd be bloody useless – no threat to him at all. Caitlin didn't deserve to live like this.

"I can wait 'til morning. Honest. I left my toothbrush in your bathroom last time, anyway. I guess I was hoping you might let me come over again."

FIFTY NINE

I pulled on my shorts and wandered to the bathroom, hoping that I might wake up more thoroughly if I splashed some water on my face. I'd shared a glass of whisky with Caitlin last night, which had dulled the pain a bit, but this morning it was back with a vengeance. Enough to make me want to slide down the stairs on my bum to go get the pain pills from my car. Maybe if I asked Caitlin nicely enough, she'd take pity on me and...

"Good morning, Nathan. This is Jake, he lives in one of the ground floor apartments and you now owe him a case of beer."

I blinked. Caitlin grinned and the man she'd called Jake stuck his hand out.

When I shook it, he said, "I was just helping Dr Miller here bring some bags up. This is the first I've heard about beer, though." He stared at my cast. "Now I know why you can't carry your own stuff. How the hell did you get up here in the first place with that?"

"Slowly and painfully. Thanks, mate. I was ready to offer her a lifetime of servitude if she'd bring my bags up. Beer's probably easier. What sort of beer do you want?"

Jake snorted. "I prefer to eat bread, not drink it. I'm more of a whisky man myself." He eyed my bags. "Well, you're welcome, I guess. But after I've spent all day sorting out the world's IT problems, one server at a time, I don't think I'll care much. You obey your doctor's orders."

"I'll arrange something after work. Thanks again, Jake," Caitlin called after him as he disappeared down the stairs.

I raised my eyebrows. "You got your IT guy to bring up my bags?"

Caitlin laughed. "Not my IT guy. He does systems for huge companies. If the hospital system went down, they'd call someone like Jake. And he volunteered to help me – he spotted me pulling your stuff out of the boot of your car, took pity on me and decided to be gallant. I think I might have an unopened bottle of cognac in the cupboard – I'll drop it on his doorstep on my way to work. And you –" her tone softened as she smiled "– you take care of yourself. Don't injure that leg any more than you already have. I'll be back around dinner time. Help yourself to whatever you want from the kitchen. If you need me for anything, send a text message to my phone – I'll get back to you on my lunch break." She pulled her jacket on, kissed me so swiftly I didn't have a chance to reciprocate, and closed the door behind her.

Deciding a shower would be better than trying to follow her down the stairs for another kiss, I rifled through my bags for some clean clothes and limped back to the bathroom. It wasn't until I spotted the plastic bag in my wet pack that I remembered the dire threats of what would happen if I showered my splinted leg. I was supposed to bag the whole thing up like crime scene evidence. Shit. I should've asked Caitlin for help before she left.

Maybe the bath... A glimpse of white caught my eye and I looked more closely at the shower cubicle. One of Caitlin's plastic chairs sat in it, facing the door, with a second one shrouded in the shower curtain. I laughed softly. She'd already considered my problem and solved it without a second thought. Shoving the shower curtain open, I saw a note on one of the chairs:

DON'T GET YOUR CAST WET. ♥C

Showering with only one good leg was a nightmare, but thanks to Caitlin's forethought, at least it was bearable. She'd even left towels within easy reach. I could've kissed her, but she was busy at work, seeing to some other lucky patient. When she got home, I promised myself.

I decided to give shaving a miss, despite the itchy stubble, so I dressed and limped to the kitchen to hunt up some breakfast. I wished for a croissant and the sumptuous cooked breakfast from the guesthouse, but toast and vegemite was the best I could find. At least it was better than the hospital fare – a cold, pale, floury mush that was marketed as scrambled eggs. I'd seriously contemplated eating cornflakes again.

Easing a couple of chairs out, I propped my useless leg up on one and sat on the other while I waited for my laptop to boot.

Back to uni next year. Shit, I'd be an old man compared to the other undergrads. Alanna would be pleased – the female students would finally be safe from me. I'd be over thirty by the time I graduated. Better late than never. And maybe, just maybe, I could earn enough of Caitlin's respect back so that she'd consider me as more than a patient. I'd never deserve her, but there was always the faint hope that she'd be willing to settle for less. It'd mean telling her everything. I knew that, and I wasn't anywhere near ready for it. If she knew that I'd seriously considered raping her, she'd run screaming and rightly so. No. I could never tell her. Everything else, maybe, but not that. That one little secret wouldn't place her in any more danger – I knew I'd die before I'd hurt her again. Or let anyone else hurt her.

Maybe I should study criminology and counter-terrorism instead. Now there was a crazy idea.

Shaking my head, I clicked on my favourite browser, only to get an error message telling me I wasn't connected to the internet. It took me ten minutes of swearing at my laptop and changing the settings before I realised that I wasn't at home…and Caitlin's wifi was asking for a password that I didn't have. I tried guessing, but when my first two attempts failed dismally, I decided I'd be better off just asking Caitlin.

I checked my watch. Lunchtime was hours away and I was itching to start planning my future. Maybe her password was as simple as the random code on the bottom of the modem, like ours was. I figured it couldn't hurt. I remembered her mentioning the spare bedroom, where I'd seen a desk last time I stayed, so that was my first guess.

Sure enough, there was a modem, but there were half a dozen different alphanumeric codes to choose from. With only one try left, I wasn't game to gamble.

Sighing, I set the modem back on the desk beside Caitlin's laptop. Hmm, I wonder…

She had given me permission to use it last night, I reasoned, and I was only searching the internet, not raiding her encrypted files for her deepest, darkest secrets. Besides, I probably knew them anyway, as the darkest thing in her past was surely me and all that I was responsible for.

I pressed the power button and waited, finding it funny that Caitlin had the same laptop as I did. Mine was six years old and definitely the worse for wear, but hers looked in much better shape. Newer, I guessed, given she could afford it.

I started with criminology, but just the thought of forensics put me off. Shit, there were so many options! Five universities in this state alone, plus plenty in the eastern states and overseas. With Caitlin here, though, I didn't want to be too far away from her. I'd missed her too much. That still left me heaps to choose from, and pages of information to scroll through.

Considering everything that piqued my interest, I slowly read through the results before rejecting the options that would take too long, not get me a job or just weren't me. Biology degrees looked boring – chasing after animals or spending hours on my knees, looking at plants or puddles or things that were too small to see. Microbiology…shit, I'd go crazy, cooped up in a lab. If the other staff didn't go insane first, from having to work in a confined space with me. Pharmacy…far too tempting. Despite the number of sleeping pills I took just to sleep, I wasn't addicted to anything yet, but if I had access to that sort of supply…I'd be bound to try self-medicating and that could only end badly. Psychology was bad for two reasons – it'd take years longer than anything else and I didn't really want to know the technical names for what was wrong with me.

Gradually, I realised that the only options I wasn't ruling out were physiotherapy courses. Caitlin was right – it was perfect for me. I clicked on the course requirements, tapping my fingers on the desk as I waited for the page to load.

My stomach gave a fierce growl and I glanced at my watch, wondering if it was time for lunch yet. A second check at the time on the laptop told me the watch was accurate – and it was nearly two in the afternoon. A few hours and Caitlin would be home…and I could kiss her for providing me with the perfect solution for my future. But first…lunch.

I made myself a sandwich and ate it by the window that overlooked the hospital where Caitlin worked. Maybe we could meet up for lunch sometimes if we worked together. Maybe…

I should contact the course coordinator and the admissions office, to find out what I'd have to do in order to start studying physiotherapy next year.

I shoved the last bite of lunch into my mouth and returned to the laptop. Yep, there were the numbers. I pulled my phone out of my pocket and swiped the screen. Nothing. I tried again. Nope. I pressed the power button, watching the screen slowly glow into life before it flashed a low battery warning and blinked off. It shouldn't have been such a surprise – I couldn't remember the last time I'd charged it. Maybe before Caitlin had called an ambulance to pull me out of that godforsaken hole in the ground. No wonder the battery was flat.

I laid the useless phone on the desk and decided to email them instead. Clicking on the email address opened up my email program, which always took a while to load as it checked for fresh messages. I sat back to wait, scanning the screen for all the unopened emails I'd received while I was in hospital. Advertising for products I didn't need, surely, and maybe a few I might want. Nothing came up. Not a single ad.

I peered at the last read email on the list and my heart froze. The subject was Alanna Miller and the sender…shit, the sender was me.

My hand shook as I opened it. And the next one. And the one after that. There was a whole list of them, all opened. Every single one was full of my inane ramblings in the middle of the night as I'd written my emails to the only person I could confide in – Alanna, the sister I'd never see again.

As I read and reread the words, remembering the descent into darkness each one represented, it slowly dawned on me that there were worse things than my nightmares.

The emails had been opened and read.

On this laptop.

Alanna's old laptop.

In Caitlin's apartment.

She knew.

SIXTY

I trotted eagerly up the last few stairs, relieved to be home and looking forward to spending an evening with Nathan. I'd been lonely for too long, but it was more than that, too. We fit. Whatever was wrong with us, we'd fix it together, or at least we'd try to. And there'd be no one else coming after us, ever.

Well, except maybe Jake if he didn't like cognac.

I glanced down and the bottle was gone from his doormat, so presumably he or his girlfriend had accepted my thank-you gift. Maybe Nathan and I could have some of the top-shelf whisky in the liquor cabinet tonight.

I unlocked the door and pushed it open. "Nathan?" I called. "I hope you don't mind – I brought pizza. After the day I've had, I don't want to cook and there's this specialty pizza place up the road that does the best pizzas, so I asked for their signature one for you. It looks better than mine, and that's saying something." The whole place was dark — he hadn't turned any lights on. Maybe he'd decided to have a nap. "Nathan?"

Clicking the light on with my elbow, I crossed to the dining table and set down the pizza boxes. He wasn't in the lounge room and I could see his made bed in the guest room. My room was empty, too, so I tried the spare room next.

Nathan was hunched over, his head resting face-down on his crossed arms on the desk surface. I reached for his shoulder. "Nathan, are you all right?"

He lifted his head and stared at me with bloodshot eyes. "You knew," he whispered, then staggered to his feet, backing away from me as if I frightened him. "You fucking knew!"

My smile faltered, but I forced myself to keep it in place. "Knew what?"

Nathan waved at the laptop, then his own head. "Everything. Everything I did. All those times you asked me to tell you about my nightmares and you already knew! You read my emails to Alanna!"

"I wanted you to tell me yourself. To help you recover. It's what she would have done."

He strode forward and ripped the name badge off my shirt. "You're not her! You're not!" Tears streamed down his cheeks, confirming my suspicions as to why his eyes were so red. "Why did you take her name, of all the ones you could have used?"

"I didn't have a choice. It was one of Mott's sick jokes. At first, I wanted to change it, but as time wore on, I realised it wasn't an insult but an honour. She was a better person than I was and she would've made a better doctor than I am. She wouldn't have run away to Melbourne when you needed her. She'd have fought for you. I bet she did fight for you, to her very last breath. And I wish they'd taken me first and that she'd been the one to survive, because you'd tell her what was hurting you and why and you'd let her help you instead of shutting her out the way you do to me!" I wiped the tears from my face. Anger and grief had no place here tonight – I needed to stay calm if I wanted to help him.

"You didn't know her." His voice sounded dead, lifeless…devoid of all feeling. "How would you know anything about what she was like? You never met her. And she wasn't stronger than you. You survived and she…didn't."

I swiped the touchpad on the laptop and the screen burst into life. A few taps opened the last email his sister had ever sent. The one about him and me.

"I survived because I had her brother to be my hero, to save me from his sister's fate. I survived because of her sacrifice. And I did know her, Nathan. She told me I'd be perfect for you and she wanted to be the one to introduce us. I guess in her own way, she did. Even in death she was looking after you." I pointed at the screen. "Read it."

Nathan's eyes darted suspiciously from me to the laptop before he capitulated. I stood silent while I waited for Alanna's words to sink in.

"You're trying to tell me that was you?" If anything, his suspicion had deepened.

I wet my lips. "I got there early. I was the only one in the lecture theatre and she mustn't have seen me, because she raced through her whole presentation with her eyes closed. When she opened them, then she saw me. We talked for a few minutes and she asked me why I wanted to study medicine. I remember the words, because I used them myself plenty of times: one day I could save someone's life and that will make it all worth it. And she said I sounded just like her. Then she mentioned you and your reputation." Laughter bubbled up. "I didn't think you were my type." I closed my eyes. "And on the beach, when you told me your name, all the pieces fitted together. I knew your sister and I knew who you were and I believed you'd gotten mixed up in something that wasn't of your making. And I trusted you."

He couldn't seem to get the words out. "You trusted me? You…knew. Me and her and…what I did. My worst…my darkest…"

I nodded.

"You should have left me in that pit to die."

"No. You're not one of those bastards, Nathan. If you were, I would have killed you a long time ago. I made that decision in hospital and I've never regretted it. Alanna was right and I bet whatever afterlife she's in now, she's enjoying watching us as the longest-running soap opera she's ever seen. She wouldn't begrudge you happiness without her, Nathan, and I agree with her. You saved my life and you'll never hurt me."

I needed to touch him, to reassure him and maybe myself, too. My eyes never leaving his, I closed the distance between us and kissed him, wrapping my arms tightly around his neck so he couldn't pry me free. He didn't respond and I pulled back.

"Yes, I've seen the darkest depths of your soul. And they're not as fucking dark as you think, Nathan. I wouldn't love you the way I do if they were. D'you hear me? I love you, Nathan."

His eyes blazed, but I didn't fear him. Never Nathan. I stood my ground as he reached for me, grasping my already ripped shirt and tearing it further until it slipped to the floor, ruined. "Angel," he said hoarsely, his gaze lifting from my breasts to my face. His kiss was sudden and fierce, inflaming my passion even as it fuelled his. He backed me up against the window, his body a rigid wall of muscle pinning me in place. No softness at all – especially not where it counted. I fumbled to undo his pants to free him, but he grabbed my hands and pressed them to the glass above my head. "No. You first, angel."

His hand slipped into my pants and I cried out as his fingers expertly found their target. My legs turned to jelly so it was only his hold keeping me upright.

Nothing could stop us now – not that I wanted him to.

"Release the girl and back away slowly, hands in the air."

Fuck.

SIXTY ONE

I raised my hands and slowly turned around, trying to keep my body between Caitlin and the dickhead who'd decided to interrupt us. Caitlin and I were doomed. Fate hated us and if I even got close to a chance of happiness, it was shot to hell by yet another bastard like this one. Fuck, he was even wearing a balaclava.

"Step away from the girl," he repeated, his voice slightly muffled by the mask.

Reluctantly, I took a step closer to him. A flash of silver sailed past me and thunked into the door frame behind him. We both stared at the knife, pinning his shirt to the wall, and he reached up to touch the blood welling up from where it had grazed his arm.

Balaclava Bastard raised shaking hands and I realised he was unarmed. What kind of idiot burst into a house and tried to break up a busy couple without a weapon? Even I was a match for him with my broken leg if I could tackle him to the floor. I limped toward him. I was going to punch his fucking lights out.

He let out an agonised wail as his body grew rigid, shaking a little as I noticed the fine wires snaking into his shirt. His eyes rolled up and he slid down the wall, his weight pulling Caitlin's knife free to clatter to the floor before he hit it like a sack of potatoes.

Caitlin darted in and kicked the knife out of his reach, but it wasn't necessary – he slumped over, unconscious. She nudged his thigh a couple of times, but he didn't respond, so she knelt beside him and yanked out the hooks that had anchored the taser to his chest. She took a moment to examine his arm, too before she rose. "Watch him," she said grimly, wiping her knife on his shirt before tucking it back into the sheath strapped to her arm. "I'm going to get something we can restrain him with."

Restraints? Oh shit. Oh shit. I tried not to think of all the sadistic things that went with restraints. I desperately needed a distraction. Pizza. That was safe. And whisky, maybe. And wondering who the hell this idiot was.

I yanked the balaclava off his head and stared at his red face. It was hard to tell, but he looked familiar. If only I could remember where I'd seen him before.

"Who the hell is he?" Caitlin stood in the doorway, staring at the unconscious man.

I shrugged. "I don't know. I was hoping you would."

"Never seen him before. Here." She tossed me a roll of electrical tape. "Roll his sleeves and his pants legs up. Bind his wrists behind his back, then tape his ankles together."

I frowned at the tape. "Sticky tape? He'll break out of

this in seconds."

Caitlin laughed. "No, it's heavy duty electrical tape. This stuff takes off hair and skin. We had a case in ED a few weeks back where some guy tried to wax his privates with it. Nasty job, putting skin grafts there."

I shuddered. "You mean you want me to put it on bare skin around his wrists and his ankles?"

"Yep. It'll hold him." She glared at the man. "And when he wakes up, he can tell us who he is and why the hell he's here in my house."

"Shouldn't we call the police?" I ventured.

She considered for a moment. "Afterwards. Maybe. If he wants us to." She waited for me to finish taping his wrists before reaching into his pocket. Flipping through his wallet, she pulled out a driver's licence. "Says his name's Otto. Nope, I don't recognise him. You?"

Otto? I stared at the man, then the card Caitlin held out. "Yeah. I used to work with him. He stopped coming to his shifts and never answered his phone. He was supposed to be working the night of your second concert, but he never turned up. He was a security guard."

She rose. "That means someone hired him and he'll tell us who if we meet his price."

"You're going to bribe him for information?" I looked around, but Caitlin had left the room.

She returned a few minutes later with a stack of towels. "No. I'm going to threaten to cut things off until he tells me." She held my horrified stare. "What? I'm a doctor. I can stitch things back on. If I want to."

I fervently hoped I never pissed her off enough to warrant attention from her knife.

Caitlin threw the towels at me. "Here, spread these out on the floor under him."

To keep the blood off her floorboards? I knew Caitlin could be cold, but this took things a little too far. I'd worked with the bloke. Surely she wouldn't...

She upended a pot of water on his face and he came up spluttering. I shoved another towel under his head to mop up the water.

Caitlin unsheathed her knife, holding the serrated blade up to the light. "Now, you're going to tell me why you're here or I'm going to use this."

Otto's eyes widened, fixed on the knife. He couldn't seem to get the words out fast enough. "He paid me to keep an eye on you. I had to stay in the shadows, out of sight, and make sure nothing happened to you. He said you weren't allowed to know I was there. If you saw me or if you got hurt, I'd lose my job."

"How long have you been keeping an eye on me?" Her voice was dangerously calm.

"I don't know. Since...since you started working at the hospital. I watched to make sure you made it home okay and then watched the place at night. Just at night – that's all he wanted. And if you went out, he wanted me to stay watching the apartment. There were a couple of Arab guys who came once or twice, watching your place, but they never went in. He said not to interfere unless you were in danger, and they left before you got home, so I stayed in hiding."

Her knife stilled. "Who's he?"

"Jay. He said his name was Jay. I never met him – we only spoke on the phone."

"Do you have his number?"

Otto jerked his head to the side. "Pocket. It's in my pocket."

Caitlin nodded to me and I extracted his phone, scrolling through the numbers until I found one for Jay. I held it up.

Caitlin snorted. "Give it to me."

She put the phone to her ear. After a few seconds, I heard someone answer.

"No, it's me," she bit out. "And you'd better leave the state tonight because if I get my hands on you, I'll castrate you for sure this time. You set a fucking stalker on me. After all the trouble I went through, you had someone do surveillance on my house. At night. You know how many nights he followed me home and how many times I nearly attacked him? I can take care of myself."

A whiny voice said thinly, "I was trying to protect you. Didn't want you to be scared."

"You should be scared. Next time, run all security through Trevor. And if you send anyone else to my house – especially at night – I'll call the police." She ended the call and threw the phone at Otto's crotch.

I winced as it landed.

"Your job here's done. I don't want to see you near my home or my work again, unless you're a genuine patient," Caitlin said. "What are you going to do if I tell him to let you go?"

"Get the fuck out of here," Otto replied, looking shaken. "He doesn't pay me enough to get stabbed and tortured. Sorry, lady, you're on your own. He can shove his job up his arse."

Caitlin nodded to me and handed me the knife. "Cut him free."

Carefully, I sawed through the tape on his legs, then his hands. After what she'd said about it ripping off skin, I wasn't game to try it.

Caitlin held up her taser. "Now get out."

Otto winced as he clambered to his feet, but he didn't hesitate. He took off at a run, out the door and down the stairs.

Caitlin sagged to the floor with a sigh. "God, I hope that means this is over."

Cautiously, I wrapped my arms around her. "It will be. And if he's crazy enough to come back, I'll be here." I glanced at her ripped shirt. "I'm sorry about your shirt. In the heat of the moment and all..."

She shrugged. "It was ripped anyway. I'll buy a new one." She sighed as she rose. "I should probably go put some clothes on. After that, I'm not really in the mood any more."

She glanced at my pants, but I didn't have to. I already knew that my libido had left the building.

<h1 style="text-align:center">SIXTY TWO</h1>

"How was your day at work, dear?" Nathan fought to keep a straight face as he stirred something in a pot on the stove. I wasn't game to ask what.

"Um, exhausting. I hate working with Dr Proctor."

Nathan pulled a beer out of the fridge and handed it to me. "Is he a real arsehole?"

I laughed. "No, he's a proctologist."

Nathan appeared puzzled. "But doesn't that mean…"

I grinned. God, the beer tasted good. "Yeah. And he deals with the emergency cases, mostly. I figured my rotation with him would be all about removing appendixes, but the things people stick up their –"

Nathan burst out laughing. "Shit, I forgot about those. I was lucky, but Alanna told me she had to remove goldfish once. Half a dozen of them and some had been dead for days."

"Urgh. Well, in the last week, I've had to deal with a mobile phone, a mouse, some condoms, a tampon and an electric toothbrush. The last one needed stitches."

Nathan winced.

"Today's one was the worst, though. You know that plaster stuff you buy at the hardware store to fill in cracks?"

He turned pale. "No. No one would be that stupid…"

I nodded. "Oh yes, someone was. He'd been fixing up some cracks in the wall with the stuff while renovating his house, and sex toys being expensive and embarrassing to buy, he figured he'd save a bit of money and blushing and make his own. Custom shape and size, too. So he got a turkey baster and the plaster and…"

"NO! Oh God, NO!" Nathan shouted, covering his ears.

I wished I could cover my imagination just as effectively. The bloke had waited three days before he'd worked up the courage to walk stiffly into hospital and whisper to the triage nurse what his problem was.

"What's for dinner?" I finally asked, pointing at the pot.

He peered into it. "Um, I was thinking pasta, but the water's not boiling yet, so nothing, so far. I found some pasta, but I have no idea what to put with it. Everything's pretty empty." He grinned at me sheepishly. "What would you like?"

I shrugged. "We could go out." My eyes followed his to his walking cast. "Okay, maybe we could get something delivered? And I'll order some groceries and have them delivered tomorrow. I'm sorry, Nathan, I'm not used to taking care of someone who can't leave the house. I don't know how you managed with me five years ago. I swear you had to be some sort of saint." I dragged my laptop bag from under the dining table and set it up. "All right, let's order some pizza and then you can help me pick out groceries for the next week or so." I buried my head in my hands. "I'm sorry. You must think I've had my head up my arse all week."

He snorted. "Well, no, by the sound of things it wasn't your arse at all."

"Oh God." Once the helpless laughter started, I couldn't stop.

When I paused to catch my breath, Nathan said, "I never thought of online shopping. Now you make me feel like an idiot. I should be paying for it, too, and rent for taking up space here and using all your electricity and water."

"No need, honestly. I own the place outright – no rent or mortgage to pay. Paid for by that TV interview we did together, years ago, so you don't owe me anything. Food and power and stuff…well, you're not working and you're injured because you were helping me, so room and board are the least I can do for you. I'm just…" I shook my head, attempting to clear it, but it only started to hurt. "Tired. I should hire a housekeeper."

Nathan limped into the dining room and my chair protested squeakily when he rested his weight on the back of it. "I could be your housekeeper while I'm here. I've already met your cleaner and if you show me where you want me to get your food from, I can order it for you. And cook it, I guess, if you tell me what you like and I know how. But if you expect me to wear a uniform or something frilly with a short skirt…stuff it. I don't do dresses."

I could hear the hope in his voice. Staying here alone wasn't helping him, with me never home. Nathan needed to do something, not sit around and be useless. I'd be lost without him, though. Life was so much brighter with him to come home to. Even if I hadn't slept with him yet. He hadn't mentioned it after the night we'd gotten rid of my stalker. I wanted to, but I was scared I'd hurt his leg worse if we did and we'd waited five years – what was a few weeks more? "What about going back to uni? Have you…decided that's not what you want?"

Nathan chuckled. He was standing so close behind me I could feel the vibration through the chair. "Actually, I've been talking to Curtin for a few days now. Nothing's official until January, but I've spoken with their admissions office and the head of the physiotherapy school. They've both told me I'm close to qualifying for their graduate degree, with the credits for my unfinished medicine degree, so I'm pretty much guaranteed entry no matter what. If I start in January, I'll be fully qualified within two years. Maybe less, if I can get credit for some of my anatomy units." His arms slipped around me in a tentative hug that tightened when I didn't resist. "Thank you. I'd never have thought of it if it weren't for you. No more breaking up drunken brawls outside the Arena. No more night shift. And no more cadavers, thank God."

I rose and returned his hug. "That's wonderful, Nathan." When I looked into his eyes now, I saw more than hope. I saw a sense of purpose that I'd never seen before. "You're too good to be my housekeeper."

"It's something to do while I'm cooped up here. It's not like I can play the piano or the guitar, or go for a run.

Daytime TV's awful on a good day. And it doesn't matter how many books you have in the house – I've never been a reader."

I took a deep breath. "Okay, but only do the groceries and cooking. And when you're healed up well enough to come with me, we'll head down south for the rest of our holiday. We'll take a day to go to the house where it all happened, and when the day is over, I'll put it up for sale. The rest of the time will be our own to have a proper holiday. Maybe your last before your course starts, because I've heard physio is almost as full-on as medicine. That reminds me…you should be doing physio for that leg. Are you doing the exercises the hospital gave you?"

Nathan shifted his gaze so he didn't need to tell me he wasn't. I already knew, anyway.

"I'll get you an appointment at the hospital physio. I want to see you well, Nathan, and if I have to drug you so you cooperate..." I threatened.

His hands flew up in surrender. "All right, all right, Dr Miller. I'll do it. But you might need a crane to get me back up those stairs."

SIXTY THREE

This time, we agreed, we'd do things differently. We'd go to the house first and all the memory-tainted places around it, and then, when we'd finished the difficult stuff, we'd get to be tourists. And when we got home, having banished every damn demon from our combined pasts, then we agreed that we'd finish what I started when I ripped her shirt.

Caitlin plugged her mp3 player into the stereo and sang along quietly as we drove. I even found myself tapping my fingers on the steering wheel. This time would be different. No bunker meant the worst memories could be avoided. We'd go in, check the place out, go to the beach and be back in Busselton by dinner. I could almost taste the fish and chips already. And with all the physiotherapy she'd made me do the last couple of months, I'd be able to walk that jetty as if I'd never broken my leg.

We passed the resort and I nodded at the road to the

beach. "We could go to the beach first and then the house if you want."

She shook her head firmly. "No. First the house, then the beach. Checking out the house is more of a priority. We need to get it over with."

I nodded and kept driving, for I knew she was right. By tonight, we'd have finally put those demons to rest and the future would be brighter. I was certain of it.

I wasn't counting on the roadblock.

And not in the metaphorical sense, either – big metal barriers across the whole damn road, blocking both lanes. The big letters proclaimed that the road was closed for a prescribed burn in the national park.

"Ooh, that's good," Caitlin said. "With all the fire danger signs we saw last time we came down here, I wondered how the house would survive, so close to all that bush in the national park. If they're controlling it now, we won't have to worry about bushfires burning down the house in summer if we haven't sold it by then."

"Sure, but it also means we can't get to the house today if the road's closed," I pointed out. "What do you want to do now?"

She seemed stunned for a moment, but she recovered surprisingly quickly. "The beach road was still open, right? And we did see that track that ran from the house to the beach. So we park at the beach and walk up to the house." Her eyes burned with determination. There would be no getting out of this. I'd have to go inside that house of horrors one more time. At least Caitlin would be there to hold my hand. Shit, if anyone else knew how terrified I was of walking into a perfectly ordinary house. To stand in that kitchen and see the light switch which my hand had covered in her blood…but Caitlin understood. The only person who could. If she could do this, so could I.

I negotiated a sloppy u-turn, leaving behind a spray of gravel as we sped in the opposite direction. The beach turn-off was only a kilometre or two up the road, so it was a few minutes before we bumped along the narrow road to the beach.

Bitumen gave way to gravel as I pulled into the parking lot. Oh God – at least it was still daylight. I hadn't been here since the night Caitlin and I had been shot. When she'd taken a bullet for me and saved my life – and nearly lost her own. A sacrifice I didn't deserve. Not then and definitely not now.

Warm fingers pulled mine from my death grip on the steering wheel. She squeezed my hand and gave me a shaky smile. "Is this the car park where I…where we…where the ambulance was?"

Be a man. She deserved to know.

I nodded as we exited the car, waiting until she stood beside me before pointing out the places that haunted my worst nightmares. "I parked there, under that tree, so the car would be mostly hidden. The ambulance was there, on the sealed road, but the police cars were in the car park, here." I dragged my feet to where I fancied the gravel was a little darker than the rest. "This…this is where we were shot. There was so much blood, I didn't know if I could stop it before you bled to death. Why did you do it? You were safe – the police, the ambulance guys, they were all there to save you. Why would you risk your life for one of the men who'd hurt you? You'd have been safer without me. No one was going to miss me."

"Nathan." It sounded like a warning. "One of the cops was crooked, working with them, and the rest of them were still alive. Without you to protect me, I'd have died anyway. You'd promised to help me and that made you important. And you never hurt me. Whatever else you did didn't matter any more, because you were going to make things right. Not just atoning for whatever your sins were, but easing the pain of everyone else's, too. You were a scapegoat. A saint. And my hero."

I snorted. "Some hero. Would you like to see where I dumped your body on the beach, almost gift-wrapping you for the bastard who almost killed you while I was looking for a first aid kit in my car?" I strode toward the track, not waiting for a reply.

"Nathan, wait."

I didn't.

"Oh, fine. But I want to take the beach gear with us. After I'm done with the house, I want to wash off every bit of dust and dirt in the water. I won't want to wait for you to get my stuff out of the car." She tugged at the boot of the car, but it wouldn't budge. "Nathan! Open this damn car or I'll swim naked."

For a moment, I smiled, until I remembered where we were. I lifted the remote and lights flashed as the car unlocked for her. She hefted the heavy bag out of the boot and slammed the lid shut, shouldering her burden with fiery determination.

Ah, shit. I couldn't let her carry that, the gentleman buried deep inside me protested, and I crossed the car park to help her. I lifted the bag easily onto one shoulder and led the way to the beach.

My pace didn't slow when I hit the sand, grinding it beneath my shoes as if I could turn it into finer powder and obliterate the memories the grains held. I stopped when I was level with the bowed driftwood fence post that haunted my nightmares. "Here. This is where your so-called hero left you to be raped one last time, when he'd promised to protect you. That's what you wanted to see, right?" I glanced at Caitlin.

Tears flooded down her face as she hugged her chest tightly. She didn't make a sound.

Oh shit, I was a callous bastard. I wrapped my arms around her, willing her to cry into my shirt instead. "I'm sorry. I'm sorry. I shouldn't have said that."

A sob escaped, but I caught it before she buried her face in my chest to smother the rest. I felt her shaking and my heart sank further.

Caitlin mumbled something and pushed me away. She sniffed fiercely and said, "This is where Mike raped me for the last time, before he breathed his last. And it's where I first knew you'd never hurt me because you killed for me when I couldn't do it. You killed to protect me. That night you became my hero. Here on this sand." She dropped to her knees and stroked the white drifts left by the last tide, before lifting her sandy fingers to point to the spot I could identify as well as she did. "There's where he stood until you shot him. He didn't believe you'd do it, but I knew better. I begged you to end it and you did." She rose. "You think you're a coward, but you're wrong. You've just seen more than any man should and still you fight. Even when you're scared shitless."

My mouth went dry and I couldn't answer. No. She was wrong — seeing good when there was nothing left. There was no heroism in seeking vengeance — just cold, congealing anger and emptiness inside.

Caitlin grabbed my hand. "Where's the track to the house? Show me. We have more demons to kill. And I can't do this alone."

For all her fierce words, I could feel the terror trembling through her fingers. I nodded and led her along the ghostly sand.

SIXTY FOUR

I stopped beside the last track before the end of the beach. "It must be this one. It's overgrown and it's a long time since I used it, but this has to be the way. It runs through the national park for a bit, then forks and you can go up to the house or deeper into the park…" I trailed off and began again. "I used to walk the beach at night. I'd go up to where Alanna's body was found and then come back, pacing up and down the beach. Sometimes for hours."

"Can you tell me where she was found? I mean you said it was near the spot where you…where you brought me. How much further along was she?" The fear in Caitlin's eyes surprised me. Almost as if she didn't want an answer to her question.

I died a little inside as I lifted my arm. "Up that way, near the café. There's a good surf break there, right beside the resort. An early morning surfer found her and raised the alarm. It was too dark for him to see much, but he saw enough to call the police. Shit, I can't imagine the shock of finding a corpse where you least expect one to be..."

"Let's try the track. If it's the wrong one, we'll come back and try the next one," Caitlin said calmly and I found myself nodding, plodding along beside her.

The breeze died as we entered the dunes, in an unearthly stillness that felt like it was waiting for something. We crested a slight rise and the air seemed to move again, bringing with it the smell of smoke as bushland burned. The easterly wind carried a hint of heat with it, too, as if the fire wasn't far away, though the hot desert winds were rarely cool.

Caitlin inhaled deeply, smiling as I stared. "What? It's a prescribed burn – I'm sure the national parks people have this completely under control – and there's something amazing about the smell of Aussie hardwoods burning. It doesn't hurt them – most Aussie trees come back bigger and stronger than ever before. And the heat makes them…frisky. They go a bit nuts and release their seed after the fire. Talk about red-hot sex." The smoke grew thicker as we continued walking. "How much further to the house?"

I nodded. "Over that hill and we should see it."

I wanted to slow down, but Caitlin's pace only sped up. "I want this over with, Nathan. The sooner we sort out this house, the sooner we can sell it. One more demon put to rest."

How could I deny her the chance to banish a demon? To hell with my fears. What she wanted mattered more and if she needed me, I'd be there for her. Always.

SIXTY FIVE

I reached the top of the hill and stopped dead. "Oh shit." The trees on the ridge were towering orange torches. There was only a paddock full of stubble between them and the house, and the easterly wind to urge them on. "Looks like the controlled burn's definitely not controlled any more."

"We need to get to the beach and the safety of the water," Caitlin said urgently, unable to take her eyes off the orange wall rippling on the horizon.

I shook my head, shouting to be heard over the roar of flames devouring everything in their path. "It's too late. That wind's driving the fire straight toward the dunes. We'll never make it to the beach. There's nowhere to go."

Caitlin turned on me. "You mean we should just sit here and wait to be burned to death? You might be suicidal, Nathan, but there's no way in hell I'm going out without a fight. That forked track goes north into the national park.

Maybe it'll take us to the next beach, or at least a clearing where we'll be safe. It's our best shot."

"NO!" Panic rose up in my throat, tasting of bile, but I swallowed it down. "The other track goes to the bunker. The dark pit where you almost died. That's it." I swallowed. "Angel, it's our only chance."

Her eyes widened in fright. "I don't have a torch. We'll be trapped down there in the dark, waiting for the fire to go past and die down. The whole place could collapse and we'd die there. No. There has to be another way…somewhere else…"

Her fingers gripped mine and she dragged me forward, heading back the way we'd come as sparks flew around us, heralding the firestorm behind.

I was going to burn alive, and then I was going to burn in hell. Terrified, I ran with Caitlin, not daring to look behind. I could feel the heat pursuing us.

A deep boom from the direction of the road was followed by an expanding ball of flame behind the house, raining shrapnel around. The sea mine had still been explosive after all.

A flurry of flaming leaves flew past me, scorching my shirt until I slapped the smouldering cotton out.

Caitlin screamed and I forgot my shirt. The remaining leaves had settled on her and her dress was on fire. I sprinted and slammed into her, throwing her to the ground. Stunned, she didn't even fight me as I rolled us across the ground to extinguish the flames. When they were out, I pulled her to her feet, but she sagged in my arms.

Oh shit. Her eyes were closed – I must have knocked her out, or she'd passed out from the pain of her burns. I had to get her somewhere safe so I could see how badly she was hurt. Behind me, the wall of flame roared ever closer, cutting off my path to the house. If there was a house left behind that smoke.

Trees crackled as the flaming leaves from previous casualties set them alight before a grass tree flared up like a petrol-fuelled bonfire. The bunker. Oh God, it was the only place left. If the fire didn't kill me, she would. "Wake up, Caitlin, please."

She didn't wake. Déjà vu – for the second time, I carried her unconscious body down the track to the bunker, knowing that when she woke up, she'd be hurt and angry and I'd deserve to burn in hell for what she'd suffer. Better than both of us burning right now in the hell roaring toward us, though.

My feet carried me down the steps of their own volition. I wouldn't save my own skin, but caring for Caitlin was automatic. I couldn't not do it. And I knew the bloody bunker could save us.

When I reached the cool darkness at the bottom, I leaned against the wall, letting it take some of Caitlin's weight as I yanked my phone out of my pocket and tapped the screen to give me some light. I needed a clear patch with no rubble where I could lie her down. Oh God, what I needed was the mattress that'd been here while we were holding her captive. The one she stabbed when she should've stuck that blade into me.

The room where they'd held her. There'd been a clear space there, surely – one I'd cleared the first time I set foot in there.

I kicked broken bricks out of my way as I carried my

precious burden into her former prison. The door lay on the ground now, where it couldn't shut her in. I laid her on that, figuring it was probably the cleanest place in the whole bunker – the only place that I knew hadn't drunk her blood or Alanna's.

I shone my phone around, looking for a mattress or anything else suitable, but this room held only rocks and nightmares. There were others, though.

Swallowing, I headed back into the main room that held the stairs to the surface. A shower of burning debris landed on the concrete steps, chasing the darkness away until it was extinguished as its fuel turned to ash. My eyes had caught a second doorway in the concrete wall, one I'd never seen before. Like I'd ever wanted to explore this place properly.

I stumbled across the rubble-strewn floor and held up my phone to illuminate the mystery chamber. A pile of broken jarrah in the corner marked it as the twin to the sleeping quarters where I'd left Caitlin. And resting against the wall was a mattress. Ominous dark stains on it marked it as the same one I'd carried down here for her comfort before, and now it would help her again. Or at least, I hoped it would. As I dragged it across the concrete, I scanned it for signs of mould or inhabitants. I didn't want her sleeping on a nest of venomous snakes. Caitlin's life had been poisoned enough by her experiences between these cursed walls.

I wondered if there was any ammunition left over from the war, when this bunker had been built. Maybe a bomb or two to blast it into oblivion if we survived this, seeing as the sea mine was gone. So no one would ever suffer here as Caitlin had. Hell, if there were explosives hidden in the rubble and we didn't survive, maybe the fire would ignite them anyway, lighting a fitting pyre.

No. Don't think of that. Caitlin had to survive. No matter what I'd done, she didn't deserve to burn.

SIXTY SIX

Clenching my phone in my teeth, I lifted up her ruined dress to see the damage to the skin underneath. Would the flashbacks ever cease? Here I was, undressing her after knocking her unconscious. This time I'd done it by accident instead of tricking her into taking sleeping pills, but the similarities were just too numerous to name.

I pawed through the beach bag, praying she'd packed a first aid kit. Or anything I could use to help her, really. Shit, what I'd give for the first aid kit I kept in the car. I'd have killed to be able to run back and get it, just as I had that fateful night, but I couldn't leave her this time. Trapped by fire, I'd have to use what I had and hope we'd survive.

I found a bottle of water and some towels. Better than nothing, I told myself, laying one towel on the mattress and leaving the other for later.

The dress had to come off, along with her singed bra.

Her knickers seemed to be fine, but I slid them off her, too, so I wouldn't wet them when I poured the bottled water over her to wash away the soot and soothe her burns.

I ripped a chunk of cloth from her dress and doused it with water, carefully cleaning away the dark patches on her skin as I examined her. Some places appeared an angry red – like a particularly bad sunburn – but the absence of blood and blisters gave me hope. Maybe I'd saved her in time.

Next, I examined her head. Blood matted her hair and I cautiously probed her scalp, looking for the source of it. I found a lump which was oozing blood, but it had almost clotted already. She wasn't going to bleed to death, either. Her pulse and breathing were strong enough to reassure me that she was okay, for the moment. Until she woke up, of course, and tried to kill me for dragging her down here and stealing her clothes. Well, it wouldn't be the first time…

At least I could make her comfortable. I poured the water over the pink patches of skin, hoping it would give her some relief, then shifted her onto the mattress so she could rest somewhere softer than the door that had kept her prisoner.

I shrugged out of my shirt and folded it into the beach bag. She'd need it to cover herself if and when we left here, as all she had left was a pair of undies.

Watching her, I debated whether to try going to find help or even my first aid kit. It's not like it mattered if anything happened to me.

But if I did get caught in the fire, no one would ever know Caitlin was here, needing help. And if she woke up in the dark alone…

Shit, no. I settled down to watch her sleep, trying to

keep my eyes on her face and not the beautiful body that had first tempted me all those years ago. Of all the times for my dick to consider resurrection…

I swore and reached for the other beach towel, flicking it out of its neat folds until it covered her completely. There. Now I wasn't perving on the girl I couldn't have.

As if to bolster my self-control, my phone emitted a warning beep that said the battery was dying. I should've charged it last night, but who'd have guessed I'd be using it as a torch in a bushfire today? Not me. I sighed as the faint phone light faded, leaving us in darkness.

Now I couldn't even watch her. And if she woke up in the dark and thought she was alone…there'd be screaming for sure.

I felt for her body, my fingers encountering the thick flannel of her beach towel coverlet. I tucked it around her and stretched out on the edge of the mattress, resting my arm on top of the towel. If she woke up, at least she'd know she wasn't alone.

SIXTY SEVEN

"Where are my clothes?" Caitlin shrieked. "I'll fucking kill you!" She lurched to her feet, a hunched shadow staggering toward the doorway and the light outside. The inferno outside.

"NO!" I shouted, striding across the rubble to tackle her before she could walk to her death. She struggled in my grasp and I tightened my hold. "There's a fire outside, remember? It's not safe. We have to stay here until it's burned out."

"I can't stay here in the dark," she whimpered. "Turn some light on. Your phone. A torch. Something. I can't. I can't. Not in the dark." She slumped against me, sobbing, and I guided her back to the mattress.

I didn't dare loosen my grip on her, though. "The battery died about an hour ago. There's no mobile access underground and all that trying to connect must have flattened it. Yours, too. I checked. We just have to hold on until it's safe."

"Hold on to me. Don't you let go, Nathan. I'll go crazy in here alone. I need you close to me." As if to illustrate her point, she squirmed closer to me, pressing her face into my chest.

Oh God, I felt her bare nipples harden against my chest and that wasn't all that was hardening either. Shit, no. Of all the times to magically recover from impotence, this had to be the worst timing in the history of fucked-up timing…

"Yes," she whispered. Her hands slid down my sides, dragging the waistband of my shorts with them. My shorts and my undies slid down to my knees, my dick rising from the dead like a zombie before swelling harder still against the soft skin of her belly.

I groaned as her fingers stroked me, hesitantly at first and then firmly, decisively. "Angel, no. We can't do this here. In the bunker where you nearly died, on a mattress stained with your blood, with a fire raging above that might still kill us…"

"Sure we can. With death so close, how can you think about anything but sex?" The way her hands were squeezing me, I couldn't think of anything else. She continued, "Make love to me, Nathan. Chase the terrors away and make me forget where we are and I'll do the same for you. Stop overthinking this."

"I almost raped you here. In this room. I can't. I can't!" I wailed. I was lying through my teeth. If her hands continued their delicate ministrations, I was going to explode.

"You wanted to sleep with me. That's normal, Nathan.

You want to do it now – I can feel it." Another squeeze that made me moan. "It's not rape if I'm willing. If I'm begging you for it, and I will. Please, Nathan."

I shook my head. "You don't beg. You're too strong and too proud to beg."

Her lips touched my cheek. "No one else, maybe, but I'll beg and plead with you. When I lose to my own weakness, your strength shines through. It did then and it will now. Be my hero again, Nathan. Please." She wiggled against me, driving me mad. "Drive every memory out of my head so all I can think of is you and what your body is doing to mine. And how I want more." She pushed me onto my back, her soft curves still pressed against me. And one was softer and hotter and wetter and…

I moaned again as she eased my tip inside her, pushing slowly until she'd enfolded me completely in the one place I swore I'd never go. "Angel, oh angel…"

She tightened around me and let out a moan of her own. "You don't know how long I've wanted to feel this. Make love to me, Nathan, please. Please. I need you."

Her hips rocked and I thrust up to meet her. Once, twice, a third time. Each time, she gasped and clenched around me. I wanted to see her face. I needed to know if she truly wanted this.

I reached up for her breasts, caressing the soft swell of them until I encountered her rock hard nipples. If I couldn't see them, I needed to taste them. Fastening my hands on her hips, I sat up with my next thrust, angling deeper to her humming satisfaction. I ran the tip of my tongue over her breast, then sucked on her nipple.

Caitlin gasped and I froze, wondering if I'd stuffed up

and gone too far. Her fingers wove through my hair, pressing my face into her soft flesh. "Don't stop, Nathan. Please do that again."

I grinned and gave in. Those perfect globes had tempted me since the day I met her and I fully intended to worship them properly. But for every stroke of my tongue, she was tightening around me, grinding her hips against mine until there was no way I'd last another minute. Unless I took charge.

I tipped her back, wincing as I slipped out of her, but I didn't release her nipple until her head touched the mattress behind her. I knelt between her parted legs and sucked in a breath.

"Nathan…"

I heard the reproach in her tone, but I didn't pause to make excuses. "If you want me to make you forget everything, from your surroundings to the past to your own damn name, I need to call the pace, or I won't last long enough. It's been a long time, angel, and I need you to trust me." I stroked her damp thighs, tracing the wetness to its source. Her heat enveloped my fingers. "What do you say, angel?"

"Yes. If you have to, then yes." She was breathless with desire. Caitlin. My Caitlin.

I grinned into the dark, unseen, and caressed those smooth legs, lifting them over my shoulders so her bum lifted off the mattress. Closer, closer…I could feel the heat radiating off her and the smell of her was intoxicating. I wanted another taste.

She cried out as my tongue slipped inside her, rasping over sensitive skin on the way in and out, and I paused again.

"More. Oh, please, don't stop – ah!"

I alternated between my fingers and my tongue, relying on the pitch of her cries to know how close I'd brought her to the precipice of pleasure. When her thighs tightened against my shoulders, I increased the pace, knowing I had her. This time, she screamed my name for joy, not pain, before she begged for more. More that I delivered sooner than she'd expected, I thought as her cries turned to moans that egged me on. I wanted to hear her scream my name again. That meant making her come harder – so hard she almost crushed my fingers as her core clenched.

I laughed, pulling my fingers free with considerable effort. "What's your name again?"

"Caitlin. Caitlin Lockyer. But you can call me whatever you want. Oh God, just don't stop!"

I plunged my tongue inside her, devouring her until she was too breathless to scream again. I wasn't much far behind her, either. "Tell me your name," I panted.

"Caitlin. Angel. Alana. Fuck, I don't know. I'm not sure if my body will hold together if you do that again. I think I might fall apart."

"One more then," I breathed against her thigh, my fingers already stroking.

"Nathan, oh, Nathan…only if you promise me. Promise me…"

"What?" I asked, knowing I could keep her on edge with just my fingers, though I craved one more taste before we were done. Just in case it was the last.

"Promise me that next time, you'll come with me." She reached between my legs and squeezed.

Oh God, not in her hands. Inside her. I needed to be inside her.

I freed up my fingers, taking one last, languorous lick. I didn't want to wait either. I'd wanted her from the minute I first saw her.

She scrambled into my lap, a hot, wet dream come true.

"Angel, oh God, angel...Caitlin!" I howled, unable to resist her, the magical minx who milked me for my last drop.

SIXTY EIGHT

Is there anything more terrifying than waking in the pitch
dark with someone's arm draped across you and not a scrap
of clothing or covering between you? Maybe for normal
people it wasn't frightening at all. My fear only lasted the
few seconds it took to swallow my building scream, because
I found my lifeline out of the dark when Nathan's sleepy
voice mumbled, "Are you all right, angel?"

The hard, naked body was his, enfolding me in his arms.
The ache between my thighs was his doing, too, as my body
reminded me what this man had done to me in the dark.

I closed my eyes and breathed in his scent. Sweat and
smoke and sex. I wanted all of it one more time before he
left me like he did every other girl, the morning after sex, or
so his sister had said. If this was my last chance, then I
wanted it again. That toe-curling, gut-wrenching, breath-
stealing moment when Nathan's mouth and hands and rock

hard muscles were my everything as I screamed his name for joy into the darkness. I couldn't see, but, by God, I sure could feel. One more round with him in the dark and I'd never want to have sex with the lights on again. Heightened sensation as touch and smell and sound and taste.

I ran my hands across his chest, then my tongue. The taste of salt lingered as I pressed closer to him, realising that I wasn't the only one aroused by our intimacy. Goosebumps broke out on my back as the chilly morning air touched my skin. I shivered.

"Angel? Are you all right?" His voice became more urgent.

"I'm a little cold," I admitted, taking a deep breath before I told him what I wanted. Needed. "Nathan, I want you to make love to me again like you did last night. Light a fire in my blood and cover me with your body and kiss me."

He peeled his body from mine and the cold turned my nipples to pink pearls. I wanted his mouth to warm them again, before slipping lower, but the only contact between us was his fingers resting lightly on my hip. "Are you sure you're ready, angel?"

I grabbed his hand and dragged it between my legs, inhaling sharply when his fingers drove deep inside me, coaxing a whisper of desire into a roaring flame. "Yes," I whimpered as he pressed harder, tracing circles that spiralled around my nerve endings, drawing me deeper into a whirlpool of sensation that sucked the world away and left only us. "Oh, yes!" I shouted.

God, why was he hesitating? I could feel the hot, hard length of him against my thigh, when I wanted him inside me. He was so hard I swore I could feel his beating pulse under my fingers as I tried to pull him in.

"Angel…" he moaned.

"I'm no angel, Nathan," I replied, driving my hips forward to meet his powerful thrust. "But I'll ride you to heaven any time."

SIXTY NINE

For the first time in longer than I could remember, I stayed awake willingly. All I wanted was to savour the sensation of this incredible woman in my arms, terrified that she'd vanish if I let go. That this would have been just another fucked-up dream. Caitlin's breath tickled my neck every time she exhaled, but I wouldn't have traded it for the world. I didn't dare move.

Her even breathing ended in a gasp, then a moment of her holding her breath as she ran her fingers lightly down my chest.

"If you keep going, you'll find out I don't sleep in pyjamas," I remarked, longing for her to take up the challenge.

Another gasp and Caitlin snatched her hand back. The warm body at my side shifted so she wasn't touching me any more.

Over. It's over. But what a magic night it was, I told myself, even as I ached for more.

"Where are my clothes?" she asked sharply.

I shrugged, then realised she couldn't see me in the dark. "Your dress was burned, so some of it stayed outside and what was left of it I threw in the corner somewhere. Your bra, too. Your undies…um, I think I stuck them in your beach bag or next to it."

"Beach bag?"

I felt around for it and dumped it on her legs. "This. It had towels and stuff in it."

"And my bathers. Guess I'll be putting those on now."

I heard rustling for several minutes until she said, "Okay. I'm decent. Is it safe to go outside? Is the fire gone?"

"I don't know," I admitted. "I didn't want to leave you alone here to find out."

She threw some fabric at my face. "Well, put something on so you can come investigate with me. I'm not leaving you here alone, either."

I pulled my shorts on and managed to clamber to my feet. I shouldered her bag, hoping we hadn't left anything important behind. "All right. I'm as decent as I'm going to get. Let's go see what hell looks like."

I insisted on going first, seeing as I was way more expendable than she'd ever be. I stepped into daylight and couldn't stop staring. The world was completely leached of colour – nothing but black, white and grey, from the burned trees and ground to the ash covering everything. Wisps of smoke curled up from raised mounds that might once have been trees or bushes or God knew what, for I didn't and I wasn't game to find out. If it hadn't been for this godforsaken bunker, we'd have been two more smoking mounds.

I dropped to my knees, thanking whatever powers in the universe that had let me live – let us live – instead of burning to death as a prelude to eternity in hell.

"Nathan? Is it safe to come up?" Caitlin called.

I opened my eyes. "I think so. There's nothing left that can burn."

Caitlin emerged and my breath caught in my throat. To hell with the burned landscape – Caitlin in a skimpy bikini was heaven itself and she was walking toward me, stepping carefully in her thongs between the still-warm piles of ash. She was the hottest thing I'd ever seen.

She folded her arms across her chest. "I wish I still had my dress. I feel naked out here like this, and I can feel the heat from the ground on my bare skin."

I held out my shirt, hoping she wouldn't take it, but she did, quickly buttoning it over her bikini.

"Looks like we won't be selling the house after all."

I turned to see where Caitlin was pointing. It took me a moment to realise that the huge, smoking pile of scorched sheet metal was what was left of the house – it had collapsed under the weight of its tin roof. I pulled her into an embrace, hugging her for the sheer joy of it. I'd never have to enter that house of horrors again because the inferno had claimed it. I was free. We were free.

She pulled away far too quickly for my liking. "I guess insurance claim forms will be easier and there's still the land." Caitlin swivelled to face the ocean, though we couldn't see it from here. "Come for a swim with me before we go find out what happened to your car?"

My car. Alanna's old car. Oh shit. I swallowed. "Sure."

I stumbled after her as she led the way to the beach. The fire had cleared a track broader than Bussell Highway, so it wasn't hard to find our way. When she reached the peak of the last dune, Caitlin gasped. I crossed the distance between us to stand at her side and found my mouth dropping open, too.

Behind us was nothing but devastation, yet the final slope down to the beach was untouched. When we reached the sand, none of the damage was visible – almost as if the fire and the disaster it had left in its wake had never happened.

Caitlin pulled my shirt over her head and dropped it on the sand, wading into the water until it reached her waist. She ducked under a wave, rubbing handfuls of sand against her skin to scrub the soot off her and probably the memory of my touch, too. I strode in after her and followed her example.

What I really wanted to do was pull her down onto the sand and make love to her like I had last night, like I wanted to every night of the rest of my life, but I wasn't willing to risk rejection again. She'd already pulled out of my embrace once this morning and the sun wasn't even properly up yet. I turned my back, trying not to think of her breathtaking body in the barely-there bikini, and splashed myself with enough cold water to cool off an elephant.

"We should go back to the guesthouse for breakfast, a proper shower and some clean clothes," I said, starting toward the beach.

"Sure," she responded and I heard her splashing steps

behind me.

SEVENTY

She didn't say another word to me the whole drive back in my miraculously untouched car. If it weren't for the smell of smoke in the air, I'd have begun to wonder if we'd imagined the fire, but I knew we hadn't. We parted in the passageway, each to our own separate rooms. I ached to join her in the shower, but I didn't dare offer.

Five minutes later, showered and dressed in fresh clothes, I pulled my door shut and set off for the kitchen. Behind me, I heard Caitlin's soft footsteps. Impulsively, I turned to offer her my hand. "I didn't think I'd ever get to eat breakfast again, let alone with you. It feels surreal, doesn't it?"

She laid her fingers cautiously on my palm, watching as I enfolded her hand in mine. "Yes. It must be strange, seeing a girl the next morning after…after what we did last night. If your sister was telling the truth, a first for you, I think. I hope you don't mind. I can have breakfast at a different time tomorrow if you like." She lowered her eyes as she trudged down the passage, pulling her hand free.

I stopped to untangle the confusion in my head. What in hell had my sister said to her? Oh! It clicked and I laughed. "Angel, I'll join you for breakfast every day for the rest of your life if you'll let me."

It was her turn to stop. "But you don't…"

"Just because I've never slept with a girl more than once, you think I'm going to leave you? None of the other girls were you, angel. I waited five years for last night. And tonight, I want to do it all over again – but in a proper bed, like you deserve. You seriously think that after one night with you, I wouldn't want more?" I lowered my voice. "Angel, tonight I'll be the one begging."

Her eyes widened as if she didn't believe me. Still chuckling, I headed for the kitchen and the smell of coffee.

"Good morning!" Beth looked like she'd had way more sleep than Caitlin and me, judging by her cheerful smile.

I mumbled a response and heard Caitlin do the same.

"Have you heard about the fire?" Beth continued, setting out bowls of yoghurt and fruit. I pushed the bowl of strawberries across the table to Caitlin, knowing they were her favourite. "A routine burn-off in the national park got out of hand and burned through half the houses in Osprey Bay, up near the resort. Then the wind changed and they had to close off all the roads as it burned out of control in the national park. They're flying in firefighters from the eastern states and we'll be full by tonight. I've had to turn some down already and I haven't even checked my email this morning!" She laughed, shaking her head. "They say no one's been hurt, thank goodness, but they aren't letting anyone back in yet, so no one's checked the houses that burned."

"No, we hadn't heard," I managed to say through a mouthful of toast. "We went for an early swim this morning. Haven't had time to check the news."

Caitlin's eyes were firmly fixed on the bowl of strawberries and yoghurt in front of her.

"We could share a room if you need it for firefighters," I added quickly, trying not to grin when Caitlin's surprised gaze turned to me. "Just make up the sofa bed for me."

Caitlin swallowed. "That won't be necessary. We should probably head home early, anyway. If the place is full of firefighters, we'd probably get more rest and quiet at home."

I opened my mouth to protest, but Caitlin's wink made me close it again. Her foot stroked my thigh under the table, awakening some other muscles in anticipation of further stroking.

Fortunately, Beth had missed the exchange. "If you're sure. You have paid for both rooms for a week. I'll refund your money, of course."

"Of course," I said smoothly. "The sooner we get that fire under control, the better, right, angel?" I felt her foot slide out of my aching lap.

Caitlin slipped another spoonful of yoghurt into her mouth and nodded.

SEVENTY ONE

"Let me see how your burns are healing," I suggested.

Caitlin shrugged and pulled her shirt over her head before stretching out face-down on the couch.

Aside from the scars on her back from five years ago, I couldn't see any sign of damage. I leaned over to kiss the back of her neck. "Beautiful. You're not going to scar at all."

She glanced over her shoulder. "You know, there are easier ways to get me to take my top off. Just ask, Nathan."

I opened my mouth to ask for more than that, but something on TV caught my attention.

"Residents of Osprey Bay are allowed back for the first time today. Scenes of heartbreak and devastation as some homes were completely lost..." the news anchor said.

On the screen were pictures of the burned-out houses. It looked like Laura's house had copped the worst of it, so that picture featured the most, from varying angles.

Caitlin's phone rang and I leaned across her to snag it from the table so I could hand it to her.

"Hello? Yes, I'm Dr Miller, the owner of 100 Osprey Bay Drive." She listened for almost a minute, nodding slowly before she replied, "Sure, I can tell you my policy number." She rattled off the number as if she'd memorised it. Several more minutes of occasional "yes", "mmhmm" and "sure" responses, she thanked them and ended the call. The phone clattered to the coffee table as she turned her puzzled expression on me. "Apparently, there are some issues with the local council and the national parks office over who was responsible for the fire, so the insurance company wanted to explain the delays. The odd thing is that they've sent in a demolition crew, but the council aren't allowing them on the site because of all sorts of things. First they said hazardous materials and asbestos, and now there's some question as to whether the land's safe because of caves beneath it. Apparently a section of ground collapsed under a truck. The whole area's been declared unsafe until a specialist team has come to assess it so demolition will be delayed until then." She grabbed her t-shirt and yanked it back on.

"Does that mean you can't sell it?" I asked.

"Well, not yet, seeing as there's a burned-out house on it, but there aren't any caves there. The whole property's sand – the limestone doesn't start until the other side of the road, where that ridge is. If there's anything unsafe underground, it's got to be crater where the mine blew up or the bunker. And if a truck's driven over it and the roof's collapsed...why would they say it's a cave?"

"They're old Defence ruins, so maybe Defence is checking it out for more explosives. Or it could be ASIO, given the history of the place..." I began thoughtfully. "Either way, it's a secret they want to hide. Maybe even bury."

"You know, I hope they do bury it." Caitlin laughed. "So it really is over. The fire took out the house, the demolition crew destroyed the bunker, and ASIO or Defence will cover up the whole mess and bury the past for us. But if that bunker hadn't been there, if you hadn't known where it was...it's a miracle we survived. It's over. I can't believe how relieved I feel. It's wonderful!" She grabbed me in a tight hug, which I was only too happy to return.

"Shall we have a drink to celebrate?" I asked.

She grinned. "Absolutely. I'll get a couple of beers and we can watch the sunset from the balcony."

We settled down to drink.

Caitlin sighed contentedly and said, "You know, if you'd agreed to enter the witness protection program with me five years ago, we could have been sharing beers on my balcony in Melbourne all this time."

I snorted. "No one ever offered me witness protection. I evidently wasn't worth protecting." I stared at her. "But if you'd wanted me to come with you, all you'd have had to do is say so. I would have dropped everything for you."

Caitlin's mouth hung open. "But Mott...he was supposed to tell you. To arrange for a transfer to Melbourne to be with me. That's what you came to the church to say. That you were sorry because you couldn't accept the offer."

I shook my head slowly. "Mott didn't offer me a damn

thing. He fired my arse and took my gun off me the day before we went to the morgue to identify the bodies of your kidnappers. The only transfer I got was to the unemployment list."

She took a deep draught of her beer and was silent for a while. Conscious of having killed the conversation, I began babbling about the weather.

Two beers turned into four and the sun was almost out of sight when we waited for the first star to appear so we could make a wish.

"I wish..." we both began before laughing.

"You first," I offered, wondering what she looked so eager to wish for.

"No, you," she replied, reddening.

"Ladies first," I insisted. I didn't want to admit that I couldn't decide on just one wish.

Caitlin got up. "I have an idea. I'll be back." She crossed to the sliding door and reached into her apartment. From the table beside the door, she took a notepad and two pens. Returning to the tiny table beside me, she tore off a page and handed me a pen. "How about we write them down?"

"Sure," I said, clicking my pen in readiness. I stared at the paper. I had too many wishes that I knew could never come true. So much of the past I wish I could change. To write down only one…

Caitlin's pen skittered across the page until she threw it down. "Aren't you done yet?" she asked.

I covered my page with one hand. "It's hard to think which wish is most important," I admitted.

She folded her page in half, leaving it on the table. "Well, I'll go take the empties inside and get a couple more, shall I? While you're still thinking." She grabbed the empty beer bottles in the crook of her arm and slid the door open. I heard the glass clink into the bin.

Still I stared at my blank page. I glanced over at her crisply folded sheet. I reached over and snagged it as curiosity got the better of me.

I wish I'd told you I loved you five years ago.

Instead of helping, those simple words shot a hole through my heart. If I'd known she'd felt that way five years ago, I'd have stopped at nothing to keep her. Another wish joined the clamour in my head.

I stared at my paper. I wanted to wish that the painful events in our past had never happened. I wanted Alanna to be here, to introduce the two of us. I wanted Caitlin and me to fall in love like two normal people in one of the romance novels Chris read when I wasn't around. To live happily ever after. Not...any of this.

I wanted to take another deep draught of my beer, but it was empty and Caitlin hadn't returned. What was taking her so long? I glanced inside, but I didn't see her, so I stepped back into her apartment. I headed for the fridge and got out two more beers – the last of our six-pack. I started searching through the drawers for her bottle opener.

Maybe she'd gone to the toilet, I reasoned. I figured she'd be back soon enough and I'd have her drink ready and waiting.

I heard a sob – unmistakably hers. I looked around, trying to find the source. She sat hunched over the dining table, her dark hair blending with the dark cloth as she rested her head on her folded arms. Her shoulders shook with another sob.

"Angel, are you hurt?" I asked as I cautiously approached her.

"No," she whispered without lifting her head. She hunched her shoulders over, as if protecting herself from me or the rest of the world. "All this time, I thought you'd chosen your job over me. That you rejected my offer because you didn't want me. Shit, if that bastard Mott wasn't dead, I'd want to kill him twice over…and bring him back to life to do it a third time. If I hadn't been so trusting…if I'd asked you…I wish I could go back five years and do everything differently." She started to sob.

I couldn't stand to see her like this. I laid careful hands on her shoulders and started to rub them. Gentle strokes, just like I'd learned in that massage course with Alanna, so many years ago, easing away the tension until I felt her start to relax.

"I read your paper," I confessed.

I felt her shoulders tighten, but I kept up my massage until she dropped them again.

"I have so many wishes about the past – about things I can't change," I continued. "I'd like to wish that they'd never seen you, or that they'd never seen my sister. Or my parents had never annoyed so many people. I'd like to wish we'd met under different circumstances, so I'd have had a chance with you. I can wish for all those things and never get any of them. Or I can make a wish for the future and do my damnedest to make sure it comes true." I leaned over and touched my lips to the back of her neck. "I wish you'd let me carry you off to bed, right now, and make love to you all night. I'd like to kiss you, caress you, taste you and feel you wrapped around me in every way you're willing to be. I'd like to hear you scream my name the way you did the last time you let me pleasure you – as if you want me and you want more. When we're both so satisfied and exhausted by such an incredible night, I'd like to hold your naked body in my arms and sleep beside you until morning. When we wake together, I'd like our first thought to be how much we'd like to do it all again – even if it's not straight away, but some vague time in the future."

She sat, still and silent.

Now I'd started, I wanted to say it all, so I told her the rest. "I know I don't deserve you, but I wish I could have you, for a night or for a week or forever. If I could wipe all the horror of the past away, I would, but I'd still want my one wish. I love you, angel, just like I did then. More, maybe, because I know how amazing you really are, taking the broken pieces and making a man out of me again." I closed my eyes.

I heard the scrape of her chair across the tiles and I felt the leg crush my toe, but my pain and protests died as her mouth fastened over mine. Salty with tears, the taste of her tongue on mine drove me mad. I lifted her off her feet, cradling her in my arms, desperate to prolong that passionate kiss.

She broke for breath, but I just wanted to savour the feeling.

"What will you do if I agree to grant your wish?" she asked breathlessly.

I laughed. "I'll give you the best night I can manage – all of it. Just say the word, angel."

"And if I want more than one night? Every night afterwards?"

"Then I'm yours for as long as you want me. A night, a month, a year, a lifetime. I owe you my life and I want to give it to you, one glorious day and night at a time. Do you want me, angel?"

"Yes," she murmured, kissing me again. "Yes, Nathan. You're my hero and you always will be."

ABOUT THE AUTHOR

Demelza Carlton has always loved the ocean, but on her first snorkelling trip she found she was afraid of fish.

She has since swum with sea lions, sharks and sea cucumbers and stood on spray drenched cliffs over a seething sea as a seven-metre cyclonic swell surged in, shattering a shipwreck below.

Demelza now lives in Perth, Western Australia, the shark attack capital of the world.

The *Ocean's Gift* series was her first foray into fiction, followed her suspense thriller *Nightmares* trilogy. She swears the *Mel Goes to Hell* series ambushed her on a crowded train and wouldn't leave her alone.

Want to know more? You can follow Demelza on Facebook, Twitter, YouTube or her website, Demelza Carlton's Place at:

www.demelzacarlton.com

Books by Demelza Carlton

Ocean's Gift series
Ocean's Gift (#1)
Ocean's Infiltrator (#2)
Ocean's Depths (#3)
Water and Fire

Turbulence and Triumph series
Ocean's Justice (#1)
Ocean's Trial (#2)
Ocean's Triumph (#3)
Ocean's Ride (#4)
Ocean's Cage (#5)
Ocean's Birth (#6)
How To Catch Crabs

Nightmares Trilogy
Nightmares of Caitlin Lockyer (#1)
Necessary Evil of Nathan Miller (#2)
Afterlife of Alana Miller (#3)

Mel Goes to Hell series
Welcome to Hell (#1)
See You in Hell (#2)
Mel Goes to Hell (#3)
To Hell and Back (#4)
The Holiday From Hell (#5)
Melody Angel's Guide to Heaven and Hell